William Allingham

Varieties in Prose

Volume 1

William Allingham

Varieties in Prose
Volume 1

ISBN/EAN: 9783337368852

Printed in Europe, USA, Canada, Australia, Japan

Cover: Foto ©Andreas Hilbeck / pixelio.de

More available books at **www.hansebooks.com**

VARIETIES IN PROSE

BY

WILLIAM ALLINGHAM

VOLUME I

RAMBLES

BY

PATRICIUS WALKER

PART I

LONDON
LONGMANS, GREEN AND CO.
AND NEW YORK : 15 EAST 16th STREET
1893

INTRODUCTION

IT is by my Husband's wish that I publish this collected edition of his prose writings.

Many of the 'Rambles' and some of the Essays have previously appeared, in whole or in part, at different times. All of them were arranged and prepared for publication by my Husband shortly before his death, and they now go forth exactly as he left them.

My warmest thanks are due to our old friend, Mrs. ALEXANDER CARLYLE, for her valuable help in reading the proof sheets, and seeing these volumes through the press.

HELEN ALLINGHAM.

CONTENTS

RAMBLES BY PATRICIUS WALKER.

RAMBLE THE FIRST.

IN THE NEW FOREST.

(1872.)

Fox-hunting—William the Conqueror—Brockenhurst Church—Swine-herds—Mark Ash—Gilpin's *Forest Scenery*—Oaks—Queen's bower—Insect Life—Birds and Squirrels—Gypsies—Foresters—The Local Dialect—Rev. William Gilpin—Three notable Trees—Boldre Church-yard—Lyndhurst—Forest Frontiers—Christchurch—Flowers, Plants, and Animals.

A MEET of foxhounds in the New Forest on a fine open winter morning is a pretty enough sight, even to one who is no sportsman.

On some lawn or rising ground, encircled by far-spreading russet or leafless woods, you see the mounted groups of red-coated gentlemen, with a sprinkling of ladies, graceful in flowing dark skirts; lively boys on their ponies, and pretty little long-haired girls; black, brown and gray-coated riders too, lawyer or doctor, tradesman or farmer; whoso-ever, in short, chooses to come on the outside of a horse to share in this aristo-democratic amusement.

The little old whipper-in (we have no huntsman), with ruddy face and lively eyes, sitting his big horse as though he lived there, and in fact the most and best of his life is in the saddle, calls now and again or cracks his whip at the hounds

1

if restless ; but usually they are standing about, or stretched
on the sward, or nosing and questing quietly round within
a small area.

The master bides somewhat aloof, the cares of sove-
reignty visible on his brow ; now and again doffing his hat
to a fair equestrian, or exchanging a grave word with some
personage of importance. Carriages drive up on the road,
and gentlemen go over to greet their friends. Other spec-
tators there are, but not many ; by no means like the
enthusiastic crowd of miscellaneous pedestrians that come
out to see the hounds in Ireland, and often follow them, too,
for the best part of the day : here are only a few foresters
and boys, smock-frocked, apathetic, and perhaps half a
dozen young women and children from the nearest cottages.

Now we move to the cover ; in go the hounds, 'feather-
ing' (waving their feathery tails) among the gorse and
rusty bracken. 'Ho, Rallywood!—Ho, Trojan!'—a hound
gives tongue—'challenges.'—'There goes Diamond—hark
to Diamond!' Forty canine voices make the wood resound:
Reynard darts across one of the Forest rides—'Tally-ho-o!'
—he bursts into the open, the whole pack at his heels, and
away we go. But 'tis not mine to attempt the description
of 'a run ;' it has been done a thousand times, and done
well. The New Forest is a good place for 'seeing the
hounds work,' as they stream together over the open moorlands, or come to a check in some gorse-brake or plantation.
The riding is the easiest possible, no jumping of any sort
unless you like ; much of the ground is open moor (you have
very seldom to go over crop), and through the woods run
numerous grassy avenues, called 'rides,' where you may
gallop as on a lawn. Two things a stranger has to guard
against—getting into a swamp, and losing his way : let him
turn and twist about a little, and then find himself all alone
among the trees and underwood, at some point where three
or more forest ways diverge, and it may prove no easy

matter to choose aright. As to the swamps, if you are so ambitious as to keep well forward without knowing the ground, you may be galloping along comfortably this moment, and the next floundering in a treacherous muddy abyss, firm to the inexperienced eye. You plunge from your saddle; alas for the shining white breeches! but all is a trifle if you can safely land your struggling and frightened horse, without recourse to spades and ropes. These swamps, clogging and chilling the legs of the hounds with wet mud, are the cause, as some think, of that lameness to which the Forest hounds are peculiarly liable. Others attribute it to the prickles of the abundant dwarf furze (*Ulex nanus*). The winter in this region is commonly so mild and open, that the sport often goes on when frozen-up elsewhere, so it is naturally a favourite habitat of hunting men.

A French lady detested war, 'because it spoiled conversation'—people could talk of nothing else. If you are fond of hunting-talk after dinner, you can enjoy plenty of it in society here; and there might be worse—it smacks of open air and living nature; but to a stranger, who is not an enthusiastic sportsman, a little of it suffices. He knows nothing of such a gentleman's bay mare, or of Captain So-and-so's 'brother to Rattler;' the copses, gorses, farms, roads, spinneys, hills, bottoms, brooks, enclosures, &c., are mere names, not in his mind's geography.

The Conqueror and his sons were mighty hunters—not of fox and hare; but the oft-told tale of the destruction of many villages, churches, and houses in making this New Forest, is like so much other 'History.'

The poor chalk-gravel soil of the district (*Middle Eocene* of the geologists), could never have supported many inhabitants. *Ytene* ('Furzy'—'the Furze-land'?) was clearly a wild, moory, woody district in William's day, with a small scattered population. He made it a Royal Forest, and increased the severity of the old forest laws of the Danish and Saxon kings. The inhabitants naturally disliked the afforestment, and stories of the new king's inhumanity were told and retold, gaining in bulk and definition as the facts retired into the past, till the First William became in monkish chronicles (subsequent, not contemporary: there is nothing of it in the Saxon Chronicle) a royal Dragon of Wantley, to whom houses and churches were geese and turkeys. He destroyed 'twenty-two'— 'thirty-six'—'*fifty-two* parish churches,' and when his two sons in succession lost their lives in this wicked New Forest, it was clearly by vengeance of Heaven.

Of the buildings named in the Norman Great Roll, which the Saxons called 'Doom-Book' (Judgment-Book—Rate-Book), and sometimes, to express their fears, 'Doomsday Book' (a title absurdly kept up, and officialised), two kinds are commonly found to this day, whether the same walls or not, in the places indicated—churches and mills.

Here at Brockenhurst (is it 'Badger-wood,' or 'Brookwood,' or 'Broken-wood'?) is one of the Doom-Book churches. Looking southward from the railway platform you may see its weathercock just clearing the tree-tops of a wooded hill, and five minutes' walk will bring you to the circular graveyard surrounded by shady roads, with its elephantine oak-bole,

> A cave
> Of touchwood, with a single flourishing spray,

and the stately pillared yew-trees, iron-red, whose dark boughs almost brush the spire. Both these trees, very likely, were here when the Norman commissioners wrote in their list, 'Aluric tenet in Broceste unam hidam . . . Ibi ecclesia. Silva de 20 porcis. Tempore Regis Edwardi valebat 40 solidos, et post et modo 4 libras.'[1] Their spelling of the names of places, by the bye, gives little

---

[1] *Domesday Book*, Hampshire, Ordnance Survey Office.

guidance; they knew the views of Rex Willelmus to be practical, not antiquarian: yet the antiquarian facts now are of the greater interest. The southern portal, with some other parts of the church, also its font, appear to be of the original Saxon building, some 800 years old or more.

Build not, good squire, worthy parishioners, a new church, high or low! repair the old with loving care and reverent anxiety: there is a charm, there is a value inexpressibly precious in ancientness and continuity of remembrance. The world is poorer and smaller by the loss of an old thing visibly connecting us, poor fleeting mortals, with the sacred bygone years; leaving a door open, as it were, into the Land of the Past. Build us not in, beseech you, on that side, enjail not our imagination (which is no foolish or trivial part of us) with new Lymington bricks, or even from the fresh cut quarries of Portland or Caen. Is every town and village in England to be made like a Melbourne, a Farragutville, a Cubittopolis? It is deeper than a question of taste, this of *blotting out traces of the great Past* from our visible world, destroying them for ever, with all their softened beauty, and mystery, and tender sadness.

The worst thing to do with a venerable relic is to erase it from the earth. The next worst thing (often almost as bad as the first) is to 'restore' it. Sometimes we are told that though a new edifice is necessary (a statement more readily made than proved) the old building is not to be pulled down. But who ever saw a forsaken edifice of the humbler sort that did not quickly fall into neglect? Besides, the mystic charm of an ancient thing *in use* is enhanced a thousandfold. What interest have antiquities in the glass cases of museums, compared with those that meet you in daily life, in streets or rural landscapes? Keep, Old England, thy old churches (albeit old forms of worship have changed, and will change), and old manor-houses too, and

town-halls, and ivied walls, and shady winding roads; these
things, believe it, tend to nourish all that is wholesome and
beautiful in conservatism, and to foster a love of the
country of our ancestors, which is also our own, and will,
we hope, be our children's.

From the churchyard, through a veil of boughs, you look
down the slope of Brockenhurst Park, and away to a wide
semicirque of woods, sweeping round the northern horizon
from east to west. Within the forty miles' circuit of the
Forest is many an open heath, many a thick wood of oak
and beech, many a green avenue and shadowy glade. Main
roads, smooth as in a park, run through it to Southampton,
to Lymington, to Christchurch, to Sarum—for this ancient
name holds its place on the milestones and fingerposts. In
most parts you may turn off where you will into heath or
hurst, without fence or other hindrance. There are many
new plantations of oaks, with alternate fir-trees to nurse
them; but through these also, lifting the gate-latch, you
may pass unchallenged. This wild liberty is the great
charm of the region. No longer under fierce forest-law are
you liable to be seized for wandering in the King's Forest,
perhaps to undergo ordeal of fire to prove your innocence of
poaching, perhaps to *lose your eyes* on the charge of slaying
venison or wild boar. You may wander for hours and meet
no one but a chance woodman or earth-stopper, or a swine-
herd in acorn-time; or, more rarely still, a truffle-seeker
with his little dogs.

The foresters have an old privilege of turning their swine
into the Forest for six weeks in autumn. One man under-
takes the care of a herd of several hundred hogs. Having
fixed on a sleeping-place, at first he feeds them a few times
and teaches them to attend his horn. Signor Gryll, though
shy and reserved, is not stupid, and knows what is good for
him. On the second or third evening, when the horn

sounds through long glades and tangled underwood, gilded perhaps with last sunlight, the hogs come trotting into the rendezvous by twos and threes, by dozens and scores, and soon lie stretched heads and tails, acorn-glutted, under dim forest boughs, only a grunt heard now and again, not unlike the human snore; while, in little wigwam close by, snores humanly their temporary lord and master, his magic horn by his side. Such a group as this, by sunset or moonlight, may the autumnal forest-wanderer, musing haply of dryads and hamadryads, of fairies and wood-sprites, chance upon beneath a spreading oak,—hogs not elves, yet picturesque after their own fashion.

The oaks of the New Forest (chiefly *Quercus robur*), slowgrowing on a gravelly soil, are not lofty nor thick-leaved; they are gnarly and close-grained, with boughs much twisted and writhen. But here and there rises a kingly tree, like that of Knightwood, a huge straight lofty bole, with mighty spreading branches, each a tree in bulk. Some three miles or so from Lyndhurst, near the road to Christchurch, stands this Knightwood Oak, strong and vigorous, and may stand for many a century to come.

Hot was the summer day, and shoulder deep the eaglefern that clothed hill and hollow, and muffled up all paths, when my friend (a magician he, who better than west or south wind can make an oak-tree talk in melody)—my friend and I pushed through from Knightwood to Mark Ash, the greatest beechen shade in the Forest. Huge and weird are its brindled beech-trees Underneath, dim at noonday, our feet rustled in the withered relics of a former summer: we paused, and the lonely wood was silent. The mighty growths stood well apart, each trunk rising into many great stems that lifted high overhead their canopy of interwoven green. Amid this company of vast and ancient trees, arrived at through a labyrinth of tangled woodland, we seemed to be at the core of some boundless primæval forest. The sunlight striking through its lofty branches on the floor of brown fallen leaves could not enliven it. There was something ominous and awful in the place. One half-expected at every turn to encounter some unexampled sight. Those hogs, if they strayed hither, would seem to be of the crew of Comus, or his mother Circe. Here, as we reclined under the shade of melancholy boughs, my companion took out a well-worn little pocket-volume, and (himself a famous poet) read aloud from ' As You Like It.' We agreed that Oliver's lioness and serpent are very strange beasts and that Shakespeare's Arden is a forest in dreamland. No serpents here ; but as we waded through the tall bracken spreading like a sea round Mark Ash, my Companion stopped suddenly and said, in deep, tragic tones, ' I believe this place is quite full of vipers !' and as we went on, he expatiated in vivid language on the various dreadful consequences that might ensue from a bite. We were only bitten by gnats and forest-flies ; and with all my walking in wild places, I don't think I have seen more than half a dozen vipers in my life. A country doctor in a district full of copses commons and woods, told me he had had only two cases of viper bite in sixteen years, neither of them serious.

The name ' Mark Ash,' like Bound Oak (Boundary Oak), indicates some special tree once used for a mark. We saw no ash in this beech wood, and ash-trees in the forest are very few.

Mr. Gilpin, in his ' Forest Scenery,' is hard upon the beech—calls it an ' unpleasing ' tree, ' an object of disapprobation.' To the worthy vicar of Boldre belongs the merit of having loved and sought after landscape beauty at a time when few had any eyes for it ; but he always criticised nature with reference to his own little drawings in brown ink, and to what could be agreeably expressed by such means. A quality called *Picturesqueness*, defined according to certain limitations of his own, was what he

looked for and found or missed in every visible object or
scene. . The horse-chestnut is 'a heavy disagreeable tree,'
—'the whole tree together in flower is a glaring object,
totally inharmonious and unpicturesque.' He is severe on
the willows—'the weeping willow is the only one of its
tribe that is beautiful.' The cedar is interesting, the more so
on account of 'the respectable mention which is everywhere
made of it in Scripture;' but the hawthorn 'has little
claim to picturesque beauty,' nay, it is 'sometimes offen-
sive;' while the poor bramble (whose sweeping curves
tufted with leaf-sprouts, appear to some eyes the perfection
of elegance) is denounced as 'the most insignificant of all
vegetable reptiles.' But all this is natural enough in one
who looked up to Horace Walpole and Reverend Mr. Mason
as his arbiters of taste; it is on a level with the former's
gothic architecture, and the latter's poetry, which the writer
of it so honestly believed to be immortal. Yet it is giving
a false impression of Gilpin to put foremost his absurdities.
His little books on scenery may still be looked into with
interest, for his love of nature was genuine; he expresses
himself in pure and accurate language of its kind, and the
brown sketches are often clever and pleasing. Henry
Thoreau, of Massachusetts, whose notes upon nature in
his own region are so fresh and vivid, took much interest in
old Mr. Gilpin's writings and sketches.

In *picturesqueness* Gilpin ranks the oak highest, and here,
no doubt, most will agree with him. That is to say, the
oak in maturity and in old age; as a stripling, like many
things that advance slowly to their perfection, it is ungainly.
Not far from the stalwart Knightwood Oak, stand his
famous elder brethren, named 'The Twelve Apostles,'
reckoned to be the oldest trees in the Forest. Their
situation is not impressive; they grow scattered about a
space of flat open ground, cultivated as a farm. Their
heads are gone; they are shattered stumps, though still

alive; forlorn and decayed giants. The new crop of winter wheat springs green around one, whose gnarly roots clutch the soil as with monstrous claws; the farmer's cows scratch their sides against the rhinoceros bark of another; this one is a hollow tower; that a pillar of ivy. The *handsomest* oak in the New Forest (they say) is one near its western boundary, at Moyle's Court.

That which as yet holds first place in my regard stands in the beautiful wood with a beautiful name—'Queen's Bower' —stretching downward one great arm across the clear brook (a rare and precious thing in the Forest), that plays over gravel, and 'winds about and in and out' among alder and hazel. This oak, though not hollow, is evidently very aged. Its short bole, massive as the pillar of some rock temple, is tinted with delicate gray lichens and embroidered with creeping lines of ivy. Tufts of polypody flourish in the ample space whence the heavy branches diverge all at once —an enviable reclining place, but not so easy to mount to as you may think it. Profane not the lichened and ivied bark by such an attempt, but lie down on the sward, under these wide-stretching twisted boughs, with the brook at your feet, and watch, if day and season allow, the trembling sunlights and cool translucent shadows, the dancing parties of whirli-gig-beetles (*Gyrinus natator*), the troops of 'water-mea-surers' (*Hydrometra*) jerking themselves on the glassy surface, the little fish coming and vanishing, the jewelly dragon-flies, some azure-bodied, some green, darting up and down the streamlet's course—veritable flying dragons to the insects which they seize and devour. One will sometimes even pounce on a passing butterfly, carry it to some twig, tear off its wings and gobble up its body in a minute. These fair ferocious creatures, blue or emerald, borne on wings of violet gauze or silver netted with black, the French (is it partly satiric or moral?) name *demoiselles*; and our own poets have sometimes called them 'damsel flies.'

The abundance of insect life in the Forest in summer-time, interesting as it is, proves now and again inconvenient: clouds of gnats in the air, armies of ants and ticks in the grass, corsair wasps and hornets, gadflies as big as humble-bees, crawling 'forest-flies' to set your horse wild—of these there are enough and to spare. The special 'forest-fly' (*Hippobosca*) is of a dirty reddish colour, about as big as a middle-sized house-fly, very abundant, hard to hit, and harder to kill. They are said to prefer white and gray horses, and they swarm on them by hundreds. They bite, but that is not the worst; they crawl—equally, it is said, forward, backward, or sideways—and *tickle* as they crawl. Olive oil defeats them when and where it can be applied. A strange horse coming to Lyndhurst races will probably have some of his running taken out of him by the fret caused by these troublesome natives. Horses bred in the Forest don't seem to mind them; and you will see many a herd of forest ponies, many a grave mare and frisking foal on the wood-lawns, feeding and moving about as comfortably, to all appearance, as if they had never heard of a *Hippobosca* or *Œstrus equi*. The horse-gadfly lays her eggs on the horse's hairs, *within reach of his tongue*; he licks off the sticky stuff and swallows it; out come the grubs, and fasten and feed on the coat of his stomach till they are an inch long, and of an age to drop off and be carried abroad; falling on the ground, they burrow awhile, then rise into the air as gad-flies, continue their species, and die. The sheep gadfly punctures the sheep's nostril and lays her eggs there. The worms creep up into the cavities of the skull, and feed, descending in due time for a short open-air life. While these creatures are crawling up or down its nostrils, the sheep jumps about and sneezes violently. The cow-gadfly is the big bee-like one; it lays its eggs under the skin, making a puncture which sends the cow galloping with tail up. While a cow is thus disturbed by the pricking of her hide, it is remarkable that a number of large grubs feeding on the inside surface of a horse's stomach don't appear to do him the least harm or annoyance in the ordinary course. When they go astray, in their fleshy pasturage, fasten in a wrong place, then they do harm, and may give their host the 'bots.' Possibly the human entozoa are countless, and only do harm in exceptional cases—when they go astray. Is not the multiplicity and variety of animal life as astounding to think of as the starry universe overhead? And is not man's mind incomparably greater and more wonderful than all the phenomena of which it takes cognisance?

Here, on a summer's day, under the Oak of Queen's Bower, its cool brook running by, the sunshine tempered with curtains of foliage, is the place of all others to fleet the time as in the golden age. There are no ants or ticks in this close sward; the merry wild bees hum past on their errands; from afar comes the soft voice of the cuckoo. And now let us rise and wander through the close beeches of Liney Hill and the graceful glades and lawns of Whitley Wood. Perhaps that sluggish hawk, the honey-buzzard, may be seen slowly skimming round; he rifles the nest of the wild bee in some hollow bole or high fork, not eating the honey but the bee-grubs. The human forester, when he can find it, takes the honey for his share. Here are fir-trees; at a dropping cone I look up and see the squirrel that has thus betrayed himself climbing from branch to branch, and keeping as well as he can on the further side of his tree, but the bushy tail (his helm in leaping) is not easily hid. When unalarmed he ascends his tree in spirals, by an easily inclined plane; if pressed, he jumps rapidly from tree to tree, uttering a creaking little cry of fright. That loosish bundle of sticks in the larch-top is one of the nests or 'cages.' The Forest-boy often wears a squirrel-skin cap, with the tail set as feather; and about Christmas-time these rough young sylvans go squirrel-hunting with 'squoyles,' short sticks knobbed with lead, and knock down scores of the bright-eyed little red creatures. Verily, man is the fiercest of animals; he spares nothing. The gypsies bake the squirrel whole in a ball of clay among their wood embers, and do the hedgehog same fashion, a way of cooking common to wild no-housekeepers in various parts of the world, and said to give a better result (keeping in the juices and flavour) than more elaborate processes. The fallow-deer of the Forest were killed off, save a few stragglers, some twelve years ago, with loss of picturesqueness and old-world associations, but to the advantage of the young oaks, and of the hollies, too, which now grow tall and strong and enrich the woods in winter.

There are yet some Gypsies, or 'Egyptians,' as old Acts of Parliament call them, in the Forest; for the most part, of the tribes calling themselves 'Lee' and 'Stanley.' When I say 'in the Forest,' I mean traversing and flitting about the district, and camping therein oftener than elsewhere. You may suddenly light, even in the depth of winter, on their squalid encampment on some sheltered piece of sward, or among the gorse and underwood on the fringe of a common; low, savage tents, mere cross-sticks and patch-work; with a population no less uncouth—weird old women, naked children, young women, boys and men, brown-faced, black-eyed, black-haired, dirty; not fierce but wild-looking, like untamed animals as they are; their attire, however old, brightened with some gaudy-coloured kerchief. With the tents is probably found a covered cart like a Cheap Jack's, three or four asses and a rough pony or two tethered close by; while a wood fire, with a large pot slung over it, sends up its blue fume.

At first glance, these people much resemble those dark-complexioned natives of the West and South of Ireland, who are said to be in part of Spanish breed; more closely viewed, they have often a strikingly Hindoo appearance, carried safe across the four centuries or so since they started westward from upper India, urged perhaps by famine or war, and became a wandering tribe. It seems likely that towards the confines of Asia and Europe they split into at least two streams of vagabondage, the northern one creeping into South Russia, Bohemia, and so westward; the southern stream making its way to Egypt and on into Spain. In Bohemia and Egypt they first came particularly under the notice of Westerns, — were probably numerous there; hence the terms 'Bohemian' and 'Egyptian' or 'Gypsy,' applied to them in ignorance of their real history. A learned indefatigable Teuton, Dr. Pott, has packed into his thick volume, *Die Zigeuner in Europa und Asien* (Halle, 1844), a huge mass of information about these folk and their speech, a wonderful little people, keeping their oriental race and manners so long distinct among the surrounding European millions, and using, however largely corrupted, a real language of their own.

The gypsies who chiefly frequent the New Forest, probably but a few scores in count, possibly a couple of hundred, seem to be steadily diminishing in number. In *their* struggle for life the new element of rural police bears hard on them; they must 'move on,' and are, nominally, only allowed to stay one night in a spot; but this rule is often evaded. Tired of moving on (involuntarily), many English gypsies have moved off, of late years, to America and Australia. The 'Stanleys' and 'Lees' of the Forest keep mainly to the traditional businesses of making baskets, brooms, clothes-pegs; some go round mending rush-bottom chairs, some play the fiddle in taverns. The men are to be seen at fairs with donkeys and forest ponies for sale, while the women and lads do the honours of 'Aunt Sally,' or some other popular game. The local magistrates and rural policemen give no unkindly report of the gypsy people; consider them in no way dangerous, and moderately honest.

They are seldom 'pulled up,' and then but for minor offences, and when they are fined the money is always forthcoming. A gypsy is seldom without ready money, and they help one another freely in case of need; nor are their old or sick ever thrown upon parish relief. They keep no pigs and have no forest privileges; they steal wood, but are not suspected much of poaching; now and again, however, a clever greyhound is seen in their company. Their *horse-stealing* notoriety has faded away. Within the last twenty years, I am told, many of the New Forest gypsies have become much less peculiar and exclusive in their habits; their men and women marry non-gypsy mates, and half-gypsies are growing commoner than the true breed. People unmistakably of the dark strain are to be seen at work in the harvest gangs; and now and again, not often, you find one of them a sailor in a yacht or merchant ship. But there are still some who pride themselves on keeping un-mixed their ancient blood; and a few years ago, I am informed, a gypsy girl of remarkable beauty, one of the Stanleys, refused, on that ground, to marry a well-to-do farmer of the parish of Fawley. It is extremely hard to get any trustworthy account of their more intimate life—for they never apply to the law, and seldom quarrel seriously. What is their education? Does one now and again rise in social rank? Is there any lady, for example, in our day (I have heard rumour of such things), in whose cheek, as in the little Duchess's in that wonderful poem, 'the tinge' might be recognised?

In addition to other good authorities I have consulted an experienced rural postman of the Forest, who is also a gamekeeper; he still, he says, comes pretty often on a gypsy camp; they sometimes, though rarely, get letters; he thinks that very few of them can read or write. He believes they have no religion. The old and young go begging; some of the old women tell fortunes. What puzzles him most is what they do with their dead; he never saw or heard of a gypsy's funeral. He has often met five or six of them in a public-house talking to each other in their own lingo, and sometimes quarrelling in their drink; but they very seldom get taken up. The regular gypsies never sleep in a house winter or summer.

As to creed, marrying, etc., my own impression is that they have certain traditional tenets, unknown to the exoteric world, and most likely not very important in any sense; while as to outward observances they take the easiest way that serves, according to time and place, and glide along like a snake through a coppice, with eyes constant to the practical objects of getting what they want, and of shunning danger. Here they always profess to belong to the Church of England, and *sometimes* use its forms of baptism, marriage, and burial, but I think never attend service. The author of 'Westward Ho' told me that a Curate of his at Eversley, who had a theory that gypsies are descendants of one of the Lost Tribes, announced one day with much delight that he had persuaded some gypsies to let him baptize a new baby of theirs, and they requested to have it named 'Rizvah,' obviously Hebrew, or of Hebraic origin. The Rector a day or two after, paid the camp a visit, complimented the mother on having her child christened, and remarked on the curious name. 'Well, your good Reverence, you see 'twas born yonder up at the Rizvore (Reservoir), so we just thought——' Be sure the Rector enjoyed giving this information to his philological Curate.

One Sunday evening in late autumn, I was roving, lonely and moody enough, under a gray sky and thinning yellow leaves, and found myself about sundown in Whitley Wood. Turning a clump of hollies, I came suddenly on two gypsy tents. There was an old woman, over seventy she said, with cunning mahogany face, and hair still black; her son, a good-looking man of five-and-thirty; his wife, who was nursing her *tenth* child; and the other nine children, all living and well, were swarming about, or not far away. There were also an elder married pair, who, I found, had no children. The father of the ten, Tom by name, happened to be an old acquaintance of mine. I had found him, some years before, lying ill and all but speechless with quinsy, and had done him some service. It had struck me then how miserable the case of a sick gypsy; but further reflection suggested that probably, in most cases of illness a ragged tent would be better than Guy's or Bartholomew's, and no treatment than too much. Great hospitals are good means of training doctors, rather than of curing patients. Still, Tom in his quinsy seemed in need of medical aid, and I had sent him some.

The older married woman had a closed book in her hand. 'It's a Bible, your good honour; parson in north parts o' the Forest giv' it us t'other day; and we was a-readin' till the daylight failed.' They had begun at the beginning, and had found some things that puzzled them, and which they were discussing when I came up. 'Who was Cain's wife, your honour?' I could not tell them. 'And who was Cain afraid of when he asked to have a mark put on him lest people should kill him? The world was empty.' Answer: 'We are to suppose that Cain had a long life before him, and people quickly increased in numbers.' Elder gypsy man (tentatively): 'Your honour, I was in a shop in Southampton last week, and I heard a gentleman say, 'The Bible's a bad book,' says he. P. Walker: 'It was not a wise thing to say.' Younger gypsy woman (trimming sail): 'Maybe he'll find his mistake out when his last hour comes.' And so we talked awhile—a conversation in itself extremely unimportant, but it was curious to find these vagrants, too, amusing themselves with a discussion of Biblical difficulties. My good offices to Tom's

2

quinsy were remembered, and made a new gift on my part inevitable; so, shutting it into the baby's hand, and receiving a number of blessings in return, I took my departure through the dark alleys of the wood.

In any case, you must not hold converse with a gypsy without having a coin ready as tag to the interview. It would be entirely against good manners to omit it. In their mixture of independence of bearing and freedom in conversation, with readiness to accept a gift, they are very like Irish folk, who in this, as in so many characteristics, are curiously unlike their Saxon co-mates.

This Irish readiness to accept a gift, is not mean or greedy. You, with whom they have entered into friendly human intercourse, have evidently much more money than they; and it is but natural, and for the pleasure of both parties, that there should be some overflow from the *plenum* to the *vacuum*. They accept it freely and avowedly as a gift, and with a well-implied understanding that in the case of contact with an emptier than themselves, they are in turn ready to play donor. And so they are. If you give nothing, no insult follows; at most, if expectation rose high, there may be some cunning little touch of satire. If they have done you some actual service, they are by no means anxious to be paid for it, in the hard shape of an equivalent. They wish the transaction to be gift for gift, and are usually quite willing that you should be the obliged party if you prefer it. This is entirely a distinct feeling from the universal English love of a fee, 'a tip,' which so disagreeably astonishes American visitors to the old country. The Saxon by no means looks for a pure gift in any case. That, to his habit of mind, would mean beggary. But he thinks 'nothing for nothing' an obviously just principle. 'If I do anything for you, what will you pay me?'—and if you withhold the pay, he growls and threatens.

Indisputable and priceless are the sturdy qualities of the

Saxon; those of the Kelt are tenderer and finer. To this day exists an astonishing incompatibility between them, who have lived together so long, and a deep-seated difficulty of mutual understanding. People easily misconceive and dislike the very virtues of those who are of temperament and habits unlike their own.

The Gypsies, for their part, try to pick up a penny or a shilling howsoever they can without much risk, and to secure such creature comforts as their shifting and shifty manner of life allows. Though now, perhaps, slowly merging into the general mass of the population, they still may be counted a strange little tribe in our midst, with a very curious wild flavour. Among the most usual places in this district for gypsy encampments are Norley Wood, and Shirley Holmes, near Lymington; The Nodes, near Hythe; Bartley Regis, in Ealing parish; Crow's Nest Bottom, near Bramshaw; Minstead-manor-bounds on the west side; Marbro' Deep, near Holmsley. Several large parties were seen encamped, during the icy weather of a recent cold January.

The Foresters of the humbler class are on familiar terms with the 'Gyps,' or 'Gypos,' but can tell you little about them, having (like perhaps most poor people) but little observation or curiosity outside the circle of their immediate interests, still less reflection or speculation; and when they do receive impressions, lacking words to convey them.

The Foresters are not distinguished for mental gifts or for excellence of manners; and indeed the same might be said of the inhabitants of some of the adjacent towns, who now and again recall to the stranger's mind that alliterative epithet which is sometimes applied to Hampshire people. Would it be fanciful, or a too hasty induction from limited experience, to set down the Wilts and Dorset folk as gentler and more kindly? Though it is a good while since Cerdic landed on its coast, Hants (the fair Isle of Wight included)

is still very Saxon in manners and temperament; and the
word Saxon has in these respects carried one consistent
reputation from the earliest times; till that absurd modern
phrase, ' the Anglo-Saxon race,' came into fashion and
glory in newspapers and stump-oratory. The Angles and
the Saxons were much of a muchness; and what of
the Scandinavians, and the Normans, and the Britons
themselves ?

The dialect of the Forest and its vicinity is ungainly in
sound, harsh and drawling, with no tone in it, and spoken
mainly with the teeth shut :—' Hev'ee zeen t' fox, Jurge?
they'se lost he, I bet!'—' Na-a-a! I zeed 'en goo into vuzz
at t' carner o' thic 'ood.'—' Big 'un?'—' Ya-a-as!'—
' Where bist gwine now then?' — ' Whoam.' — 'Thee's
betterr come with I.' The ' r ' has not a burr, but a thin,
slurring sound. They have a good many words not usual in
book English, and some of them expressive; for example—
' flisky,' small, like small rain; ' louster,' noise, confusion;
' slummakin,' slouchy, careless, untidy; ' wivvery,' giddy,
as when the head swims; ' mokins ' are coarse gaiters;
' humwater' is a cordial with mint in it. They call the
bog-myrtle or sweet-gale the 'gold-withy,' and the white-
beam ' hoar-withy.' The word ' idle ' always means light-
minded, careless, flippant, which is traceable to the Anglo-
Saxon meaning.

When Mr. Gilpin (of the ' Forest Scenery,' etc.) came to
this locality in 1777, as vicar of Boldre parish, including a
large slice of the southern part of the Forest, he found the
people rude and semi-savage, a wild flock, poachers,
smugglers, despisers of laws and morals; and during his
stay among them of twenty-seven years he faithfully sought
to improve them, not without effect. William Gilpin, a
lineal descendant of Bernard Gilpin, called ' The Apostle of
the North,' was born in 1724, at Scaleby Castle, near

Carlisle, the house of his grandfather, 'a counsellor of note,'[1] whose eldest son, being a bad manager, ran into debt, and was at last obliged to sell the family place. The second son, John Bernard, entered the army, and when a captain of foot got command of a company of Invalids at Carlisle, where he settled. He had married at· the age of twenty, his wife being eighteen, and they 'lived together in conjugal felicity fifty years,' says the tombstone at Carlisle. Their son William entered Queen's College, Oxford, January, 1740 (N.S.); B.A., 1744; ordained 1746, and made curate of Irthington; M.A., 1748. In 1752, age twenty-nine, he became principal assistant at the school of the Rev. Daniel Sanxay, Cheam, Surrey, who in a year retired in Gilpin's favour. He now married. His own account, dated thirty years later, is simple and pleasing :—

'When my uncle was in possession of Scaleby Castle, before his affairs went wrong, he took a little niece, a fatherless child, to bring up. He had no children of his own, and his wife and he considered her as such, nor were any father or mother fonder of any of their own children than they were of her. She used often to be at Carlisle to play with her cousins, and her cousins were as often at Scaleby to play with her. She was a pretty little girl; and everybody said she was a very good little girl. In short, one of her cousins, though only a schoolboy, took a particular fancy to her. He soon after made his father and mother his confidants; and they were far from discouraging him. They probably thought (as I do now) that early attachments, though not favourable to ambition and worldly schemes, are far from being unfavourable to virtue; and my father, good man (which alone would endear his memory to me), painted her picture and sent it me to Oxford; though the poor girl herself was then ignorant of the occasion. In process of time, however, the plot began to open. The two cousins became acquainted with each other's sentiments; and though (as neither of them had anything to depend on but themselves) it was several years before the drama was concluded by a marriage, yet at length this step was thought prudent by all their friends; and they have now (1791) lived together about thirty years, without having been almost as many days separated. No marriage could be more happy. All their schemes succeeded; and they are now, in

[1] From letter of Rev. W. G., quoted by Rev. Richard Warner in *Literary Recollections*, London, 1830, vol. i., p. 316, etc.

their old age, in affluent circumstances, and have six fine grandchildren
to bear their name after them. They have often said to each other, they
never knew what could be called an affliction : and only have to hope
that God will be pleased to work with them by felicity, as He often does
with others by calamity.'[1]

In his school he seems to have been a sort of minor
Arnold ; took great pains with the morals and religion of
his pupils, had a constitutional code, and in certain cases
tried a culprit by a jury of his fellows, ' bound by honour.'
' I never knew,' he says, ' an improper verdict given.'
Two daughters were born to him, who died young, and two
sons, of whom the elder went to America, married and grew
rich, settling at Philadelphia. The second son, another
William, went into the Church, and succeeded his father as
master of Cheam School in 1777. The father, fifty-four
years old by this time, had kept the school for twenty-five
years, and now retired with about 10,000*l.* saved. His
many excellent qualities, both as man and teacher, made
many of his old pupils friends of his for life, and one of
these, William Mitford, Esq., now presented him to the
vicarage of Boldre. He had thus, altogether, an income
of perhaps 700*l.* a year. In this large parish, fifteen to
eighteen miles in circuit, Mr. Gilpin went about actively,
visiting the poor cottagers and helping them as well as he
knew how. As a preacher, he had an impressive earnestness and simplicity ; and it is related that he once com-
pelled a certain rich married farmer to give up a mistress
whom he kept, to the general scandal, and, moreover, to
appear in church led in by the two churchwardens, and to
repeat after the curate a paper of confession and contrition,
after which the vicar preached a grave, appropriate sermon.
Mr. Gilpin was large built and rather corpulent, with a
good voice and dignified presence, fit for a head master, fit
for a vicar. His face, somewhat fat, with a roundish bald

[1] Same authority.

head (I have seen his likeness in crayons, hanging in Wal-
hampton Park, a house which he often frequented), chiefly
expresses a grave and cheerful benevolence, spiced with
some hint of mental alacrity.

Before coming to Boldre he had published a book, 'Lives
of the Reformers,' including an account of his ancestor
Bernard. After being released from the school, he indulged
his love of scenery and sketching by making frequent tours,
generally, or perhaps always, accompanied by his wife, in
some of the most beautiful parts of England and Scotland,
a very uncommon kind of amusement in those days; and
produced in succession the following publications, which
soon gave him a considerable reputation, and are still sought
after and valued: 'On Picturesque Beauty' [Scottish High-
lands]; Ditto [English Lake District]; 'Forest Scenery;'
'Essays on Picturesque Beauty;' 'Picturesque Travels and
the Art of Sketching Landscape;' 'On Prints;' 'The
Wye;' 'Picturesque Remarks on the West of England;'
all embellished with aquatinta engravings after the author's
drawings. He also published 'Sermons;' 'An Exposition
of the New Testament;' 'Moral Contrasts;' 'Amusements
of Clergymen;' 'Life of John Trueman and Richard Atkins,
for the use of Servants' Halls, Farmhouses, and Cottages;'
and an 'Account of William Baker,' one of his humble
parishioners. He was very careful and deliberate in the
production of most of his books, keeping them in MS.
beyond the Horatian period, and meanwhile submitting
them to private critics, and often retouching.

His life at home was simple, pure, and economical; he
seldom dined out. 'I never was fond,' he says,[1] 'of eating and drinking; but, from habit, I have now taken a
thorough dislike to them both, and never dine pleasantly
but on my own bit of mutton, and a draught of small beer
after it (for I never drink wine), and so the job is over.'

[1] Letter of his, quoted by Warner, i. 359.

His delight was to stroll after breakfast into the grove behind his vicarage, note-book in hand; to improve his little grounds and garden; to visit in turn his parishioners, rich and poor, especially the latter (not forgetting their bodily wants); to address kind words of greeting, inquiry, admonition, or encouragement to every one he met in his walks; to come home to his bit of mutton, his dear good wife and family, and his pen and ink drawings in the evening. His style of art was not the exact and realistic, but the bold and generalising — verging often on what Mr. Ruskin calls the Blottesque; his illustrations of the Highland and other scenery only possessed—and according to his convictions were right, inasmuch as they only possessed —a kind of broad and sweeping resemblance to real scenes; and his very numerous later drawings were nearly all fancy sketches, exemplifying the true rules of 'picturesque beauty,' as he conceived them. These sketches — made with a reed pen and a brownish 'iron-water' ink, and afterwards 'toned' with a yellow wash—he used to give away freely to his friends, until it came into his mind that he might in this way make some money for the benefit of his poorer parishioners. He had already, out of the profits of his books, built and opened a school at Boldre for the children of day labourers—twenty boys to be taught reading, writing, and ciphering; twenty girls, reading, sewing, and spinning. To this school he wished to leave a permanent endowment, and also an aid to the school at Brockenhurst, and sold for these ends a collection of his drawings, received 1,200*l.* for them, and placed it in the Three per Cents. The sum being still insufficient to carry out all his intentions, he went to work again with his reed-pen, at the age of seventy-eight, and in two years produced a large number of drawings. These, 'the last effort of my eyes,' were sold by auction at Christie's, and produced no less than 1,625*l.* The schools were endowed accordingly, and the Boldre children, in addition to being taught free of all charge, receive yearly—the boys a jacket, pair of breeches, and a green vest; the girls a green frock and black petticoat. The school-house, shadowed by a pair of tall lindens, stands on the road-side, between the church and the vicarage, and the school, locally called 'The Green School,' is still alive, but not flourishing. The true causes of this unhealthy condition are not easy to get at, but certainly the lamp which old Mr. Gilpin left trimmed, with a careful provision for keeping it alight, now burns but languidly.[1] *Make his will* as he may, the possibility of a man's extending his power, according to any formal plan, into future generations, is always very problematic.

There are three notable trees, now flourishing in Boldre parish, which are connected with this good old vicar's memory. You may see them in the course of a moderate walk. About a mile from Lymington, well sheltered among soft woody slopes, stands the comfortable vicarage of gray and red bricks, with trim flowery lawn guarded by Scotch firs, and slanting little meadow, beyond which rises the grovy hill in whose wood-walks Mr. Gilpin used to stray. Near the south-west corner of the house stands conspicuous an unusually fine Occidental Plane-tree, tall, shapely, healthy, which the vicar used to admire more than seventy years ago, and has celebrated in the 'Forest Scenery.' This Plane was the vicar's favourite *home-tree*.

In his walks, he was fond of visiting a Yew, some two miles distant,—

'A tree,' he says, "of peculiar beauty. . . . It stands not far from the banks of Lymington River, on the left bank as you look towards the sea, between Roydon Farm and Boldre Church. It occupies a small knoll, surrounded with other trees, some of which are yews, but of inferior beauty. A little stream washes the base of the knoll, and winding

[1] Measures are now (December, 1872) being taken to revive it.

round, forms it into a peninsula. If any one should have
curiosity to visit it from this description, and by the help of
these landmarks, I doubt not but he may find it at any time
within the space of these two or three centuries in great
perfection, if it suffer no external injury.'[1]

There it stands at this day; now, in winter-time, sombrely
conspicuous as you approach it among the naked gray
boughs of the oak-coppice.

The third tree connected with Mr. Gilpin's memory is a
Maple. 'One of the largest maples I have seen,' he wrote,
'stands in the churchyard of Boldre, in the New Forest.'[2]
This churchyard is beautifully situated on a hill about half-
way between Brockenhurst and Lymington, and so thickly
surrounded by large elms that the square embattled church
tower is not visible in the summer landscape, and scarcely
in the winter. But *from* the churchyard you have glimpses
through leafy screens, or thinner network of bough and twig,
of the wide stretching woodland in which it stands. The
church, the oldest part (they say) Saxon, another part thirteenth century, patchwork as it now is, retains on the whole
a quaint and pleasant rusticity. A year ago it still owned
an ancient window, but that has now been *gutted !*—filled
up with clean handsome new stone (och hone!), and the
gayest of bright London glass (alas!). There is something
that deserves philosophical investigation in the attitude of
John Bull's mind to his national relics of antiquity. He
holds hard to the customary and familiar, and is thus inclined—not æsthetically or sentimentally, but in a cat-like
manner as it were—to keep old things as they are; but he
has also a passion for trimness and tidiness, a practicality of
mind that is vexed by any appearance (however beautiful
or in itself harmless) which is at all connected with notions
of disrepair, neglect, poverty; and against this love of com-

[1] *Forest Scenery*, vol. i., p. 95.
[2] Ibid. vol. i., p. 57.

fortable trimness, no matter how ugly, the feeling of cat-like conservatism counts for nothing almost, if they come into competition—is daffed aside (if any one appeals to it) as a whim and folly. It cannot be too often repeated, until it is generally felt and acknowledged, that all the significant public relics and traces of the past, great and little, are *sacred things*, not ours to destroy (whether by demolition or ' restoration '), but ours to preserve for those who now walk the earth, and for those who are to come after us. Absolute, inevitable necessity can alone justify our laying one violating finger upon any such connecting link in the life of a nation and of mankind. But to return to our churchyard Maple. Maples in England are seldom more than bushes; this is a good-sized tree, about six or seven feet round, and something like a dwarfish old oak. Under its branches is the plain square-cornered tomb of William Gilpin and his wife, with this inscription :—

' In a quiet mansion beneath this stone, secure from the afflictions, and still more dangerous enjoyments of life, lye the remains of WILLIAM GILPIN, sometime vicar of this parish, together with the remains of MARGARET, his wife. After living above fifty years in happy union, they hope to be raised in God's good time, through the atonement of a blessed Redeemer for their repented transgressions, to a state of joyful immortality ; there it will be a new joy to meet several of their good neighbours who lye scattered in these sacred precincts around them. He died April 5th, 1804, at the age of 80. She died April 14th, 1807, at the age of 82.'

His last illness was very short, and his healthy, virtuous, and happy life closed in peace. It is wholesome and pleasant to reflect on such lives, of which there are always a great many in the world, most of them undistinguished by anything publicly memorable. Mr. Gilpin, in one of his letters, speaking of a visit which he received from his son from America, says : ' His chief employment while he was here, was transcribing a family record, which I drew up some time ago, of my great grandfather, my grandfather, and father, who were all very valuable men ; and I en-

couraged him in it for the sake of William, Bernard and
Edwin, whom it may hereafter have a tendency to excite to
honourable deeds. Indeed I have often thought such little
records might be very useful in families, whether the
subjects of them were good or bad. A lighthouse may serve
equally the purpose of leading you into a haven, or deterring
you from a rock. I have the pleasure, however, to reflect
that my three ancestors (beyond whom I can obtain no
family anecdotes) were all beacons of the former kind.'

One can fancy Mr. Gilpin going benevolently about (his
mind and note-book at the same time busied a good deal
with his next work on ' Picturesque Beauty '), now stopping
a farmer or a schoolchild with friendly smile and word, now
carrying good advice and coin of the realm into some poor
cottage, distributing orders for coals and blankets in the
winter, consoling the sick, admonishing the lawless, etc., etc.
—he also (no way disgracing his ancestors) a ' valuable '
man and most kindly. Yet, with all his benevolent and
pious activity, it may perhaps be doubted whether our good
friend had much real insight into human character, or much
real intercourse of mind (rare between those of different
grades) with his humbler parishioners. There is not seldom
found an amiable blindness in such men as he—amiable,
perhaps, yet not commendable ; for that course which is
sure of applause as ' practical benevolence ' may often (from
defect of clear perceptions, and consequent sound conclu-
sions) do injustice, and on the whole be harmful to society.

Some twenty paces westward from the vicar's tomb (I
have paid it many a visit) stands a headstone with the
following inscription—the vicar's composition : ' Here rests
from his Labour WILLIAM BAKER, whose Industry and
Frugality, whose Honesty and Piety, were long an Example
to this Parish. He was born in 1710, and died in 1791.'
This is the Baker of whom Mr. Gilpin also published an
' account,' for the wider dissemination of that old peasant's

good example; but Mr. Warner, the admiring friend and sometime curate of Mr. Gilpin, conscientiously makes the following mortifying disclosure :[1]—

'William Baker was an old rustic, resident in a wild part of the parish of Boldre. In one of his walks Mr. Gilpin had lighted upon his cottage. On entering it he found its inhabitant, an aged, but stout and athletic man, eating his humble dinner. All within was neat and clean, and something indicative of strong sense and a cheerful mind appeared in the countenance of the old peasant. In conversation he proved himself well versed in the Bible; full of maxims of prudence and economy; and apparently of the most open, blunt, and independent character. Highly interested by his visit, Mr. Gilpin frequently repeated it; and from the conversations which passed during this intercourse, he drew up that beautiful account which he published in the work above-mentioned. The misapprehension of Baker's real character was not done away till some time after the death of the old man; and, considering it as exemplary at the time of his decease, Mr. Gilpin wrote a short epitaph, and had it engraven on Baker's tombstone, as a salutary monition to the parishioners of Boldre [sly, stolid rustics with thoughts of their own!], who were in the same humble class of life with the deceased. At length, however, he was undeceived; and had the sorrow rather than the mortification to find that Baker had been, through life, a worthless and flagitious character; that age, instead of curing, had only altered the nature of his vices; and that by all, except the pastor, he had ever been known and despised as a consummate rogue, an oppressive extortioner, and a base hypocrite.'

That headstone must have weighed more or less on Mr. Gilpin's mind after the discovery. Could he—ought he to have added a postscript? *Requiescas*, if thou canst, old William Baker! thy pastor did not, I suspect, mean to include *thee* in that friendly hope on his tombstone of meeting 'several' of his good neighbours who lie near him. Living and dead thou hast cheated the good vicar; and by means of this graven testimony dost perennially cheat the churchyard moralizer. I have no doubt that Mr. Warner is substantially accurate in the matter, but I should like to hear some more particulars of this cunning old William. In Boldre Church is preached every 18th of March, 'the

[1] *Literary Recollections*, vol i., p. 343.

Wild-beast Sermon,' founded many years ago to commemo-
rate 'for ever' the escape of a Mr. Worsley from the jaws
of a lion in Africa.   In Boldre Church Robert Southey
married for his second wife Miss Caroline Bowles, of
Lymington—a literary marriage.   He was then a worn-out
man.   Over-industry in literary labour is apt to tell dismally
both on the man and on his work.   How much too much
Southey read and wrote!   How sure he was of literary
immortality!   How faded already are his name and influence!   Yet one is grateful to him for 'Kehama' and
'Thalaba,' not as poetry but as wild stories—

> Sail on, sail on, said Thalaba,
> Sail on, in the name of Allah!

This church stands near the middle point of the southern
boundary of the Forest.   Northward for fifteen miles or so,
stretch the old woods, the moorlands, the new plantations,
with a few farms and domains interspersed—some 70,000
acres in all, producing to the Crown a profit of about
10,000*l.* a year.   It is a free and pleasant space to ramble
in, although (to be accurate) the New Forest is without any
very remarkable beauties.   There are no romantic hills or
glens, only two or three brooks, and those not of the best,
no ponds, no rocks (a great want).

Near the north-eastern corner of the district lies Romsey,
with its massive Norman church and adjacent park of
Broadlands, where Lord Palmerston was lately master;
near the south-eastern corner is the old-new town of Southampton (water-gate to Egypt and India), its suburban
houses visible from some points, in front of the chalk downs
that overlook Winchester.   Beaulieu Heath stretches south,
to ruined Beaulieu Abbey, of John's and Henry III.'s
time, its prior's house now the Duke of Buccleuch's.   Elsewhere, looking northward, one may see the slender far-off
signal of Sarum, a stone flower, graceful, to use Emerson's
image, as the great-mullein stalk—the highest spire in

England. Ringwood is on the western boundary, and the beautiful pastoral vale of the river Avon running down to Christchurch and its venerable priory church. I was in that church one evening, near Christmas-time, and stood listening in its huge dusky nave while the singers practised their anthem in the dim-lit organ-loft. Beside me glimmered a white marble cenotaph, like a *Pietà*, a woman bending over a dead youth. There was not light to read the inscription, but I knew it well enough, and that it commemorated a certain poet drowned in the Bay of Spezia : the inscription partly in his own words—

> He has outsoar'd the shadow of our night,
> Envy and calumny, and hate and pain ;
> And that unrest which men miscall delight,
> Can touch him not and torture not again.

The house of his son, the Baronet, is not far off; and in Bournemouth churchyard is the grave of Sir Percy's grandfather, William Godwin, whose dust came hither from St. Pancras churchyard by strange adventure, and now lies quiet amid a crowd of more orthodox tombstones.

Lyndhurst is the Capital of the Forest, and whoever shall chance to be invited to one of those country houses that pleasantly dot the neighbourhood of Lyndhurst, most urbanely rural of villages, let him count it good luck.

Over and above the delights of a cultivated and friendly society, there is plenty to interest the sportsman, the naturalist, or the general rambler and inquisitive person. In ' Rufus's Hall,' at the Queen's House (built in the reign of James or Charles), he may attend a forest court, and hear the trial of some poacher or woodstealer, no longer liable to lose life or eyes ; and may, perhaps, learn a new meaning to him of the word *mote*, namely, stump or stool of a felled tree. An easy walk will carry him to the beechen shade of Mark Ash, or the mossy lawns and winding paths of Whitley Wood, or to the vale which tradition points out as

the scene of the Red King's death. From certain parts of
the higher ground he may look southward over seven or
eight successive ridges of woodland to the wavy soft blue
hills of the Isle of Wight.   He may gather in their seasons
many a fern and flower—sundew, and great trefoil, and deep
blue gentian, on the marsh; 'tutsan,' a St. John's wort, on
open ground, whose berries, the people say, are coloured
with Danes' blood; the lung-wort or 'snake-flower,' rose-
blossomed wild-balm, and among the bracken of Knightwood
the tall gladiolus; may hear the tap of the woodpecker, the
rustle of the harmless snake, perhaps the warning hiss of
the viper; the fern-owl at dusk 'whirring in the copse;' the
hoo! hoo! of the brown owls somewhere amid the branchy
wilderness; and (suppose it spring) the songs of the rival
nightingales with their deep trills, their *tio-tio-tio-tix*, and
their 'one low piping sound more sweet than all.'   He may
visit the heronry on Vinney Ridge, and watch the wide-
winged parents floating round the tree-tops as they feed
their young with eels carried from the mudflats of the
Solent; may with good luck see the honey-buzzard, the
crossbill, the kingfisher, in their haunts, and Epops himself, once King of the Birds.   Or, some long summer afternoon, and far into the weird twilight—the moon perchance
beginning to rise—he may pursue through many a glade and
vista the shadowy vision of a beauty imagined but never
wholly realised on earth.

> Beautiful, beautiful Queen of the Forest,
>   How art thou hidden so wondrous deep?
> Bird never sung there, fay never morriced,
>   All the trees are asleep.
>
> .   .   .   .
>
> Now her flitting fading gleam
>   Haunts the woodlands wide and lonely;
> Now a half-remember'd dream,
>   For his comrade only.
> He shall stray the livelong day
> Through the forest, far away.

RAMBLE THE SECOND.

AT WINCHESTER.

St. Giles's Hill—College—Cathedral—Destruction of Old Things—St. Swithin—Keats—Rev. Thomas Warton—Culture.

FROM St. Giles's Hill one looks down on the famous old city. Its Cathedral among lofty trees, Wykeham's College with the lads at cricket, the water-meadows leading to St. Cross, the swelling green downs with one grove, a 'peculiar coronet,' on St. Catherine's Hill, show fair in the May sunlight. Methinks a flagstaff would stand well at one angle of the low cathedral tower. Brisk and clear runs the shallow river below, by small gray and red houses and their gardens, mill-sluices, the quaint little flint-built church of St. Peter's Chesil, and a vine-clad remnant of the city wall.

I pass under the college archway and courts gray with time, green with new foliage, and see, with a natural sigh, the fine lads strolling careless in cap and gown. But, surely, regrets for the past, if natural, are vain—if vain, not to be dwelt on ; if dwelt on, foolish. Are these boys all happy, too? Many a 'fag' (the fagging is severe, and often cruel) is longing for manhood and freedom. Even in play hours he must submit to the will and caprice of an oldster. 'Good for him on the whole—prepares him for the battle of life.' Perhaps so ; but perhaps (along with 'cram,' chapel, and other things) it prepares him to *make* life a battle—a scene of fierce unscrupulous rivalry, instead of peaceful effort and mutual help. Life brings its combats, its battles, to be well fought out when each crisis comes; but it ought not to *be* a battle. The laws of war are not the laws of life.

The book-shop outside the gate is full of college boys; at the next-door pastry-cook's the younger ones swarm like bees. Up those steps, the dining-hall still sets its tables with the old-world square wooden trencher, but also now-a-days with knife and fork; and tea flows morn and even, where beer in their father's time was the only lawful liquor. A famous novelist of our day (who deals much in cathedrals) said to me, 'We had no tea or coffee'—he was a Wykhamist—'but beer, as much as you liked—beer at breakfast, beer at dinner, beer at supper, beer under your bed.' Beer sounds barbarous for boys; but clean home-brewed is a different thing from the tavern-keeper's mixtures. Our novelist is a burly man, and so was Cobbett, who detested 'slops.'

Some of the big lads are at cricket, and with a will. Terribly swift the athletic bowler swings in his heavy ball overhand; his well-greaved opponent sends it whizzing off the bat. The sport is now made a serious business. It takes money to rig out a cricketer (amusements, like most other things, tend in England to become more and more costly); he goes forth like Trojan or Achaian warrior, emulates 'professionals' in his style of play, and in public matches calls in their aid—these professional gentlemen, by the bye, being much akin to horse-jockeys and pugilists. To-day in our railway carriage was a gentleman summoned by telegraph to his son at this school; a cricket-ball had broken the boy's nose, and his father meant to take him to a London doctor by the evening train. To many, perhaps to most of our boys cricket and boat-racing are the serious parts of school life.

Full-clothed in freshest verdure tremble the lofty lindens of the Close; firm as a rock stands the gray fortress-like

Cathedral, its oldest stonework undecayed as though built yesterday. A side-wicket admits to the vast interior, with massy pillars, and roof high-embowed over the coffins of old kings: solemn and monumental the weighty transept arches and plain thick pillars of Norman work. Noble, too, are these clustered columns of the nave; yet I wish, on the whole, that Bishop William and others had withheld their hands from *perpendicularity.* The nave windows are to me of ugly form, the tracery of the great west window stands an offence, which its fine glass hardly condones. And this glass is but a patchwork. Upon Cheriton Down, one March day, of 1644, the Roundheads smote the Cavaliers, and, leaving many brave men dead and dying on the hill, came grimly down into Winchester, and smashed the Cathedral windows and monuments. The gathered bits of glass, *disjecta membra* of saints, kings, queens, bishops, warriors, a fragment of a motto, a corner of a device, broken as they are, make splendid this tall, greenish-bluish west window.

The outside of a great old cathedral, seen from different points of view, with various relations of parts and various groupings with surrounding objects and the landscape, I always find both impressive and entertaining, the interior nearly always disappointing. English cathedrals particularly, differing as they do in details, are much alike in the general interior effect, and that effect is monotonous. In magnificence of space, one's imagination is never fulfilled; and in that other kind of impressiveness which we desire of a great building, *mystery,* they are usually wanting. The baldness of the empty nave, after the first glance, is chilling and disheartening; the choir, on the other hand, has a petty and parochial look. Often the finest thing is some oblique glimpse across the angle of a transept. Considering the money, time, earnestness, and architectural skill employed in raising so many huge perennial structures, one wishes there had been more variety of plan, more invention.

I picture to myself, for one example (in the architecture of dreams), a church of long *low* arcades, converging to a great central space of loftiness almost immeasurable to the eye. In architecture, methinks, *the delight of smallness* in porches, pillars, doors, windows, stairs, arches, etc., is not enough considered. I found at Venice (and Mr. Ruskin, I remember, approved the observation), in the Doge's Palace, in St. Mark's itself, and throughout the city, the *delight of smallness* often emphasised.

But whatever we may desire, it were unreasonable to look for much originality in the plan of this or that building among many, all the produce of one spirit, that of Papal Christianity, which of all the virtues cultivated conformity, submission, imitation, as the most necessary, or rather as the groundwork of the rest, and which in every plan (architectural or other) started with certain data—inevitable fixed points. One should rather wonder, perhaps, to find in Papal architecture, so much variety. The art of painting has fared much worse; witness those leagues of Madonnas, Holy Families, and great and little saints, that weary our soul in the galleries.

Passing strange are these great Papal temples, so alien to modern thought, so unfit for Protestant worship, maintained under such singular conditions—beautiful anachronisms, venerably incongruous with the life around them, standing whole and massive, with gray tower and shapely pinnacle, among the landscapes of England.

The western porches of the Cathedral have been *done-up*, and look as pretty as a wedding-cake; the college chapel has been done-up; old St. Cross is partly done-up—well or ill I say not, but done-up they are; and whoever likes clean white stone-work, like a door-step on Sunday morning, and fresh paint, and the brightest coloured glass that an eminent London firm can manufacture, and no trace left that can be obliterated of Time's finger, in tint or line, must be pleased with what he finds going on in nearly every old place in England.

Yet what boots grieving? The use and significance of a structure gone, how should the thing escape ruin of one kind or another? The piety and humanity that founded St. Cross—church, almshouses, dole of food to the way-farer—sad ghosts of these haunt their ancient cloister. The realities have fled away, to find (we will hope so) new and fitter mansions. Here is no visible ruin as yet, for this endowment remains a legal and arithmetical fact, with some significance to the thirteen old men, much to the wealthy nobleman, their 'master.' Of antique faith and bounty, many costly relics crowd this land—structures made for perpetual homes of living worship and beneficence, and secondarily as hints to men unborn to remember now and again their brother's name, the founder, with a little prayer breathed to heaven; but now more like tombs of old good intentions and pious plans, fallen into neglect and well-nigh forgetfulness, along with the men in whose minds they were once warm and potent. Nor even as tombs (under costly guardianship) can they escape disfigurement—preserve the venerableness and beauty of aspect so precious in many ways, and so touching.

When everything old has been thoroughly destroyed or 'restored' (that is, defaced), what a pretty world it will be!

There are few old-looking towns left now in England; some years hence there will be fewer, or none; though some old houses, perhaps even a few old back streets may linger. The busy builder and contractor, with his bricken Snug Street, and stuccoed Victoria Terrace, his elegant modern residences in the outskirts, and splendid business frontages in the High Street, is taking good care of this, in co-opera-tion with the pullers-down and doers-up (corporate and individual) of every old public edifice. *Villages* retain and will retain more of the crust of antiquity, where the modern spirit does not think it worth while to set up its plate-glass and stucco, where gain and display, both in their ugliest forms, do not rule everything.

Yet even the villages can't always escape, nor the village churches. I know two village churches in Hampshire near one another, each of which has lately been disfigured by the substitution of an ugly modern window for a beautiful ancient one. These new windows, filled with gaudiest glass, are both put up in memory of one deceased lady, whose wealthy husband, in consultation of course with the legal guardians of those edifices, could discover no better manner of displaying at once the strength of his grief and of his purse, than by the destruction of two delightful bits of architectural skill, tenderly tinted by the slow hand of time, hallowed by the associations of centuries, linking the living to their fathers and predecessors ; and the setting up in permanence of two pieces of vulgar and pretentious ugliness. Supposing these latter windows perfection in their kind, it were monstrous to substitute them for the antique. I could not find that anybody, of any class, was pleased or satisfied with the alteration. Vanity and purse-pride, ignorance and bad taste, met by apathetic complaisance in those who might have known better, and egged on, doubtless, by the mercantile cunning of the tradesman who profited by the affair— these were the motives, and here is the result. I speak of this, and sharply, with some hope of inducing those who have influence and right judgment, not to forego, in similar cases, their duty to themselves and their neighbours; and to the world, present and future. [1]

By an archway, where the little church of St. Lawrence lurks behind the houses, we pass into the High Street of the White City (taking the old British name to have been *Caer*

---

[1] Some years after this was published arose the Society for the Preservation of Ancient Buildings, owing its birth and continued existence mainly to the energy of Mr. William Morris.

Gwent), and see its Gothic market-cross in a corner, beside
the shop of a serious bookseller who is always to be found in
ecclesiastical precincts.

St. Swithin, the weather-famous, besides his share of
patronage in the Cathedral, has a little parish-church of his
own, built by King John over the postern of St. Michael.
Swithin, Bishop of Winchester, dying *circa* 865, his body (as
the story goes) was buried at his own request, out of humility
perhaps, not in the Cathedral as usual with bishops, but in
the churchyard, where the drops of rain might wet his grave;
afterwards, when he was canonised, the monks resolved to
move his bones into the Cathedral, and the 15th of July was
fixed upon for the ceremony; but on that day, and for forty
days in succession, it rained so violently that the plan was
given up as displeasing to the saint, and they built, instead,
a chapel at his grave, where many miracles were wrought.
Such the tradition, with its postscript that, ever since, the
weather on St. Swithin's Day, be it wet or dry, will hold for
thirty-nine days following.

Many people, by the bye, forget certain effects of the
great change in the English calendar made in 1752 by cutting out eleven whole days, in acceptance of the 'New
Style,' introduced by authority of Pope Gregory XIII. in
1582, and adopted by all Catholic nations; but, though it
had not merely the Pope but the sun on its side, resisted till
1752 by Protestant England, as it still is by Russia. That
day of the year which we now call 26th July is that which
belonged to St. Swithin by the old way of reckoning, and to
which reference must be made if we go about to inquire, is
there any meteorological foundation for this adage? So also
that point in the earth's annual voyage which about a
century ago was called Christmas Day in England, is now
called the 5th of January. Instead of being but four days
from the shortest day, the festival was fifteen, falling thus at
a time of year when the weather is on an average colder:

'As the day lengthens, the cold strengthens.' We keep the traditions of a snowy Christmas, which is the seldomer realised because we have changed our almanac. Mayday, again, Milton's and Herrick's Mayday, is towards the middle of the month, not at its beginning. How needful it is to be on one's guard against WORDS—continually tending to slip away from facts and assume power and authority as *in their own right.*

The Irish (a people of most conservative temper in many things) still have a high respect for certain holy days as reckoned by the Old Style — 'Old Christmas,' etc. An Irish peasant hardly ever dates by months and days in his talk, but by 'set times,' saying, So long before or after Christmas, Candlemas, Patrick's Day, Corpus Christi, Lammas, Michaelmas, 'Holiday' (All Hallows) and so on; and he keeps reckoning of some, if not all, by the Old Style as well as, perforce, the New.

Looking down from this old West Gate a-top of the High Street, 'tis pleasant to see at the street's end a green hill rising bold and steep. Many a cheerful country walk stretches out from this ancient city; through the meadows, with clear streams full of gliding fish and waving weeds, across little bridges, by willows and mills; over breezy chalk-downs, wide-viewing, with farms and hamlets in their vales; by shady roads and field-paths through the corn and clover. Here wandered once on a time, solitary and somewhat sad, a certain young poet—now for ever young. In these fields, one Sunday, among the corn-stacks and orchards, he felt and sung the rich sadness of autumn. 'How beautiful the season is now,' he wrote to his friend Reynolds, 22nd September, 1819; 'How fine the air—a temperate sharpness about it. Really, without joking, chaste weather, —Dian skies. I never liked stubble-fields so much as now— ay, better than the chilly green of the Spring. Somehow a stubble-field looks warm in the same way that some pictures look warm. This struck me so much in my Sunday's walk that I composed upon it.'

> Seasons of mists and mellow fruitfulness ! . . . .
>
> Where are the songs of Spring ?   Ay, where are they ?
>   Think not of them, thou hast thy music too,
> While barrèd clouds bloom the soft-dying day,
>   And touch the stubble-plains with rosy hue.
> Then in a wailful choir the small gnats mourn
>   Among the river sallows, borne aloft
>   Or sinking as the light wind lives or dies ;
> And full-grown lambs loud bleat from hilly bourne ;
>   Hedge-crickets sing ; and now with treble soft
> The redbreast whistles from a garden-croft,
>   And gathering swallows twitter in the skies.

Young Keats's gaze that Sunday evening was upon the Winchester stubble-fields like a spiritual setting-sun, and left them lying enchanted in its fadeless light.

Thou couldst not on this earth, dear Poet, reach the autumn, nor the summer of thy life ; yet enough remains of thine ethereal musings to enrich the world and deserve our eternal love. One day, perhaps, I shall touch thy very hand, no more fevered with sickness and care.

How delightful are Keats's letters, carelessly scribbled off, simple, kindly, picturesque, with views of life and literature at once broad and subtle. No politics or gossip of the day, ' echoes of the clubs,' personal trivialities—merely the intimate chat of a poet, thinking of nature, humanity, and poetry. After all, it is permissible to believe, the poet draws the best lot from Fortune's urn. Whom could he envy ? Not alone is his delight in life the keenest, but his insight the most veracious. Yet, ah me ! how thin-skinned he is— how open to suffering—how sure to suffer, in a world such as this ? Is it partly the world's fault, for being such a world ? Was Keats, pensive amid the sheaves, a happier man than Hodge, who reaped them, and quaffed his ale-cup

at the harvest-home? 'Happier'—what is *happiness?*
Would any man deliberately give up a grain of his intellect
or sensibility to win a lower kind of happiness than he was
born capable of?—escape suffering by stupidity? Here, truly,
is a catechism of questions, and food for meditation. An interesting personality, John Keats : more of a poet than any-
one else we can think of : manly, tender, eternally young.
His fine spirit is with his lovers on Hampstead Heath, and
at the inn at foot of Box Hill, and in Devonshire Lanes, and
by the seaside at Shanklin, and in these Hampshire corn-
fields. His verse is an enchanted cup, yet beware lest it clog
and give headaches, and shun imitators who offer you word-
jugglery without feeling or thought as the quintessence
of poetry. This waxwork poetry will not die, for it never
was alive, but will come surely and speedily to the lumber-
room and dust-hole.

In these Wintonian fields roved another son of the Muses,
whose 'shade' (as he himself might have expressed it)
would no doubt disdain association with that of the author of
Endymion; I mean the Rev. Thomas Warton, Fellow of
Trinity College, Oxford, Professor of Poetry, and Poet
Laureate, which famous and prosperous man of letters came
often on a visit to his brother, the Rev. Dr. Joseph, master
of Winchester School, himself a bard of note.

> Where shall the muse, that on the sacred shell,
>   Of men in arms and arts renown'd,
> The solemn strain delights to swell ;
> Oh. where shall Clio choose a race
> Whom Fame with every laurel, every grace,
>   Like those of Albion's envied isle has crown'd ?

Hush, Reverend Shade !—yet for thy diligent annotation,
Tom, of Spenser and of Milton, pass not unkindly remembered. Strange, that along with intense study of these
masters thou couldst pursue thine own scrannel pipings
undismayed.

Probably it is rather fame than merit, in every department, that attracts nine in ten of even the *cognoscenti.*

But how comes an established fame ?—from the consistent
and accumulative judgment of a few in each generation, in
whom the divine light of intelligence burns clearest. Therefore the cultivated (who know what has been said) generally
take, on the whole, sound views of past work ; while as to
contemporary doings they are at sea, they also, and sailing
every way with the various winds of criticism.

One hears a good deal nowadays, in England, of 'culture'
and 'philistinism,'—a generation or two after the Germans
have tired of the subject. That culture is a good thing
hardly admits of contradiction, any more than that food and
sleep are good things. What our literary friends, A, B, and
C, mean exactly by the word is rather obscure. It is very
certain, at any rate, that English University Education and
culture are not, and never have been, interchangeable terms.
The *Cultured Philistine* (if that phrase may be coined) hath
ever been the favoured son of Alma Mater. Had John
Keats gone to Oxford, is it likely that he would have risen
to college honours, wealth, and power, like Thomas Warton ?
Methinks the Cultured Philistine is the very Goliath of his
people. Who is not daily afflicted by the tongue and pen
of the over-educated man, so fluent and well-worded, so
vague and unreal, so haughty and so hollow? He bullies
us, and, usually, we knock under for a time. But the roll
of literary heroes is not made up of names such as his.
Perhaps the time is coming when England (whether under
the term of 'culture' or some other term) will recognise a
a set of new ideas on education—a faith clear and high, and
in application as broad as English citizenship. The atmosphere of our generation is electrical with new thoughts,
and neither Oxford nor Canterbury, Westminster, Winchester, Manchester, nor Little Pedlington, can escape
the subtle and potent influence. Meanwhile in criticism

reigns something like chaos come again, modified by wire-pulling.

Upper Winchester, near the station, is becoming thoroughly villafied, as cockney-suburban in appearance as Haverstock Hill. But the entrance to a town from the railway-station is almost always ugly. How pleasantly Winchester must have greeted the coach-traveller, whirling up the green valley, seeing the great Cathedral grow larger through its elms, then turning a corner of the Close, a corner of the High Street, into the court-yard of the 'George.'

RAMBLE THE THIRD.

AT FARNHAM.

High Street—Bishop's Palace—'The Jolly Farmer'—Sketch of William
Cobbett's Life and Writings—His Grave—Crooksbury Hill.

WHEN you are in the long, flat, well-to-do and
modernish High Street of Farnham (Fern-ham?)
you see only the High Street, and there is not much to see
there; emerging at either end you are among hopgrounds—
myriads of brown poles in spring, multitudinous bowerage
in summer; and the hops here grow the highest and make
the most delicate beer, so the Farnham folk say, of any
hops in England.

Farnham High Street, running east and west along a
hollow, is built on either side of a main road: and this
never gives the proper *town effect*, for the road is thus the
chief thing, the street subordinate. The smallest town, or
even hamlet, wears a certain civic importance when it looks
like a goal or finish in itself, mistress of all the roads that
approach it, and older than they; not an accident or
afterthought, but an ancient centre and biding-place of
humanity, a heart or at least ganglion in the general circulation. A town with gates is most complete; but such
towns now (to fall into rhyme) are obsolete. Farnham is
but a road with houses.

At back of the north side of this High Street, hop-fields
slope upwards to a crowd of great trees stretching along the
summit of the hill. Those are the Bishop of Winchester's

45

elms; his palace-tower rises proudly amidst the circling ruins and the moat (now a hawthorn dell) of the old castle of Henry the Third's time; those are the Bishop's fallow-deer that troop in scores down the richly-shadowed park; and from his flower and fruit garden, made artfully atop the ancient keep, the bishop can comfortably overlook no small piece of his diocese in a bird's-eye view. To the left, over the wooded vale of Moor Park (Sir W. Temple's and Swift's), rises Cobbett's Crooksbury Hill, like a lion couchant, heading northwards, shagged with dark fir-trees: at our feet are the town and tall square church-tower of Farnham.

Down the hill, under those huge episcopal trees, across the High Street and bridge over the little river Wey, slow winding through poplars and willow-fringed meads, and so to a high bank bearing a grove on its shoulder, we come to where the road bends upwards left to the railway station. Facing the bridge stands a public-house, a little back from the road, built close at foot of the steep bank, and partly in a quarry scooped in its sandy front.

William Cobbett was born in this house in 1762. It was then the residence of his father, a small farmer, and does not seem to have been much altered in appearance. It is a decent-looking brown-roofed house, with two small windows on each side of the open door, and five on the second floor; the sign of 'The Jolly Farmer' set on a pole in front, and the thick grove shading it on each flank and rising high above the chimneys.

In my own home in a distant part of the kingdom, Cobbett's name chanced to mix with some of the earliest circumstances of my childhood. My father, who was then a kind of Tory, had in his younger days been a Radical reformer, and subscriber to the *Political Register*, of which paper a long row of volumes bound in red stood on a shelf in his bedroom. Always curious about books, I did not fail to turn these over, and to ask the meaning of the *Gridiron* picture, and who Cobbett was, though I could not make much of what I was told, or enjoy, until long afterwards, the variety, vigour, and amusing unreasonableness of that famous agitator.

Cobbett has left, dispersed through a hundred volumes or more, many pleasing touches of autobiography, which are now the best parts of his writing, and which might easily enough be combined into a distinct picture.

'With respect to my ancestors [he says], I shall go no further back than my grandfather, and for this plain reason—that I never heard talk of any prior to him. He was a day-labourer; and I have heard my father say that he worked for one farmer from the day of his marriage to that of his death, upwards of forty years. He died before I was born: but I have often slept beneath the same roof that sheltered him, and where his widow dwelt for many years after his death. It was a little thatched cottage, with a garden before the door. It had but two windows; a damson-tree shaded one, and a clump of filberts the other. Here I and my brothers went every Christmas and Whitsuntide to spend a week or two, and torment the poor old woman with our noise and dilapidations. She used to give us milk and bread for breakfast, an apple-pudding for dinner, and a piece of bread and cheese for our supper. Her fire was made of turf cut from the neighbouring heath; and her evening light was a rush dipped in grease.'

George Cobbett, this old cottager's son, who out of earning twopence a day as ploughboy had been able to attend evening school, was 'learned for a man in his rank of life,' understood land-surveying and had a reputation among his country neighbours for experience and understanding. 'He was honest, industrious, and frugal,' and 'happy in a wife of his own rank, liked, beloved, and respected.' He became tenant of a farm, on which he and his sons laboured vigorously :—

'My father used to boast that he had four boys, the eldest of whom was but fifteen years old, who did as much work as any three men in the parish of Farnham. . . . I do not remember the time [says William, the third (?) of these boys] when I did not earn my own living. My first occupation was driving the small birds from the turnip-seed and the rooks

from the pease. When I first trudged afield, with my wooden bottle and
my satchel swung over my shoulders, I was hardly able to climb the gates
and stiles ; and at the close of the day, to reach home was a task of infinite difficulty. My next employment was weeding wheat, and leading a
single horse at harrowing barley. Hoeing pease followed ; and hence I
arrived at the honour of joining the reapers in harvest, driving the team,
and holding the plough.'

William's love of gardening, which remained with him
through life, showed itself early. When six years old—

'I climbed up the side of a steep sand-rock [doubtless one behind the
house], and there scooped me out a plot of four feet square to make me a
garden, and the soil for which I carried up in the bosom of my little blue
smock-frock.'

One sees clearly the sturdy, ruddy, whitish-haired little
rustic, with twinkling gray eyes, in his blue smock and hob-
nailed shoes, hoeing pease, scaring the rooks, rolling down a
sand-bank with his brothers, now and again running away
from his work to follow the hounds, with the certainty of
losing his dinner, and the probability of being 'basted'
on his return ; and on winter evenings learning from his
father the arts of reading and writing.

'I have some faint recollection of going to school to an old woman,
who, I believe, did not succeed in learning me my letters. . . . [Cob-
bett sticks to the old form—learning me my letters.] As to politics, we
were like the rest of the country people in England ; that is to say, we
neither knew nor thought anything about the matter. The shouts of
victory or the murmurs of a defeat would now and then break in upon
our tranquility for a moment ; but I do not ever remember having seen
a newspaper in my father's house.'

The American war, however, gradually took hold of the
attention even of country-folk. George Cobbett was a partisan of the Americans, and had many a dispute on the
subject, over a pot of good ale, with a shrewd old Scotch-
man, the gardener of a nobleman in the neighbourhood.
The boys, who were sometimes listeners to these discussions,
always thought their father right—'There was but one wise
man in the world, and that one was our father.'

Let us now into the 'Jolly Farmer,' and drink a glass of the famous Farnham ale. It would seem that Cobbett's father not only farmed, but also kept a public-house here, but of this I am not quite sure. William, who is never tired of bragging of his father as a working farmer, is silent, so far as I know, as to the selling of ale.

Alas! they give us *Windsor* ale—have no Farnham. Why at so many places, even some that are widely noted for brewing, do they give you beer of some other town? Intervention between producer and consumer (which Cobbett used to rail against, and which is vastly increased in our day) is at work in this matter too; supporting, at the cost of the community, a far too numerous class of mere *transmitters.* One can hardly buy a fish now-a-days, on the seashore, or a pound of butter from a country dairy. Before the article is allowed to reach your hands, several people, in addition to the producer, are determined to squeeze a profit out of it.

'Yes,' the man said, 'Cobbett was born in this house, in the room above the parlour.' The front part of the house remains nearly unaltered, but another set of rooms has been added at the back. The parlour, a low room with a beam across the ceiling, has an engraving of William Cobbett, Esq., M.P., over the fireplace. A corporal of the Military Train, from Aldershot camp, who was drinking beer, knew something of Cobbett's history, and was clear as to the number of his regiment (54th), which I had forgotten.

Diligent a boy as William Cobbett was, and dutiful to his parents, he was always determined to see something of the world outside of his parish. He ran away from home three times—to Kew, to Portsmouth, to London. The first escapade he described, fifty years after, in an address to Reformers, when he was candidate for the City of Coventry in 1820:—

'At eleven years of age my employment was clipping of box-edgings

4

and weeding beds of flowers in the garden of the Bishop of Winchester, at the castle of Farnham, my native town. I had always been fond of beautiful gardens; and a gardener, who had just come from the king's gardens at Kew, gave such a description of them as made me instantly resolve to work in these gardens.'

Next morning, accordingly, the boy walked off, and towards the evening of a day in June reached Richmond with threepence in his pocket.

'I was trudging through Richmond, in my blue smock-frock and my red garters tied under my knees, when, staring about me, my eyes fell upon a little book in a bookseller's window, on the outside of which was written, "Tale of a Tub—price threepence." The title was so odd that my curiosity was excited.'

Instead of supper, he bought the little book, and carried it off to the shady side of a haystack :—

'It was something so new to my mind, that though I could not at all understand some of it, it delighted me beyond description ; and it produced what I have always considered a sort of birth of intellect. I read on till it was dark without any thought about supper or bed. When I could see no longer, I put my little book in my pocket and tumbled down by the side of the stack ; where I slept till the birds in Kew Gardens awakened me in the morning ; when off I started to Kew, reading my little book. The singularity of my dress, the simplicity of my manners, my confident and lively air, and doubtless his own compassion besides, induced the gardener, who was a Scotsman, I remember, to give me victuals, find me lodging, and set me to work.'

One day—

'The present king [George IV., then a boy of about the same age as little Cobbett] and two of his brothers laughed at the oddness of my dress, while I was sweeping the grass-plot around the foot of the pagoda.'

This queer little book, 'The Tale of a Tub,' was mainly composed within a couple of miles of Farnham, some eighty years before little William walked to Kew.

At the age of 20, Cobbett went on board the *Pegasus* man-of-war, at Spithead, and offered himself for the navy, but Captain Berkeley thought fit to refuse his request.

Next year, one May-day, the young man, dressed in his holiday clothes, was on his way to Guildford fair. He was at foot of a hill, and the London stage-coach came down towards him at a merry rate.

'The notion of going to London never entered my mind till this very moment, yet the step was completely determined on before the coach came to the spot where I stood. Up I got, and was in London about nine o'clock in the evening.'

He had but half a crown left. One of the passengers, who knew the lad's father, after vainly trying to persuade young Cobbett to return to Farnham, procured him employment in a lawyer's office at Gray's Inn — a detestable dungeon, in which he worked at 'quill-driving' for about eight months.

Walking one Sunday in St. James's Park, he saw an advertisement, 'To Spirited Young Men,' went down to Chatham, enlisted, remained a year in garrison, giving his leisure time to reading, and was then shipped off to Nova Scotia to join his regiment, where, being intelligent, well conducted, and indefatigably hard-working, he rose with unusual speed to the rank of sergeant-major.

In person, he was tall, burly, ruddy, with obstinate mouth and jaw, and shrewd, small gray eyes; on the whole, with a true, downright, positive, good-humoured John Bull aspect.

When he first saw his wife, she was only thirteen years old. Her father was a sergeant-major in the artillery, and William Cobbett was sergeant-major (perhaps the youngest in the army) of a regiment of foot, both stationed in forts near the city of St. John, New Brunswick.

'I sat in the same room with her for about an hour, in company with others, and I made up my mind that she was the very girl for me. That I thought her beautiful is certain, for that, I had always said, should be an indispensable qualification; but I saw in her what I deemed marks of that sobriety of *conduct* of which I have said so much, and which has been by far the greatest blessing of my life. It was now dead of winter, and, of course, the snow several feet deep on the ground, and the weather piercing cold. It was my habit, when I had done my morning's writing [he rose at four o'clock], to go out at break of day to take a walk on a hill, at the foot of which our barracks lay. In about three mornings after I had first seen her, I had, by an invitation to breakfast with me, got up two young men to join me in my walk; and our road lay by the house of her father and mother. It was hardly light, but she was out on the snow scrubbing out a washing-tub. "That's the girl for me," said I, when we had got out of her hearing.'

They were engaged; but, after a time, the artillery went to England, and she along with them.

Cobbett had saved 150*l.*, and this he sent to his 'little brunette' before she sailed, desiring her not to spare the money, but buy herself good clothes and live without hard work. It was four long years after this when Cobbett's regiment returned to England, and

'I found,' he says, 'my little girl a servant of all work (and hard work it was) at five pounds a year, in the house of a Captain Brissac; and, without hardly saying a word about the matter, she put into my hands the whole of my hundred and fifty pounds unbroken.' Cobbett on his part had been equally faithful; though with an episode—of friendship on his side, and a beginning of love on the other —between him and a farmer's beautiful daughter in New Brunswick, which would have been dangerous to a man of weaker will and principle. He tells this story delightfully in the 'Advice to Young Men.'

The sergeant-major, now thirty years old, obtained his discharge (this was in 1792) and immediately accused four officers of his regiment of embezzlement and keeping false accounts. A court-martial was granted, but on the day of trial no accuser appeared. Cobbett had gone to France with his new-married wife. Thence, after six months, they sailed to America. His heat of temper, I should guess, along with a real conviction of being in the right, made him put in the accusation; and his shrewdness showed him, afterwards, the difficulty of sustaining it; and so, being but a retired sergeant-major without advisers or backers, or any confidence in the powers that were, he thought the best plan was to remove himself. In 1794, Cobbett, then in Philadelphia, began authorship by writing certain pamphlets under the signature of *Peter Porcupine*. These were violently anti-democratic, opposed to all the views then popular in France and America, and made a great noise. Then, as all through his career, he delighted in opposing and attacking; and the title of one of these pamphlets, 'A Kick for a Bite' (by no means 'A Kiss for a Blow'), truly indicates his manner of carrying on a controversy. Cobbett afterwards opened a bookseller's shop in Second Street. He was recommended not to expose anything in his window that might provoke the populace.

'I saw the danger; but also saw that I must, at once, set all danger at defiance, or live in everlasting subjection to the prejudices and caprice of the democratical mob.'

When he took down his shutters, the window of the new shop was seen to be filled with portraits of royal and aristocratic personages, George III. in a prominent position and 'every picture that I thought likely to excite rage in the enemies of Great Britain.' The bold bookseller was attacked in newspapers and pamphlets, and by threatening letters, but his shop and person remained without scathe.

At this time, the first of many suits for libel was brought against Cobbett by the Spanish minister for an attack upon himself and his royal master in *Porcupine's Gazette;* this was followed by an action on the part of one Dr. Rush, who treated yellow fever by bleeding, and whom *Porcupine* called 'Sangrado' and 'quack' — probably with truth. But in this case Cobbett was fined 5,000 dollars and costs, and 'sold up' by the sheriff.

Soon after, he returned to England, already noted as a journalist, and set up in London a daily paper, *The Porcu-*

pine. This soon came to a stop; and then began in 1802 the famous *Political Register*, which appeared, first fortnightly, then weekly, and continued, almost without a break, during more than thirty years.

At first, Cobbett was a warm anti-Napoleonist, partisan of Pitt, and defender of aristocratic institutions. At the Peace of Amiens he refused to light up his windows in Pall Mall (where his shop was), and had them smashed by the mob. Six persons were convicted for taking share in this outrage; the jury recommended them to mercy, and the prisoners' counsel asked Mr. Cobbett if he would join in the recommendation. 'Certainly not, sir,' was the reply, 'I came here to ask for justice, and not for mercy.'

In the early volumes of the 'Register' some of the most amusing things are Cobbett's violent attacks on Sheridan, and also his denunciations of the study of Greek and Latin as 'worse than useless,' his ire having been roused by the frequent employment of the phrase *uti possidetis* in some of the parliamentary debates. Cobbett had his own notions of 'culture;' he never regretted the early narrowness of his education as a farmer's boy, but vaunted it to be the very best in the world. Without this kind of education, or something very much like it,—

'I should have been at this day' (he says in 'Rural Rides') 'as great a fool, as inefficient a mortal, as any of those frivolous idiots that are turned out from Winchester and Westminster schools, or from any of those dens of dunces called colleges and universities.'

Here, after Warton and Keats, we have a distinct third variety of the writing man. As to poetry and philosophy and art, Cobbett sincerely despised them. His ignorance of all that is highest in literature was immense, and he was immensely proud of it. If he could be supposed to have noticed Keats's existence, which is unlikely, one may imagine the profundity of his contempt for it. Keats could have imagined the contempt and understood it, with Cobbett himself and all his works and ideas into the bargain, in one lazy twinkle of his eye. The broad-shouldered beetle-browed, shrewd, indefatigable, self-esteeming, pugnacious, obstinate man, unlearned and unimaginative, crammed with prejudices and personal likings and dislikings, looked upon his own *practical common sense* as the final standard of everything in heaven and earth. He was in a good many ways like Walter Savage Landor, *minus* the culture.

When he set up the 'Register,' Cobbett was about forty years old, and he soon became a political power in the kingdom, and a thorn, or a whole bush of thorns, in the side of the ministry—of every ministry in turn. He was never quiet for a day, always fighting twenty people at a time, and knocking them down in succession with his cudgel, like Master Punch. In 1803 he came under two fines of 500*l.* each for libels on members of the Irish Government. Having begun as a partisan of Pitt, he changed round (it was said under the effect of a personal slight), attacked Pitt violently, and his *funding system;* backed Sir Francis Burdett, and became recognised as one of the leading 'Radicals.' In 1810, for an article on the flogging of two militiamen at Ely, he was prosecuted by the Crown, fined 1,000*l.*, and sent to prison for two years. The 'Register' for July 14th is dated from 'Newgate;' and the sturdy man is as full of courage and fight as ever.

'This work' (he says), 'of which I now begin the *Eighteenth Volume*, has had nothing to support it but its own merits. Not a pound, not even a pound in paper money, was ever expended in advertising it. It came up like a grain of mustard, and like a grain of mustard-seed it has spread over the whole civilized world. And why has it spread more than other publications of the same kind? There have not been wanting imitations of it. There have been some dozens of them, I believe: same size, same form, same type, same heads of matter, same title—all but the word expressing my name. How many efforts have been made to tempt the public away from me, while not one attempt has been made by me to prevent it! Yet all have failed. The changeling has been discovered

and the wretched adventurers have then endeavoured to wreak their
vengeance on me. They have sworn that I write badly ; that I publish
nothing but trash ; that I am both fool and knave. But still the readers
hang on to me. One would think, as Falstaff says, that I had given
them love powder. No ; but I have given them as great a rarity, and
something full as attractive—namely, *truth* in *clear language*.'

After his two years in prison, Cobbett emerged again,
pugnacious and undaunted, though now fifty years old. He
had a strong frame, perfect health, and a cheerful temperament. He rose early, took plenty of exercise, was very
moderate in diet, eschewing wine and spirits, tea and coffee,
and also vegetables (which he called ' garden stuff '), and
eating as little meat and bread as he could prevail on his
teeth to be satisfied with ; his drink beer, milk, and water.
He was very fond of farming, which he understood well, and
also of field sports, especially hunting. During the middle
part of his life he occupied for some time a farm at Botley,
in Hampshire.

In his family life he was one of the most fortunate of men,

' I have seven children ' (he wrote), ' the greater part of whom are fast
approaching the state of young men and young women. I never struck
one of them in anger in my life ; and I recollect only one single instance
in which I have ever spoken to one of them in a really angry tone and
manner. And when I had so done, it appeared as if my heart was gone
out of my body. It was but once, and I hope it will never be again. . . .
In my whole life I never spent one evening away from my own home, and
without some part, at least, of my family, if I was not at a distance from
that home.'

His wife he never tired of praising. Some one lately told
me, P. Walker, a little anecdote, belonging doubtless to the
Botley time. A gentleman, who told the thing to my
informant, was travelling to London inside the Southampton
coach. There were four passengers, one a lady. Cobbett,
whose name was in everybody's mouth, became the topic of
conversation, and was severely handled by the three gentlemen, probably Tories. ' I hear,' says one, ' that he is a
tyrant at home, and beats his wife.' On which the lady,

hitherto silent in her corner, said: 'Pardon me, sir, a kinder husband and father never breathed; and I ought to know, for I'm his wife.'

How far (if at all) can the domestic life of any public man be usefully considered in connection with his public life, as throwing light on the latter? The domestic life seems to belong to the department of biography, *as distinguishable* from history. The fact of a man being in the common meaning, a good husband, father, friend, or not good, seems in many cases to throw no light at all upon his character as a politician, a soldier, an author. To sum up the total of a man, tracing the connection between his public and private life, is a task which, if at all fit to be attempted, it would be vain to attempt without an extremely unusual command of all the facts. The rule that public men, as such, are to be judged by their public work seems, broadly, the sound one. But here is matter for an essay. Cobbett, in his political writings, continually praised his own domestic virtues. Whether or no this added much weight to his arguments on paper currency and rotten boroughs, it certainly made his writings more vivacious and readable.

In 1816, Napoleon being finally settled, the British public began to talk loudly of *Parliamentary Reform;* 'Hampden Clubs' were established in every part of the kingdom, muttering of 'universal suffrage' and 'annual parliaments.' 'Cobbett's Register' had hitherto been a stamped paper, price a shilling and a halfpenny; he now published it unstamped and at the price of twopence. The circulation became enormous, and so in proportion did Cobbett's fame and influence. He had the largest audience of any living writer, and by unfailing warmth and vigour of style, and reckless personality, in abuse of his opponents, kept his public always attentive and amused. Next year the Government, alarmed by the state of the country,

passed 'Six Acts' of a repressive character, and suspended
the right of habeas corpus. Cobbett, not wishing to be
clapped in gaol without trial, suddenly moved off to America,
where he remained till November, 1819. He resided most
of the time in Long Island, and he also travelled to acquire
a knowledge of transatlantic farming. In the meantime he
kept on sending over his 'Register' for publication in
England. When the repeal of the obnoxious law enabled
him to return, he published 'A Year's Residence in
America.'

He arrived at Liverpool in November, 1819. When the
custom-house officers examined his luggage, they opened a
certain box, and to their surprise found that it contained
human bones. 'These, gentlemen,' said Cobbett, 'are the
mortal remains of the immortal Thomas Paine!' This
business of Paine's bones (in the earlier numbers of the
'Register' he was 'that miscreant Paine') was a truly
comical attempt on the part of an unimaginative elderly
man to produce a dramatic effect in real life. It was an
attempt in the French style, and it utterly failed in England.
Cobbett made a kind of progress through the provincial
towns up to London, where he was banqueted by his reform
friends at the Crown and Anchor tavern. As to Paine's
bones, he kept on speaking and writing about them for a
time as a treasure of immense value. He proposed a public
funeral, with 'twenty waggon-loads of flowers' to strew
the way. A splendid monument was to be erected. Locks
of the deceased patriot's hair were to be soldered into gold
rings in Cobbett's own presence, and sold at a guinea each
beyond the value of the ring. But the public only laughed,
and some reported that Mr. Cobbett had been taken in by
the Yankees, and had brought away the bones of an old
nigger instead of those of his hero. Cobbett gave up talking
of his anatomical treasure, and what became of it nobody
knew.

Cobbett at this time, and probably more or less all through his career, was embarrassed in his money matters. Insolvency was one cause of his flight to America, and he seems at that time to have repudiated his debts on the ground of his having been unjustly treated by ' society as a whole.' He was then made a bankrupt. He had not long returned, before, in a new action for libel, he was cast in 1,000*l.* damages. But neither debt nor obloquy, nor any of the numerous difficulties of his life, had any perceptible effect on the spirits and industry of this indomitable man. He seems to have borrowed money largely, and raised it by hook or by crook in ways utterly mysterious to ordinary men, who fear their butcher and baker. He blazed away in his 'Register' weekly (at this time violently attacking his former ally, Burdett), and in the beginning of the year 1820 he offered himself as a candidate for the borough of Coventry, but was defeated. In Queen Caroline's case he took the queen's side with his usual vehemence. In 1822, his 'Register' for August 17th is addressed to Joseph Swan a prisoner in Chester jail for some political offence), and begins—

' Castlereagh has cut his own throat, and is dead. Let the sound reach you in the depth of your dungeon, and let it convey consolation to your suffering soul.'

Canning, 'Property Robinson,' and 'Parson Malthus,' were, among other public characters, objects of constant abuse in ' Cobbett's Register' at this time. He was incessant in vituperation of the borough-mongers and 'tax-eaters;' they were the 'basest of mankind,' 'vermin,' and even 'devils.' He was against standing armies, paper money, and national debt; modern shopkeeping and loco-motion, modern London (' the Wen ') and other over-peopled centres; he abhorred Jews, Methodists, Quakers, Bishops, and Malthusians. His opinions usually stood on a rational foundation, but were built up into ill-balanced and grotesque edifices, lopsided and uninhabitable. Take a specimen of his manner :—

'There is an " Emigration Committee" sitting to devise the means of getting *rid*, not of the idlers, not of the pensioners, not of the dead-weight, not of the parsons (to "relieve" whom we have seen the poor labourers taxed to the tune of a million and a half of money), not of the soldiers : but to devise means of getting rid of *these working people*, who are grudged even the miserable morsel that they get ! There is in the men calling themselves " English country gentlemen " something superlatively base. They are, I sincerely believe, the most cruel, the most unfeeling, the most brutally insolent ; but I know, I can prove, I can safely take my oath, that they are the most base of all the creatures that God ever suffered to disgrace the human shape. The base wretches know well that the taxes amount to more than *sixty millions* a year, and that the poor-rates amount to about *seven millions* : yet, while the cowardly reptiles never utter a word against the taxes, they are incessantly railing against the poor-rates, though it is (and they know it) the taxes that make the paupers.'

The best thing in Cobbett (for which one must love him, amidst all his faults) is his hearty compassion and kindness for the working classes and the poor, and his unwearied efforts to improve their condition. His 'Cottage Economy' is an excellent book, containing, among many other useful things, an explanation of how to prepare and use English wheaten straw for the manufacture of hats, bonnets, etc., which has helped many a poor cottager in the struggle for a living. One of his periodical publications is called 'The Poor Man's Friend,' and this phrase ought to be inscribed on his monument. Nothing made him more indignant than to see a rich tract of country, here tilled like a garden, there grazed by herds of fat oxen, the downs covered with sheep, the valleys yellow with corn, and to find on this teeming soil the labourers, and the labourers' wives and children, living from year's end to year's end on the barest subsistence, with no prospect towards the close of their hard life but the workhouse. It was Cobbett's fixed belief that all the country parts of England, including the villages and small towns, were far more populous some centuries ago, that is, in the times called 'medieval,' than they are to-day; and as one evidence of this he points to the vast numbers of cathedrals and churches, built in those good old times, which still exist all over the land. The English 'Reformation' was one of Cobbett's numerous objects of attack, and he wrote a 'History' of it, in which, as usual, his statements (seldom without a vein of strong sense and originality) were vitiated by ignorance and violence.

In 1829-30, Cobbett, now approaching his seventieth year, but as hale and vigorous as ever, went through a great part of England, chiefly on horseback, and gave political lectures in many towns and villages. His main topics were the villany of existing methods of taxation, and of the funding principle, and the effect of these on the farming interest; also the 'accursed' rotten boroughs, and the necessity of Parliamentary Reform. He was an easy and fluent speaker, self-possessed, shrewd and humorous, and spiced his discourses with plenty of amusing egotism and personal allusions to the men of the day.

'Though I never attempt,' he says, 'to put forth that sort of stuff which the "intense" people on the other side of St. George's Channel call "eloquence," I bring out strings of very interesting facts; I use pretty powerful arguments, and I hammer them down so closely upon the mind, that they seldom fail to produce a lasting impression.'

At last 'Reform' was actually carried; a reform which most of the peers, and all the bishops but one, thought almost equivalent to the downfall of the English Constitution —a reform which *now* is so antiquated, superseded and surpassed. And in the first Reform parliament, in 1832, William Cobbett, seventy years old, took his seat for Oldham. After this he made a political tour in Ireland, and was well received. In Parliament he was regular in attendance, and spoke not unfrequently, for the most part

on agricultural questions, and with good sense and moderation. But his rat-like instinct of using his teeth on something or somebody, brought him again into trouble.
Differing from Peel on the currency question, Cobbett took
the violent and absurd step of moving for an address to the
King, praying him to dismiss Sir Robert Peel from the
Privy Council. Only three members voted in favour of
Cobbett's motion, and his influence in the House was
ruined.

In these years Cobbett rented a place called Normandy
Farm, about a couple of miles from his native town of
Farnham. When he could get away from 'the Wen,' he
lived with his wife and children in this plain farm-house
among his barns and fields, in daily sight of the scenes of
his infancy, and engaged in those rural occupations which
he delighted in, as much as in his alternate business of
fierce political controversy.

In the middle of May, 1835, Cobbett, though suffering
from sore throat, attended the House and spoke, almost
inaudibly, in favour of a motion for the repeal of the malt-
tax ; he grew worse, but again came to the House on the
25th, and spoke and voted on a motion on agricultural
distress. Next morning (Tuesday) he went down to his
farm, and felt better at first, but relapsed.

'On Sunday,' writes his son in the 'Register' of June
20th, 'he revived again, and on Monday gave us hope that
he would yet be well. He talked feebly, but in the most
collected and sprightly manner, upon politics and farming ;
wished for "four day's rain" for the Cobbett corn and root
crops ; and on Wednesday he could remain no longer shut
up from fields, but desired to be carried round the farm,
which being done, he criticised the work that had been
going on in his absence, and detected some little deviation
from his orders, with all the quickness which was so remarkable in him. On Wednesday night he grew more and more

feeble, and was evidently sinking; but he continued to
answer with perfect clearness every question that was put
to him. In the last half-hour his eyes became dim; and
at ten minutes after one p.m. he leaned back, closed them
as if to sleep, and died without a gasp. He was seventy-
three years old.'

A portrait of the sturdy man's personal appearance in his
later days, drawn by William Hazlitt, is lifelike :—

'Mr. Cobbett speaks almost as well as he writes. The
only time I ever saw him he seemed to me a very pleasant
man, easy of access, affable, clear-headed, simple and mild
in his manner, deliberate and unruffled in his speech, though
some of his expressions were not very qualified. His figure
is tall and portly. He has a good sensible face, rather full,
with little grey eyes, a hard square forehead, a ruddy complexion, with hair grey or powdered; and had on a scarlet
broadcloth waistcoat with the flaps of the pockets hanging
down, as was the custom for gentlemen farmers in the last
century, or as we see it in the pictures of members of
parliament in the reign of George I. I certainly did not
think less favourably of him for seeing him.'

The 'Bush,' extending from the High Street towards
the river meadows, is a fine old-fashioned inn, with modern
comforts added. I was rather afraid of the waiter at
first; for his smart dress-coat, white necktie, handsomely
arranged head of hair, and elegant manners, made him fit
apparently to wait upon no one with less than 2,000*l.* a
year. But my dread wore off; he proved very civil, and
the bill moderate. When I looked from my bedroom
window in the morning, it was through a fringe of ivy
leaves, on the bloom of three great hawthorns, two pink,
one white, the latter with an upright but spirally-twisted
stem like a Lombardic pillar; and a pretty garden of sward,
flowerbeds and shrubberies, where the landlord was lovingly
at work with his hoe.

He told me something of Cobbett, whom he had often seen. When Cobbett was a member of parliament, and living at Normandy Farm (two or three miles from this town), did he mix with the neighbouring gentry? Hardly at all, the landlord thought—he went about his own affairs in his own way. He used to drive into Farnham in a carriage that looked as if the fowls had been roosting on it, and with a couple of farm-horses. Mr. Nicholls, formerly postmaster, has some letters of Cobbett to him, which he shows to the curious. Cobbett was dissatisfied with the mode of delivery of his letters by the post-office, and insisted upon an alteration with his usual vehemence; but finding that he was in the wrong, apologised to Mr. Nicholls, and used afterwards to send him frequent presents of fruit and vegetables from the farm. My landlord was at Cobbett's funeral, and saw Daniel O'Connell there. The funeral took place on the 27th of June, 1835, between two and three in the afternoon. The great Irish agitator did not follow the coffin into the church, but stood in the churchyard the while, amidst a circle of observers, to whom he put questions about the land, hops, wages.

O'Connell and Cobbett were not unlike; big, burly, blustering, able, noisy fellows, who made themselves heard far and wide. Each was fond of field sports; fonder still of the turbulent excitement of political contest. Each was powerful in vituperation, great in giving nicknames, full of ready coarse humour of a popular sort, merciless in antagonism, unscrupulous in invective; and, moreover, they had more than once or twice exercised these gifts against each other. Each of the men in his family circle was respected and beloved. In public life they were like prizefighters. Pugnacious and powerful, they found their arena in politics.

After my conversation with the landlord, I went over to the church, a building of rubble-masonry, done-up of course, with some remains of good early work in the

windows of the tower, which is high, square and massive.
Close to the north porch, enclosed with iron railings, is
Cobbett's tombstone, an ugly lump. The leading facts of
his life are given in a simply-worded inscription on one
side; the other side bears record of his wife, Anne Cobbett,
born at Woolwich, 1775, died in London, 1848. So wretchedly
has the stonemason (or as he calls himself, ' Thos. Milner,
Sculptor, London, 1856') done his work, that the inscriptions are already almost illegible in parts. A headstone close by, within the railings, is inscribed with 'George
Cobbett, died 1762,'—this was the old grandfather, the
farm-labourer. While I was looking, an old farm-labourer
came through the churchyard and paused beside me,—' Ay,
that's Cobbett's grave, is that. I was at his funeral, myself,
that I was: I saw O'Connell, he was an Irishman, he was:
he stood just here, he did: I saw him myself, I could swear
I did:' a very stupid poor man, and not like George Cobbett, I fancy, though in the same rank of life.

William Cobbett, the whitish-haired, ruddy-faced little
grandson, in smock-frock, scaring birds, weeding, etc., who
became a stalwart young sergeant-major, a political writer,
farmer, good family man, indefatigable and world-famous
journalist and public speaker, member of the House of
Commons, was born in that brown-roofed, low house just
across the river; and here, alongside the graves that he
often ran amongst in his childhood, his own bones are now
laid to rest.

Leaving the churchyard, I walked past the 'Jolly Farmer,' and eastward from the town, in the direction of
Crooksbury Hill, which I had seen from the Bishop's Park,
like a lion couchant, with dark fir-trees for mane; and
recalled that passage in Cobbett (one of the many which
give us a tenderer feeling for his memory), where he describes
his visit to Farnham in 1800, after returning from America.
He was then thirty-eight years old.

'When in about a month after my arrival in London I went to Farnham, the place of my birth, what was my surprise! everything was become so pitifully *small!* I had to cross in my post-chaise the long and dreary heath of Bagshot. Then, at the end of it, to mount a hill called Hungary Hill; and from that hill I knew that I should look down into the beautiful and fertile vale of Farnham. My heart fluttered with impatience, mixed with a sort of fear, to see all the scenes of my childhood; for I had learnt before the death of my father and mother. There is a hill not far from the town, called Crooksbury Hill, which rises up out of a flat in the form of a cone, and is planted with Scotch fir-trees. Here I used to take the eggs and young ones of crows and magpies. This hill was a famous object in the neighbourhood. . . . ".As high as Crooksbury Hill" meant, with us, the utmost degree of height. Therefore the first object that my eyes sought was this hill. I could not believe my eyes. Literally speaking, I for a moment thought the famous hill removed, and a little heap put in its stead; for I had seen in New Brunswick a single rock, or hill of solid rock, ten times as big and four or five times as high! The post-boy, going down-hill, and not a bad road, whisked me in a few minutes to the Bush Inn, from the garden of which I could see the prodigious sandhill where I had begun my gardening works. What a nothing! But now came rushing into my mind, all at once, my pretty little garden, my little blue smock frock, my little nailed shoes, my pretty pigeons, that I used to feed out of my hands, the last kind words and tears of my gentle and tender-hearted and affectionate mother! I hastened back into the room. If I had looked a moment longer, I should have dropped.'

However we may estimate Cobbett, his life was certainly a *happy* one. How different from that of Robert Burns! Peasants, both of them, born and bred; vigorous in body and mind; enjoying rural scenery; sworn admirers of the fair sex; eloquent, humorous, vehement, eagerly sympathetic with working people, especially the agriculturists; yet utterly unlike in their aims, in their careers, and, as we must believe, in their inmost nature. The finest sensibility to impressions, that is the quality of a poet. Sensibility to pleasurable impressions, but also to painful,—which are apt to be most frequent in this work-a-day world; and the poetic nature feeling both in extreme is specially fain to shun these and to seek those. Hence temptations; and, if there be a flaw in the *will* (whether the will be faculty or

function) alas for the poet's chance of happiness! I fear
the New Brunswick farmer's daughter would have fared
differently had her peace of mind been at Robert's mercy.
The Surrey Ploughboy had constant good health and good
spirits, a strong will (which the other sadly lacked), plenty
of work and plenty of amusement, both such as he liked
best. He never had, and never missed, the thrilling
delights of his poor Ayrshire brother, wandering lonely by
Nithside, with murmured song, or crossing the moor to
'Nannie, O,' or feeling his heart swell on the field of
Bannockburn. But Cobbett believed in himself, and
produced visible effects on the world. He was thoroughly
fortunate in his family circle. 'Cares!' he exclaims
('Advice to Young Men')—'what have I had worthy of
the name of cares?' He ended his career tranquilly at a
full age, vigorous to the last, and after having attained
the chief object of his ambition, a seat in a Reformed
Parliament.

As to his writings, their style is sturdy, straightforward,
clear, emphatic, but often clumsy, and almost always
verbose. The violence, personality, and self-conceit sometimes pass all bounds. In spite of the perspicuity, vigour,
and raciness of his pages, the general effect upon the mind
is very unsatisfactory. Strength and narrowness combined
give one a peculiarly uncomfortable feeling, as of mental
incarceration.

Still his 'Rural Rides,' 'Cottage Economy,' 'Advice
to Young Men,' are, in the main, thoroughly wholesome
reading, manly and pure, with much sweetness; often
reminding one of the smell of new-turned earth mingled
with that of spring flowers. Many of his leading opinions
—for example, those on Malthus, Public Credit, Taxation—
appear to me perfectly sound. A favourite conviction of
his was that 'England was at her zenith in the reign of
Edward the Third;' and it is rather curious to find so

5—2

different a man from Cobbett as Mr. Ruskin, telling us that in many respects 'we have steadily declined' since about that time.[1]

Much work William Cobbett certainly did do, and with great effect on the 'public opinion' of England; shoving on England with his big shoulder through thick and thin, more than perhaps any other one man, into what is called *Reform*. He was a Radical of the best type, in so far as he insisted upon truth, industry, frugality, obedience, love of goodness and simplicity, as the first things necessary, without which all politics are moonshine; and, on the whole, he fairly carried his own doctrines into practice.

The sun shone on flowery hedgerows as I turned down a byway leading to Moor Park, the Moor Park of Sir William Temple and Jonathan Swift.

[1] See *Eagle's Nest*, p. 230.

RAMBLE THE FOURTH.

PASSING Cobbett's birthplace, the 'Jolly Farmer,' and the Farnham railway station, I soon quitted the main road for a by-road on the left. The hedgerow-bank among other flowers showed an abundance of the greater celandine, with its yellow four-petaled bloom and beautifully cut green leaf. Neither this, nor Wordsworth's friend, its lesser namesake (which is of the ranunculus tribe—this of the poppy), nor any other of yellow wild-flowers equals in richness of colour the common king-cup at its best. It tells wonderfully in a field nosegay. Never king of Thule quaffed his wine from so rich-hued a goblet.

This spring [1867], though strangely broken by three or four patches of winter, has been profuse of wild flowers, at least on the south coast of England, especially of primrose, lesser celandine, stitchwort, red campion, king-cup, water crowfoot. Blue-bells were less plentiful. The hawthorns, which burst into sudden bloom, as the nightingales into song, in the warm beginning of May, stopped short, as the birds also were stricken dumb, in those three weeks of unnatural cold which made 'hoary-headed frosts fall in the fresh lap of the crimson rose,' and blighted many a walnut-tree, mulberry, and myrtle in cottage-gardens, as well as countless ridges of the 'famine-root' abhorred by Cobbett, for which he cursed the memory of Sir Walter Raleigh. The later-leaved forest trees, oak and ash, are also many of them scorched as by fire ; but *not* these two broad spreading oaks that overshade the steep lane descending to Moor Park, and under whose branches Jonathan Swift must so often have passed, during the nine or ten years of which he spent the best part at this place, between the ages of twenty-two and thirty-one. From the name of it, and from finding mention of its loneliness, I had always fancied Moor Park to be a bleak solitary place. It is but two miles from Farnham, and in a richly-wooded vale. The little Wey winds through meadow-ground, steepish slopes rising on either hand, forest-like with large oaks, horse-chestnuts, beeches, lindens, mixed with the pillared shade of dusky firs. Moor Park House is now an ugly stuccoed building, the old walls, or part of them, still forming its core. The garden slopes to the river ; the lane crosses the river by a little bridge, then, turning sharp to the right, passes in front of the white mansion and along the vale, a rural grass-grown avenue (public, but unfrequented)—the tree-shaded high bank on your left hand, the watery meadow-fields with sallows and osiers on your right, and the parallel shady slope beyond. A mile or so of this brings you to another bridge, a mill, a main road winding up the shoulder of fir-clad Crooksbury Hill ; and just beyond this bridge, in a shady park, are the ruins of Waverley Abbey. Moor Park House was lately a water-cure establishment, but is now again a private residence. Up the steep bank close by, fir-shaded, from which you can look down the chimneys, Sir William Temple's amanuensis used to run violently of a morning, in hopes of improving his health, and putting to rout his sick headaches ; and perhaps did himself more harm than good. In some solitary recess of these woods the same moody youth used to sit reading by the hour, trying to forget the last rebuke of his dignified patron, and all the countless vexations which a proud, irritable temper finds or contrives for itself.

The sunny shady hill-slope here of red-stemmed Scotch pines, and the grass-grown lane and valley beneath it are haunted for me by the figure of a tall, gaunt young man, rapid and abrupt in gesture, of dusky complexion and somewhat grim look, who hits one in passing with a glance from prominent blue eyes, suspicious, penetrating; hurries on muttering, and strides into the thicket. An odd little fatherless child at Dublin, brought up on the charity of uncles; a sarcastic, insubordinate student of T.C.D.; a discontented young man, penniless, of little promise, though conscious of capacity, and not knowing which way to turn; for his mother's sake (she herself dependent on relations) taken under the patronage and into the house of the dignified ex-courtier and man of letters, to do the part of a humble kind of secretary; vague schemes in his head of attempting literary work; an uncertain hope of getting into some sort of career by the help of his patron's influence; already, at twenty-two, suffering from frequent ill health; already a moody, despondent, irritable human being,—I could see young Jonathan Swift, haunting these lonely avenues and fir-tree slopes; and when I got home after this ramble, I tried to sift out and make clearer to myself such facts as are presented (sometimes too vaguely, and mixed up with evident inaccuracies and statements without authority) by the various biographers.[1]

The Rev. Thomas Swift, Vicar of Goodrich, near Ross in Herefordshire, took the king's side in the great Civil War, and thereby suffered much loss. At his death he left thirteen or fourteen children, but ill off. The eldest son,

[1] Two books have since appeared: 'Life,' by John Forster, vol. i, 1667-1711 (London, Murray, 1875), left unfinished at the writer's death: and 'Life,' by Henry Craik (London. Murray, 1882). They give some additional details. but no new light on Swift's character. The latter book is very positive—and, in the opinion of some, very positively wrong—on a disputed point in the Dean's history of great importance in forming a judgment upon his character. See further on.

Godwin Swift, was called to the bar, and received a legal office in Ireland. His good fortune drew three more of his brothers to that country, William, Jonathan and Adam. Jonathan, an attorney, had the place of steward or under-treasurer at the King's Inn, Dublin; but some two years after his appointment he died suddenly at an early age, leaving his widow in destitution, with an infant daughter, and the expectation of another child. This fatherless child, a son, was born on the 30th of November, 1667, *most probably* in Hoey's Court, Dublin. This was the year after that *Annus Mirabilis* of Naval War with the Dutch and Great Fire of London; on its heels came Titus Oates, Lord William Russell and Algernon Sydney, Alliance against the *Grand Monarque*, Banishment of the Protestants from France, and many other things. His nurse, a native of Whitehaven, carried him, out of affection, to that place, and kept him there during the first three years of his life, after which little Jonathan was brought back to Ireland, and at six years old sent to Kilkenny School, his Uncle Godwin undertaking the charge of his support and education. In his fifteenth year he entered Trinity College, Dublin, where he continued some seven years, gaining little credit either for conduct or study. The Student, poor and dependent (and hating his dependence and what he deemed his uncle's parsimony), was a *mauvais sujet*, irregular in attendance, given to 'town-haunting,' contemptuous to those above him, audacious in lampoon. He obtained his 'B.A.' with difficulty, and, after this, in the course of two years, incurred over seventy penalties, was publicly admonished, and subsequently, being convicted of insolence to the junior dean, had his degree suspended, and was forced to crave pardon in public. In 1689, being then in his twenty-second year, this unruly young man, a nuisance to the learned authorities, and a heartburn to his own relations (uncle Godwin was dead, but another uncle had carried the youth

on), left college without money, character, or definite prospect of any kind. Sailing to England, likely in some little
coasting vessel, young Jonathan Swift sets off on foot to his
anxious poor mother, then residing at Leicester, a tall awkward youth, with large observant blue eyes, and a drily
sarcastic tongue which he delights to exercise upon carriers,
tramps, tavern-keepers, and whomsoever the cheap wayfarer
falls in with, having, in fact, a taste for amusing himself
with low company.

Though an irregular student, the lad is, in his own way,
much addicted to books, and has read a large quantity. He
has also tried his hand at scribbling, and carries an old
pocket-book crammed with verse-jottings, not odes to the
moon or his mistress's eyebrow, but lampoons and epigrams,
personal and political—on the Queen's *accouchement*, the
Prince of Orange, the Dublin actresses, doctors, college
dons, etc., often coarse enough in phrase. He has noted
the political movements of the time ; is not only inclined to
divert himself with the manners of the lower class of people,
but to observe (if he had the chance) the ways of courts and
cabinets, and of those great folk who pull the strings of the
puppet-show. Towards intermediate mankind, the 'respectable' classes in general, all their thoughts and doings,
his attitude is one of habitual contempt, now and again
concentrated into anger. They are dunces and fools, their
manners dull, their actions base, their objects despicable.
In the year that young Swift took his B.A. degree at
Dublin 'by special grace' (1685), Charles's merriment
came suddenly to an end; and in the year of the lad's
leaving college, Irish and French were encamped before the
gates of Derry, the parliament in College Green upholding
King James as their lawful monarch, while William and
Mary ruled in England.

During Jonathan's stay with his mother at Leicester (it
could not have been more than a few months) he entertained

his leisure in a manner not at all unusual with him, by *making up* to a pretty girl of that place, by the name of Miss Betty Jones, who was of the decent middle class, and not without a share of education and refinement. Meanwhile, Mrs. Swift having made humble application on behalf of her son to the great Sir William Temple, who had some knowledge of her, and received a gracious reply, the youth set off southward, and joined the household of Sir William, now some time retired from active public life, and resident on a small estate, Moor Park to wit, which he had purchased near Farnham, in Surrey. The ex-ambassador and diplomatist was at this time a handsome stately man of sixty, with a courtesy that easily rose to haughtiness, and a love of letters that was not without a flavour of pedantry. He had transacted with success various high negotiations in his time, especially between England and the States of Holland, was twelve years ambassador at the Hague, had been in favour with King Charles, and was now in favour with King William. He was fortunate in his birth, in his marriage, and in every step of his career, and had gathered honours not only in statesmanship, but also in the field of literature. He was fond of reputation, and as fond of ease and comfort ; perhaps a little irritable ; certainly not a little vain of his diplomacy, his learning, his gardening, his person, and of all belonging to him ; moreover, a precise, methodical, and loftily respectable gentleman in every particular, no doubt worshipped by his Dorothea, and looked on with more or less of awe by every one near him. It has been said, and often repeated, that Mrs. Swift was related to Lady Temple, but for this I find no evidence. Sir Thomas Temple, Sir William's father, was Master of the Rolls in Ireland, and there had known and patronised the Swift family, many of whom were connected with the law. William Temple had lived for a time with his father in Ireland, and was returned to the Irish parliament for the County Carlow in 1661: here is foundation enough for the acquaintance of the Swifts and Temples. Thomas Swift, a 'parson-cousin' of Jonathan, was for a time domestic chaplain to Sir William.

Jonathan Swift, we observe, never had a father to guide him, never had an early home to look back to with sacred recollections. From the age of six to fourteen he was at Kilkenny school, and had rough treatment most likely. When he spoke of his early years, which he seldom did, it was not tenderly but bitterly: his uncle 'gave him the education of a dog.' Dublin College was no Alma Mater; he despised its men and broke its rules. But to the mother who bore him he was ever reverential and affectionate, visiting her regularly, it would seem, once a year, when he walked to Leicester for the purpose.

And now here is Jonathan at Moor Park, in his twenty-second year, clever, awkward, sensitive, proud, insubordinate, with a strong Dublin brogue, unused to society, ready enough to be moved to contempt or sarcasm by the formalities of polite company, yet, at the same time, very willing to study the manners and views of the great, whom he for the first time has a chance of seeing close at hand, and awe-struck, in spite of himself, by the high reputation and dignified manners of Sir William. The rough Dublin student finds himself in a totally new scene of life. But the position is far from agreeable; he seldom if ever dines at Sir William's table, and shares his conversation on a distant and dependent footing. He does his daily business as copyist and amanuensis, listens and replies with forced humility, glides moodily out of the house, avoiding alike the servants and superiors of the family, and runs up and down the steep slope behind it for exercise, or sits for hours reading in a solitary place among the woods. He is lonely, anxious, discontented, knows not what to turn to, or what is to become of him; loathes his perpetual and inevitable condition of dependence, and fancies an insult in every word or look of those about him. One comfort he has, in a dark-eyed pretty child of six or seven years old, daughter of Mrs. Johnson, the housekeeper, a widow, and 'tis said a distant cousin of the Temples. Young Swift spends many a spare hour in teaching little Esther, and though he is ever grave and almost hard in his manner even with her, there is evidently a good feeling between teacher and pupil, and no other portion of his time passes so agreeably. But this little solace is not enough to prevent his discontent and gloom growing thicker upon him, much increased by frequent fits of ill-health.

'A natural daughter of Temple's,' some call Esther, without any evidence. That Sir William, aged sixty, should bring a 'natural daughter' of six years old, and her mother, to the house with himself and his wife, to whom he was always tenderly attached, is not the most likely thing in the world.

Young Swift became so ill and restless at Moor Park, that it was agreed he should return to Ireland for change of air and scene. He went, but did not stay many months, and came back (very likely on advice of friends and new reflections in his own mind) to Moor Park towards Christmas: this being in the year 1690—the battle of the Boyne lost and won, and King James finally fled to France. Jonathan's life here went on much as before—his health no better; but by degrees the great man admitted him nearer to his confidence.

About this time young Swift received, from a certain Rev. John Kendall of Leicestershire (a relative of his) a letter on the subject of Miss Betty Jones, about whose flirtation, or whatever it was, with young Jonathan the scandalmongers of Leicester had been busying themselves. The young gentleman at Moor Park replies to this in a curious letter, civil enough towards his correspondent, but defiant of the world in general, and in particular of 'the obloquy of a parcel of very wretched fools, which I solemnly pronounce the inhabitants of Leicester to be.' He says he has behaved to 'twenty women' in the same way as to Miss Betty Jones, 'without any other design than that of entertaining myself when I am very idle, or when something goes amiss in my affairs. This I always have done as a man of the world, when I had no design for anything grave in it, and what I thought at worst a harmless impertinence.' As to marriage, he is resolved not to think of it till he settles his fortune in the world; and even then, 'I am so hard to please that I suppose I shall put it off to the other world.' He is apt to talk with women, he says, because there is something in him 'which must be employed;' and during these seven weeks that he has been lonely at Moor Park, since his return from Ireland, he has, for the same reason, 'writ and burnt and writ again, upon all manner of subjects, more than perhaps any man in England.' A great person in Ireland 'used to tell me that my mind was like a conjured spirit, that would do mischief if I would not give it employment. It is this humour that makes me busy when I am in company, to turn all that way; and since it commonly ends in talk, whether it be love or common conversation, it is all alike.'

Among his tentative scribblings in Sir William's library, and during his rambles out of doors, young Swift has jotted down many notes for an odd kind of satire on the church controversies of which he hears so much talk, and the respective tenets of the Church of England, Popery, and Dissent. He himself is thinking of entering the Established Church, not willingly, for he does not feel himself to be well fitted for a clergyman, but because he cannot see any other opening.

In 1692 he is admitted to the degree of Master of Arts at Oxford, afterwards visiting his mother at Leicester. At

Oxford he says, ' I am ashamed to have been more obliged in a few weeks to strangers than ever I was in seven years to Dublin College. . . . I am not to take orders till the king gives me a prebend: and Sir William Temple, though he promises me the certainty of it, yet is less forward than I could wish, because (I suppose) he believes I shall leave him, and, upon some accounts, he thinks me a little necessary to him.' [1]

In fact, Swift was impatient to get away, and become in a measure independent; while Sir William, for reasons of his own, put off from one time to another the carrying into effect of his promises to advance the young man's interest, and desired him to rest content at Moor Park for the present; and this state of things at last came to a rupture between them, Swift going over to Ireland in May, 1694, with the resolution to be ordained there, and ' make what endeavour I can for something in the Church.' [2] But he found unexpected difficulties, and was reduced to address a most submissive letter from Dublin to Sir William (October 6, 1694), requesting from ' his honour,' a certificate of good behaviour, without which he could not gain admission to the ministry.

' The particulars expected of me are what relate to morals and learning, and the reasons of quitting your honour's family, that is, whether the last was occasioned by any ill actions. They are all left entirely to your honour's mercy, though, in the first I think I cannot reproach myself any further than for *infirmities.*' Sir William sent the certificate, and Swift took ' deacon's orders,' took ' priest's orders ' a couple of months after (January, 1695), and was appointed (probably through Sir William's influence) to the small benefice of Kilroot (*Kil ruah*, ' red church '), worth about a 100*l.* a year. He was now twenty-seven years old. This

---

[1] Letter to his uncle William, from Moor Park, Nov. 29, 1692.
[2] Letter to his cousin Deane Swift, June 3, 1694.

Kilroot, a parish situated near Carrickfergus, in the county Antrim, was a *prebend* in the diocese of Connor (allowance for the support of a clergyman of the cathedral). The prebend is now Kilroot and Temple-corran, and the diocese Down, Connor, and Dromore.

The prebendary moped at Kilroot; Sir William missed him at Moor Park; before many months were gone Swift was again (1696) under the same roof with his patron, and with Hessy Johnson. He resigned his benefice, and continued to reside at Moor Park for the next three years, that is till Sir William's death, in 1699.[1]

Hessy Johnson, thirteen years and three months younger than Jonathan Swift, was fifteen years old when he returned to Moor Park. She had been sickly from her childhood, but now grew into perfect health, a beautiful dark-eyed, black-haired girl. In the society of this delightful girl, whose studies he directed, and who almost worshipped him; and on a footing of increased confidence with his patron, upon whose influence he relied for some suitable promotion, when an opportunity should arrive, Parson Swift must have spent three comparatively comfortable years. We do not hear him grumbling and growling. He writes a book of singular ability, full of odd humour and satiric fancy, coloured indeed with the general temper of his mind, but not so imbued with vitriolic cynicism as most of his later writings. This was the *Tale of a Tub*, published anonymously in 1704, along with the *Battle of the Books*, and never acknowledged by the author. The *Tale of a Tub*, wonderfully clever as it is, has perhaps been ranked higher as a literary work than it deserves. It has a great reputation; and some choice parts of it, like Lord Peter's declaring the loaf to be a shoulder of mutton, are often quoted. But,

---

[1] The gossiping stories of the cause of Swift's leaving Kilroot, his manner of going, his handing over the living to a poor clergyman, are the merest rubbish.

though not long, the book is seldom read through, and as a whole is not very readable. It is amorphous. Scarcely half of it is occupied with the fragmentary history of Peter, Martin, and Jack; the other half consisting of intercalary chapters in a strain of grave irony, chiefly on the petty literary controversies of the day. A notable and characteristic performance, it hardly shows a right to be classed among the finished treasures of English literature, though Dr. Johnson rated it far above all Swift's other writings, including Gulliver. The abundant images and illustrations, often ingenious and pithy, are at best the product of a whimsical fancy, not of a humorous or witty imagination; they are clever but not truthful and delightful, not exhilarating, nor satisfying. The foul smell, too, which so often exhales from Swift's pages, is perceived throughout. This *Tale*, which occupied the author several years, was written, he says, ' to expose the abuses and corruptions in learning and religion;' but it did not come out of any serious purpose, nor by the method of it could any useful result have been possibly attained. The broad Rabelaisian jesting on Peter and Jack threw no kind of light upon Catholicism or Calvinism. Swift's own convictions, now and afterwards, were of the negative kind. His notion of Religion was an Established Policy, to be defended against innovators, and he could have defended Popery with equal vigour. He perhaps *believed* in nothing save Orderliness and Industry, though earnestly *dis*believing in many things, which is more than some people do. He hated injustice and misgovernment. He despised the dullness and meanness of mankind.

The *Battle of the Books*, written during the same period as the *Tale of a Tub*, and published along with it, has all the characteristics of Swift's style, quiet and cultivated irony, happy description (as of the spider's web), and a taste for rough vulgar abuse and coarse jesting patches of which come in here and there. *The Battle*, written to please Sir William Temple, in the controversy on Ancient and Modern Learning, between Temple and Boyle on one side, and Bentley and Wotton on the other, is intrinsically worthless, and contains no atom of argument. Bentley was a man of real learning, Sir William a *dilettante*, Swift but Sir William's partisan. It is noticeable that neither Temple nor Swift, in speaking of modern writers, makes the least allusion to Shakespeare. He didn't count. In this *Battle of the Books* is the phrase, lately revived, *sweetness and light*, descriptive of the products of the Bee's industry, honey and wax, as compared with the Spider's ' dirt and poison.' It is amusing, by the way, recollecting the two essayists, to think of the contrast of Swift's straight hitting, and the modern Litterateur's beautiful sparring with no real fight in it.

It is plain that Swift, in these years at all events, had no intention of making Hessy Johnson his wife; perhaps because he had known her from childhood, and been 'always with her in the house,' but to marry *somebody* he was always intending, or rather half-intending. He longed for a wife,—he feared matrimony; he fell in love (after a manner of his own) with this girl and that,—he looked round and saw very few happy marriages, and many poor men overweighted with large families. For a long while he could not make up his mind to marry because his plans were unsettled and his maintenance too small; then he found that he was too old and his habits too fixed. But almost from his boyhood to the decline of life, Swift was engaged in successive intimacies with virtuous and cultivated women. Some of these friendships lasted through many years. Several of the ladies had more or less hope of becoming his wife; but they were all disappointed.

It does not appear at what precise time Swift first met Miss Jane Waryng, a young lady of the north of Ireland,

sister of his 'chum,' or chamber-fellow at Trinity College,
Dublin; he probably, while at Kilroot, renewed a former
acquaintance with her; and in the year of his return to
Moor Park (1696), we have a letter of his addressed to her
under the fancy name of 'Varina,' speaking of their engage-
ment, and urging its speedy fulfilment.   This letter, dated
April 29, which would seem to have been written at Belfast,
or some other seaport town in that part, is the most artificial thing I know from Swift's hand.   'It is so, by
heaven! the love of Varina is of more tragical consequence
than her cruelty, . . . a thousand graves lie open,' etc.   He
continued his correspondence with Miss Waryng all through
his last residence at Moor Park, and there is no reason to
think that his daily intercourse with Esther Johnson had
any intentional colour of courtship on it.

In May 1699 (N.S.), somewhat unexpectedly it would
seem, tho' he was over seventy years old, Sir William
Temple died, leaving his secretary unprovided with any
permanent maintenance, but bequeathing him 100*l.*, and
the privilege of editing, for his own benefit, Sir William's
writings.   Jane Swift, Jonathan's sister, writes thus to her
cousin Deane Swift at this time: 'My poor brother has
lost his best friend, Sir William Temple, who was so fond
of him whilst he lived, that he made him give up his living
in this country to stay with him at Moor Park, and promised to get him one in England.   But death came in
between, and has left him unprovided both of friend and
living!'

So now the Rev. Mr. Swift, aged thirty-two, takes his
last leave of Moor Park.

Shall we follow him a little further?

He comes to London; publishes Temple's works (the *Tale
of a Tub* still quiet in his desk); memorials King William,
and applies whatever court-influence he has, with the
object of getting some church-living, but does not succeed.

At length he accepts the post of chaplain and private secretary to the Earl of Berkeley, appointed one of the Lords Justices of Ireland, and attends his lordship to Dublin Castle. To Ireland he constantly gravitates, in spite of himself. Swift and Lord Berkeley soon quarrelled; the secretaryship was given to a Mr. Bushe; Swift lampooned the earl and the secretary, though he kept on good terms with the countess and the other ladies of the family, and amused them with *jeux d'esprit*, such as the 'Petition of Mrs. Francis Harris.' After a year or so (in 1700), having been refused the deanery of Derry, he was given, to get rid of him, a little bunch of livings, Agher, Laracor, and Rathbiggan, in the diocese of Meath, in all worth about 200*l.* a year, and went to live at Laracor glebe house, two miles from Trim and twenty from Dublin. Here he improved the house, made a canal at the foot of the garden, stocked it with pike, and planted willows on the edge. He also put the church in repair, preached every Sunday, and played the part of country vicar with at least an average assiduity. Before quitting Dublin he wrote a letter to Miss Jane Waryng, beginning, 'Madam,—I am extremely concerned at the account you give of your health; for my uncle told me he found you in appearance better than you had been in some years, and I was in hopes you had still continued so. God forbid I should ever be the occasion of creating more troubles to you, as you seem to intimate.' 'You would know,' he says, 'what gave my temper that sudden turn, as to alter the style of my letters since I last came over.' Is it owing 'to the thoughts of a new mistress?' 'I declare, upon the word of a Christian and a gentleman, it is not; neither had I ever thoughts of being married to any other person but yourself.' He goes on to speak most disdainfully of her mother and her family, calling her home 'a sink,' asks whether she is healthy enough to marry, can put up with solitude and a poor way of living, can promise to obey him in everything, show no ill humours, etc., all in the harshest tone. 'I singled you out from the rest of women : and I expect not to be used like a common lover.' Not being a common lover, certainly! Exit poor Jane Waryng, no longer 'Varina.' That Swift at one time intended to marry her is certain, unless the two letters are forgeries ; and does not this dispose of several of the biographical theories ?

Now (1700) he is vicar of Laracor ; and odd to say, Miss Johnson, late of Moor Park, Surrey, is coming over to live at the town of Trim, within a walk of Laracor. Sir William has left her a bit of leasehold land in the county Wicklow, as well as a sum of money, and for that reason, in addition to others, she may as well live in Ireland. She comes over accordingly, with an elder companion, a Mrs. Dingley, who has a small income of her own ; and the two ladies go into lodgings in Trim. Esther Johnson is now twenty, a beautiful and sensible young woman, inclining to plumpness of person, with intelligent dark eyes, black eyebrows and lashes, and black hair ; her countenance at once soft and piquant ; the forehead broad for a woman's, and of a very fine curve. Her manners are full of natural grace, with a sort of gentle sprightliness ; her conversation always agreeable ; she knows how to be silent and how to speak with pleasant effect, though not possessing nor pretending to any remarkable intellectual gifts. On Swift, her tutor, the friend of her childhood and maidenhood, she looks with constant reverence and admiration, under which lies hid a tenderer feeling. She is very gentle and submissive, but no coward : she can rebuke a troublesome fool, and even shoot, or shoot at, a midnight burglar on occasion. She is hoping (yet very doubtfully, I imagine) to be Swift's wife, although as yet he has never said or hinted anything of marriage. His manner to her, now dictatorial, now playful, anon both at once, is part fatherly, part lover-like—so far as a caress-

ing phrase or intonation, scarcely beyond. He calls her
by various pet names, ' Stella,' the most usual. But with
all their intimacy, he always reserves himself, and she is
ever somewhat in awe. Esther and her Mrs. Dingley being
settled in their lodgings in the little town of Trim, are constantly visited by the vicar of Laracor, and pay him visits
in return; and when Doctor Swift leaves home, the two
ladies come and live at the vicarage during his absence.
There is at first plenty of gossip in the neighbourhood on all
this, which the doctor much disregards, being at the same
time scrupulously careful in his demeanour to the ladies,
never seeing Hessy without Mrs. Dingley, and equally
attentive to both. It became fully understood by his acquaintance that he was Esther Johnson's friend and
guardian, and no more; and when the Rev. Dr. Tisdall
proposed for her hand, Swift, then in London, wrote to him
to say that he had no objection to the match. But Esther
had objections, and Tisdall sued in vain.

It seems to me most likely, on the whole—indeed, all but
certain—that it never at any time was seriously in Swift's
mind to marry her. *There is no proof that he ever thought of
it*, much less that he did it, as is often stated. Swift wrote
to Tisdall: ' I think I have said to you before, that if my
fortunes and humour served me to think of that state, I
should certainly, among all persons on earth, make your
choice; because I never saw that person whose conversation
I entirely valued but hers; this was the most I ever gave
way to. And, secondly, I must assure you sincerely that
this regard of mine never once entered into my head to be
an impediment to you: . . . the objection of your
fortune being removed, I declare I have no other; nor shall
any consideration of my own misfortune in losing so good a
friend and companion as her prevail on me, against her
interest and settlement in the world.' [1]   Swift's relation to

[1] April 20th, 1704.

Esther Johnson throughout seems to be in no respect mysterious, but perfectly intelligible and in accordance with his character. He was her instructor, guardian, intimate friend and companion—nothing more at any time.

Of Swift's life at Laracor, his oddities in church, his whimsical clerk Roger Cox, several well-known anecdotes are in circulation, few if any of which are authentic. He made a visit nearly every year to London, where he was acquainted with the 'wits' of the town, and intimate with some of the best of them—Addison, Steele, Arbuthnot and others, and also stood on familiar terms with several of the leading Whig statesmen. The *Tale of a Tub*, which first appeared anonymously in 1704, and afterwards in several successive editions, was much talked about, and attributed to various writers of note. Swift's intimates knew whose it was, but he never directly acknowledged it. Among the knowing, it gave him rank among the first order of 'wits;' but it also opened a breach for attack which his enemies (of whom, as a satirist and partisan, he had many) did not neglect to use.

Being deputed by the Irish bishops to move the ministry and the queen to a remission of a sum deducted by the crown, under the name of 'first fruits,' from the incomes of the Irish clergy (at first a papal impost, for crusading purposes), Swift was thus at liberty to sojourn in England from the beginning of 1708 till the spring of next year. In the interest of his Whig friends, Somers and Halifax (and of himself) he turned political pamphleteer, watched the changes of court weather, and waited confidently for preferment. Marriage was less and less in his thoughts. Conscious of his strength, proved in trials, personal and literary, with the most famous men of the time; never amorous, though much attracted to the company of women who suited his tastes; the excitements of party conflict and London society, along with the ambition of rising to a position suitable to his talents, now occupied his mind almost altogether. On Church questions Swift was always 'High,' so far as stoutly stickling for all the external possessions and privileges of the established clergy. In this he differed from his Whig friends; and finding it impossible, after more than a year's trial, to get from them what he wanted, either for the Irish Church or for Dr. Swift, he sheered off, and was ready to attach himself to Mr. Harley, when that statesman led the Tories into office.

In the spring of 1710, Swift, then at Laracor, heard of the death, at Leicester, of his 'dear mother,' aged seventy, and recorded it in an account-book, with this addition: 'I have now lost my barrier between me and death; God grant I may live to be as well prepared for it as I confidently believe her to have been! If the way to heaven be through piety, truth, justice and charity, she is there.'

Harley being on the point of coming into power, the Vicar of Laracor again hastened over to London (September, 1710), on the Irish clergy's behalf and his own; and soon set his pen busy, in pamphlet and squib, on the side of Harley's party. His political pamphlets (he often lamented afterwards to have so spent his time) were highly able and successful, and the ready, telling, and well-informed writer became a person of some importance to ministers (though, perhaps, not so high as he rated himself), and could play the patron among his acquaintance, getting this and that preferment or sinecure for people whom he knew or who were recommended to him. For himself he got nothing, being too proud to make a direct request, and his expectations and merits well known; and his recompense during several years consisted in the glory of being intimate and influential with certain great ministers, and able to behave to them with a kind of pseudo-equality of demeanour,—for after all it was a little too conscious and self-asserting. Along with these feelings, be it remembered, he had always a genuine desire to be of use to persons of desert, especially when there was friendship in the case. Swift's friendships were sincere and lasting; and though he took extraordinary pains to cultivate his intimacy with Harley and St. John as eminent statesmen, and boasted of it continually in his own manner, there went with this a real attachment to them as friends, which survived their loss of power.

This longest visit to London extended from September, 1710 to June, 1713, *ætatis suæ* XLIII-XLVI; and an uncommonly particular and interesting account of it remains in a series of private letters, partly in the form of a diary, and commonly called his *Journal to Stella.* Hester for her part must have been lonely and sad enough during this long absence, during which her years were counted from twenty-nine to thirty-three, and she felt herself passing out of the fair land of youth. She and Mrs. Dingley kept house at Laracor vicarage, their amusement, besides walking and a few books, being usually *ombre* with Dr. Raymond, vicar of Trim, and two or three other neighbours; their chief pleasure—Stella's at least—to receive and answer Dr. Swift's letters from London. The brook at Laracor, edged with willows, still creeps under its little bridge down to the river Boyne, but the site of Swift's vicarage is now 'an ill-tilled potato garden' (or was some years ago), a trace of the pond just discernible, and of the house but one fragment of a gable-wall remaining.

In reading these letters (Stella carefully preserved them; of *her* letters, not one, I think, has been found), a most vivid and real picture of Swift in middle life, mental, bodily, and circumstantial, seems to form itself in one's mind.

One intimacy which the Doctor now began does not make any figure in his *Journal,* namely, in the house of Mrs. Vanhomrigh (pr: *Vanumry*), a rich widow with two daughters. Vanhomrigh was a Dutchman, a commissary in Ireland for King William, and afterwards a commissioner of revenue there. IIis widow, an Englishwoman, came over to reside in London after his death. The beginning of Swift's acquaintance with this family is not indicated, but he probably knew something of them in Ireland.

Mrs. Vanhomrigh's eldest daughter, Esther, is a charming girl of nineteen, intelligent, accomplished, fond of reading, and Doctor Swift, in his leisure moments, takes pleasure in assisting and directing her studies. This grew by degrees into a kind of semi-pedantic flirtation on his side, such as suited his taste; for he did not relish ladies' acquaintance unless where he could more or less play the preceptor. With his acquaintance of both sexes, indeed, it was necessary to allow him a touch of domineering. Esther Vanhomrigh, for her part ('Vanessa,' he calls her, IIessy Van), grew thoroughly, passionately, irrevocably in love with the great Dean, who, when he pleased, was the most delightful company in the world, and even whose sarcasm and imperiousness had, with women, a fondling tone.

Here let me ask, how can the following odd mistake, or string of mistakes, have come to appear in edition after edition of our good Leigh IIunt's book on *The Town*? Swift's introduction to the Vanhomrighs is described; the young lady 'fell in love with him;' but 'unluckily he was married; and most unluckily he did not say a word about the matter. It is curious to observe in the letters which he sent over to Stella (his wife), with what an affected indifference he speaks of the Vanhomrighs,' etc., etc. 'When he left England, Miss Vanhomrigh, after the death of her mother, followed him, and proposed that he should either marry or refuse her. IIe would do neither. At length both the ladies, the married and unmarried, discovered their mutual secret—a discovery which is supposed ultimately to have hastened the death of both. Miss Vanhomrigh's survival of it was short—not many weeks.' In this account, for want of investigation, Leigh IIunt (one of the most

kind-intentioned of men) does Swift a grievous injustice.
The great modern humourist [Thackeray] who lectured on
Swift—with a certain strong bias of dislike ('I hate Swift!'
he said to me, in his lecture-room)—though he knew better
than to commit so great a blunder as the above, has made
several absolute assertions upon very insufficient authority;
among the rest, that 'he married Hester Johnson,' and that
she was 'Temple's natural daughter.'

The first-fruits affair long ago settled—Swift remained in
London, expecting his own so often promised advancement.
'Farewell, dearest beloved MD [Stella], and love poor, poor
Presto [himself], who has not had one happy day since he
left you, as hope saved. It is the last sally [attempt for
promotion, I understand] I will ever make; but I hope it
will turn to some account. I have done more for these, and
I think they are more honest than the last [ministry]; however, I will not be disappointed. I would make MD and
me easy; and I never desired more.' 'I will not be disappointed,' for I *shall* not, is an Irishism. Swift's turns of
phrase, as well as his jokes, are not unfrequently of Irish
fashion; and it is on record that he spoke with a brogue,
to which indeed many of his rhymes testify. Mr. Thackeray
thinks that Swift had nothing whatever of the Irishman
but the accident of his birth; but it is impossible to suppose that in twenty of the most impressible years of his
life, which Swift spent in Ireland, he could have failed
to receive some stamp of Hibernicism, and in fact it is
visible enough.

Months went on; the doctor visiting at the Vanhomrighs',
dining frequently with Harley and St. John (and drinking a
good deal of wine, as his habit was), and his friends expecting
every day to hear of his getting 'a lean bishopric or a fat
deanery,' as Lord Peterborough wrote to him about this
time. Swift replies, 'my ambition is to live in England,
and with a competency to support me in honour.' In the

same letter he says, 'I must leave the town in a week, because my money is gone, and I can borrow no more;' and, in fact, with his income of only two to three hundred pounds a year, he must often have been low in pocket. He complains of the cost of hackney coaches, and when it rains, calls it '*twelvepenny* weather.' His writings have brought him no money; he disdained to trade with the publishers, and, as we saw, indignantly refused 50*l.* offered him by Harley on account of the *Examiner.* Altogether, he holds up his head haughtily among the great folk. The 'wits' he for the most part looks down upon, tossing Steele (until they quarrelled) a *Tatler* now and again; with Arbuthnot he is friendly, and with young Pope, and intermittently with Addison.

Swift's right position would have been that of a statesman and administrator of great affairs, and he knew this very well. Hustled unwillingly into an Irish vicarage, he forced himself into notice by his personal and literary powers, and expected sooner or later to become an English bishop and lord of parliament; and expected justly too. He desired power and dignity. He was fitted to govern, and would certainly have managed his diocese with equity and care, as well as superior ability.

At last he quite loses patience with his great friends who have made so many promises:

April 13, 1713.—'This morning my friend Mr. Lewis came to me and showed me an order for a warrant for three deaneries; but none of them to me. This was what I always foresaw, and received the notice of it better, I believe, than he expected.'

Swift said of himself, that he was ' too proud to be vain,' but I believe he was vain, and rather haughty than proud—for there is much difference in these. Besides the want of means and authority, he felt mortified in the eyes of others in missing promotion, at which he was well known to have been aiming for a long while. In simple fact there were obvious reasons why it was difficult to get Jonathan Swift made into a Church Dignitary : his satiric writing on theological questions, his demeanour,—he, nobody by birth or office, yet haughty and sarcastic to all, with personal oddities and an Irish brogue,—reasons enough. And his being so much in evidence near the court (where too he had bitter enemies) probably made the difficulty greater. At court, of all places, you must be courtly, unless you be one of those two or three men in a generation who are *necessary* factors in the politics of the time.

'At noon lord-treasurer, hearing I was at Mr. Lewis's office, came to me and said many things too long to repeat. I told him I had nothing to do but to go to Ireland immediately ; for I could not with any reputation stay longer here, unless I had something honourable immediately given to me. . . . I am less out of humour than you would imagine, and if it were not for that impertinent people will condole with me, as they used to wish me joy, I would value it less. But I will avoid company, and muster up my baggage, and send them next Monday by the carrier to Chester, and come and see my willows, against the expectation of all the world.—What care I ? Night, dearest rogues, MD.' But he did care. Tho' he often tried hard to convince himself that he would contentedly retire to Laracor without more ado, and there live a peaceful life with Stella and her companion. The choice was in his hand, but ambition and vanity imposed silence on the whispers of his better will.

April 18.—'Lord-treasurer told me the queen was at last resolved that Dr. Sterne should be Bishop of Dromore, and I Dean of St. Patrick's. . . . I do not know whether it will yet be done ; some unlucky accident may yet come [he being so accustomed to disappointment]. Neither can I feel joy at passing my days in Ireland ; and I confess I thought the ministry would not let me go, but perhaps they cannot help it. Night, MD.'

April 21.—'I dined at an alehouse with Parnell and Berkeley ; for I am not in humour to go among the ministers.'

April 23.—'Pray write me a good-humoured letter immediately, let it be ever so short. This affair was carried with great difficulty, which vexes me. But they say here it is much to my reputation that I have made a bishop, in spite of all the world, to get the best deanery in Ireland. [alas! how the brag tries to seem real!] Night, dear MD.'

April 26.—'Yesterday I dined with lord-treasurer and his Saturday people, as usual ; and was so be-deaned!'

In June (1713) Swift is in Dublin, 'horribly melancholy, while they were installing me,' and soon flies to Laracor from the great, empty house, 'which they say is mine.'

In October, urged by his friend Lewis, he goes back to London : he is promised 1,000*l.* to pay off debts and expenses on his deanery ; and still has hopes of a bishopric, or at least of some sufficient dignity and income *in England.* Harley and St. John, now Lords Oxford and Bolingbroke, he strives hard to reconcile, but vainly : he memorials for the small post of Historiographer to the Queen, but it is refused him, and given to 'a worthless rogue that nobody knows.' He goes down, sadly, to lodge with a clergyman at Letcombe, in Berks. Oxford is dismissed, Bolingbroke comes into full power, and is warmer than ever in his promises to the Dean. A few days after this, Queen Anne dies (July 31, 1714), George I. is proclaimed, all arrangements go topsy-turvy, the Tories in dismay, the Whigs triumphant, and Swift returns to Ireland in August.

He is now forty-seven years old ; 'condemned to live in Ireland ; ' his ambitious hopes at an end ; angry and ashamed at having spent so much of his time in dangling at court, yet missing the excitement of brilliant and various

company; his health growing worse; his opinion of mankind sinking ever lower; his economy tightening into parsimony; his satire deepening into grim rage, his domineering
spirit becoming harsher and more tyrannical. Esther Johnson, his dear gentle old pupil and intimate friend, now past
her youth, is in a lodging in Dublin, still with Mrs. Dingley;
but his relations with her are no longer what they were.
The fair Miss Vanhomrigh, young and brilliant, with her
sister Mary, also resides in Ireland now (much, I imagine,
against his wishes)—sometimes in Dublin, sometimes in the
vicinity of Laracor, where she has inherited a small property; and to them the Dean writes often, and sometimes,
though not often or openly, visits at their house.

The letters of poor 'Vanessa' (Hessy Van) are full of
ardent affection, and the most touching expostulations
against his hardness; his are at once flattering and petting
and full of cold reproofs and gibes; and as he used to
make a pretence of holding Mrs. Dingley in something of
the same regard as Stella, so in part he manœuvres with the
two sisters, Hester and Mary.

Domestic happiness is not his, he has thrown it away;
has now less than ever any thought of marriage. He
manages carefully his deanery affairs and his income; drinks
his wine daily, probably with sedative rather than exhilarating effect; and for amusement exchanges puns and grotesque verses (not always of the cleanest) with Dr. Sheridan, a
queer, clever schoolmaster,—fated to have a grandson known
as Richard Brinsley Sheridan. His friend Lord Oxford a
prisoner in the Tower, his friend Lord Bolingbroke an exile
in France,—he himself, the new dean, a suspected Jacobite,
is sometimes hooted by the Dublin populace, and publicly
insulted by men of rank. His archbishop and he are not
on good terms; all the Irish bishops are jealous and suspicious of him,—and no love lost. Swift said once, that the
Government always appointed excellent men to the Irish Sees,

but that on their way across Hounslow Heath they were
sometimes stopped by highwaymen, who took their money,
clothes and papers, and came over to Ireland in their stead.

To the eye, Dean Swift of these years is a tall, portly
man, in clerical dress and hat, with commanding and austere
face, dusky complexion, prominent blue eyes full of scrutiny
and suspicion, or, not seldom, blazing with anger. He
never laughs, rarely smiles, yet lines of humour sometimes
flicker round the nostrils and mouth corners. Manners
abrupt, steps rapid, voice imperious. He has done much,
and attained much; but neither his work nor his position
are satisfactory—to himself least of all. As a writer he can
only rank as an able party pamphleteer, and the author of
some humorous trifles. The *Tale of a Tub* it is his interest
to deny, not to claim. Had he died now, his fame
would have been little. But he will write the *Drapier's
Letters* (because he hates injustice and misgovernment),
and become thereby the most popular man of his day in
Ireland, and *Gulliver's Travels*, the work on which his
literary fame now really rests—a *world-book*—simple, striking, unforgettable, new to every new generation. And of
these '*Travels*' the two first parts, Lilliput and Brobdin-
grag are the cream; no reader is too young or too old to
enjoy them. It is strange, by the bye, that the printer's
mistake of 'Brobdingnag' (which Swift himself pointed out
in the 'Letter from Captain Gulliver,' prefixed to the edition
of 1727 [1]) should be perpetuated to this day. Let this

---

[1] 'Indeed I must confess that, as to the people of *Lilliput, Brobdin-
grag* (for so the name should have been spelt, and not erroneously
Brobdingnag) and *Laputa*, I have never yet heard of any *Yahoo* so
presumptuous as to dispute their being, or the facts I have related con-
cerning them.'—*Letter from Captain Gulliver, etc.* [Some of those not
very rare gentlemen who have a turn for contradiction and prefer something they are pleased to think subtlety to common sense, wrote to the
literary papers to argue that this correction was merely a new joke or mys-
tification of Swift's. If so, it was certainly the poorest joke he ever made.]

unpronounceable and on the face of it blundering word
be universally dropped for the future, and the oft-mentioned
country of giants be known by its true name of BROB-DIN-
GRAG.

Swift's best verses, too, which are masterly in their kind
for clearness and concinnity—tho' wanting continuity of
flow and variety of cadence, were the product of his later
years. His verses, like the bulk of his writings, were *occasional*. He was a man of the world and of society in its
artificial sense ; his subjects are those which naturally
interested him, shaped by a clear and practised intellect,
and coloured by the disdainful and satiric quality of his
thoughts. To beauty of every kind his senses were obtuse ;
he cared nothing at all for the picturesque in nature,
nothing for real Poetry, nothing for painting, sculpture or
architecture, and in music it seemed

> ' Strange that such difference should be
> 'Twixt Tweedledum and Tweedledee.'

Beyond his ' polite learning ' of the usual sort on Greek
and Roman subjects, he seems to have cared little for
history or for general literature. During his many
years of sojourn in Ireland, the history, antiquities, language,
ethnology, natural history, of that country did not excite
in him the faintest spark of curiosity.

After allowing all his merit as a writer, it is certain that
Swift's fame is a more conspicuous edifice than could have
been built upon his literary performances alone, even though
they include that rare and happy kind of thing (whether
great or small), a *world-book*. His strong and peculiar
personal character, his distinction first in the social and
literary world of London, and then (much higher) in Irish
politics, the interest that belongs to Stella and Vanessa, his
position as a church dignitary, which lends so much zest to
his humour and to the odd stories and jests reported of him,

the terrible eclipse of his brilliant intellect, his gloomy death, and the legacy to found a madhouse,—all these strike the imagination and impress the memory of mankind. Many have been his predecessors and successors in office, but Jonathan Swift remains and will remain *the* Dean of St. Patrick's. Yet his grand mistake in life was going into the church—' allowing himself to be driven into the church for a maintenance.' [1] He heartily despised clerical men and clerical matters, save as a part of business. When once in, irrevocably, he looked upon it as his necessary business to be a clergyman, and to maintain all the established doctrines and rights and emoluments of his church, as 'one (he says) appointed by Providence for defending a post assigned to me.' [2] He was not a pious, not an amiable dean; he was unhealthy, disappointed, cynical, contemptuous, unhappy; yet also was he reasonable, charitable, equitable; still quaintly humorous amidst his glooms; after a fashion, kindly; in a large measure, honest and faithful. Not the least foggy, plausible, slippery, but clear and somewhat hard in intellect. When obliged to touch questions of theology, he handled them in a resolutely conservative manner. He constantly argued that all private men, and especially all clergymen, should submit to the existing legal forms of worship, and if they have doubts, to ' take care to conceal those doubts from others.' [3] He attacked, and would have suppressed, with equal vigour, atheists, papists, and dissenters. On Trinity Sunday he duly preached in defence of the doctrine of the Trinity; on the 30th of January he duly preached to the glory of ' that excellent king and blessed martyr Charles I.,' and in denunciation of the ' murderous Puritan Parliament,' and of such as continued to hold ' those wicked opinions.' [4] He proved

[1] *Anecdotes of the Family of Swift. Written by Dr. Swift. Scott's Memoirs.*

[2] *Thoughts on Religion.*　　　[3] *Ibid.*　　　[4] *Sermon the Sixth.*

7

to his congregation how superior the meanest Christian is to the loftiest and wisest Pagan philosopher in rules of life, and in consolations and hopes; quoting Socrates, Aristotle, and others. 'Solon lamenting the death of a son; one told him, "You lament in vain." "Therefore," said he, " I lament, because it is in vain." This was a plain confession how imperfect all his philosophy was,' etc. 'Diogenes delivered it as his opinion, "that a poor old man was the most miserable thing in life."' And, alas! Jonathan Swift, when no longer in the pulpit, said so a thousand times.

Swift was a politician, was fitted to be an adviser and still more, an administrator in affairs of public importance; shut out from these occupations, his activity domineered and ruled in the petty bounds within which it was limited in actual life, and overflowed through his pen in gibes upon the folly, stupidity and baseness, and denunciations of the injustice which he saw around him. He hated injustice, not out of pity for the misused, but from a deep principle of his nature, a kind of exact and exacting equitableness, love of rule and order, which commonly took a form of severity, and made him in the highest degree punctilious in money matters and household economy. Whatever lay next him he bent himself, with harsh effort if needed, to subdue into discipline and regularity.

I must own my real opinion, that there is but poor nourishment for the soul in any part of Swift's writings. Clear, practical sense he gives us, and a wide knowledge of men and affairs, put into form by a vigorous realistic fancy, and coloured with ironic humour; but there is nothing cordial or encouraging, no reconciling insight, no deep wisdom. This age of English literature in its whole result I confess strikes me as poor and thin, however elegantly simple and clear in its turns of expression. It is not corrupt, like the preceding period. Addison has a kind of polite religiosity of tone; he associates good-breeding with virtue; Steele, though sometimes a rather prurient moralist, draws some charming little pictures of domestic happiness; Pope's didactics and sentimentals, in his verses, letters, and everything, sound hollow, yet have a kind of improved heathenish morality *au fond*. Swift is the strongest, and the most objectionable; his satire is sincere; it was his habitual view of life. It smites forcibly the vices, failings and follies of mankind; but too often it attacks human nature itself. He does not merely say, See how far you fall short of what you might be and ought to be; how different your practices from your pretences; how you lie, cheat, grovel, and brag, advance the wrong men, make useless war, miseducate your children, misgovern your own and the public affairs; but he says also, See what a poor, weak, wretched, filthy, selfish, sensual thing is Humanity! How absurd is all your fine talk about it! What can you make of it at best? Even your virtues are contemptible. He draws the character of Gulliver with gentle and pleasing touches at first, but in this book also, at the end, rushes fiercely into a horrible coarseness. The human form divine is by him represented as 'an ugly monster;'[1] and this picture of the external fact may be fairly taken as a test and measure of his general truthfulness. As to the filthiness of Swift's pen, the foul smell that one is liable to encounter at any step in his writings, no reasonable excuse or even palliation can be offered for it. It is a shameful fact, not accounted for by the fashion of the time, for among his famous contemporaries he is pre-eminently filthy (indeed the epithet is not descriptive of any but him), and much aggravated by his position as a public authority in religion and morals. His humour took this turn from a contempt and exasperation against mankind, along with a liking to outface and overbear ordinary conventions, and was supplied with images by a fancy of depraved appetite. Like

[1] *Voyage to the Houyhnhnms*, chap. 1.

every Writer, he remains accountable before the Highest Tribunal for every word he has written.

The better part of Swift's nature comes forward in his private letters. His indignation and contempt were constant against mankind, and against classes and societies of men; but he could be attached and even affectionate to individuals. In his correspondence with Bolingbroke, Pope, Gay, and others, Swift's letters are always the best, and (while his tone to everybody is that of an acknowledged superior) they are full of sincere steadfast friendship, and often show a manly tenderness. Their gloomy ground is inlaid with freaks of quaint humour. His letters to great ladies are admirable examples of spirited politeness, and prove how well he could mingle wit and sense with courtly manners. Besides his nearer intimacies, he was never without some female friends in whose conversation or correspondence he took evident pleasure, notwithstanding the contempt with which he spoke of the sex in general.

As to Swift's relations to most people, it seems to me that he was probably a very good-natured man to those who were in want of any kind of help, at the same time that he desired to *appear* rough and ungracious, partly out of whim, partly to avoid being imposed on (which he hated), and to escape thanks and sentimentalism. His words are full of harshness, and apparent grudging; but in fact he was lifelong busy serving others, in ways suitable to his mind and temper. He says himself (in a letter to Pope) that he detested that animal called *man*, yet loved John, Peter, Thomas, and this is true. His *sæva indignatio* was against the stupidity, injustice, and ingratitude of mankind. To individuals he was constant and tender. Mr. Thackeray asks, 'Would you have liked to be a friend of Swift's?' I would, for one; would have liked better, I think, to be a friend of Swift's, than of any of his set—than of the refined Addison, the jovial Steele, the brilliant St. John, the fastidious Pope—and would have felt safer with him, in spite of the whims and harshness and domineering.

As I have said, he was a man of the world and of society in its conventional sense; but promptings of something finer within him, along with his poor success in gaining worldly advancement, made him ill content to be this. Church and State were conditions of the game in which he found himself engaged. An ideal life was above his natural aims. Religion, in a personal sense, did not affect him. Of a life of independent principle he had glimpses, but ambition, vanity, fear of poverty, and other personal motives drew him aside into repeated false steps, disappointments, and continual discontent.

In early years, he 'had a scruple of entering the Church merely for support'—but he got over this scruple on finding no hope of promotion in any other direction. The thought of poverty and dependence made him miserable. He felt deeply that 'the worst of poverty is that it makes a man ridiculous.' For this reason, not for any love of accumulation, he was frugal to parsimony; and mainly for this reason, as I think, he at last *faute de mieux* hastened 'into holy orders,' through which door he might hope for many things, not excluding political influence and office. But the satiric pen which he could not keep quiet was an ill help to church preferment, the worse for its trenchant originality, and he saw when too late that had he held on for a time as free lance, he might have reached a position in the political world more in accordance with his ambition and his powers.

His Will was strong, but he did not use it, as every man is under penalties bound to do, in striving towards the objects which in his best moments he knew to be the best. He directed it to lower aims and missed them: hence, mainly, his unhappiness. That a load of disappointment had much to do in aggravating his brain trouble, who can doubt? And that every man's employment of his Will-power plays a large part in the history of his life,—tho' often a secret part, and never one fully known—I for one do always believe. In hints of the use and misuse of Will, and the consequences, lies the chief value of Biography.

Thirty years of life still remained to Jonathan Swift, sad, sombre, deepening at last into black gloom and a state as of living death. Of these I hope to write on some future occasion, perhaps after a special visit to Dublin and Meath.

Along the grass-grown avenue I walked away from Moor Park, thinking of these things, and of little boy Cobbett of Farnham, reading the *Tale of a Tub* behind the haystack at Richmond; and thus came to Waverley; where the old dame who opened the gate pointed to an old-fashioned pretty house, half-timbered, in a little garden by the mill-dam, and said, 'That's Stella's cottage; she was the daughter of the gardener at Moor Park.' Thus valuable is local tradition. A pond with swans; a wealthy heavy-porticoed mansion; a clear, shallow little river, under lofty banks of trees, half encompassing a wide meadow; shattered gray ruins, fern and ivy-clad, shaded with ash-tree and thorn, here a triple lancet window, there a low-arched crypt: this is Waverley, a Cistercian foundation of the 12th century. Here, when Cobbett was a boy (he tells us), flourished the finest fruit-garden he ever saw in his life. It has long since disappeared; and it seems that one (I know not which) of the successive owners of the park improved away a great part of the abbey ruins. The name of Scott's famous novel probably came into his head by means of the annals of this abbey; being both a pretty name and appropriate to his hero's character. The description of Waverley Honour has no resemblance to the real Waverley.

I took the shady road up Crooksbury Hill, turned left, along the moorland, which lies behind the vale of Moor

Park, and accounts for the name, and soon saw before me the ridge of Aldershot, my thoughts again connecting Swift and Cobbett, by the link of a *standing army*—a novelty in Swift's day—and a thing obnoxious to them both, very different as they were, both as men and politicians.

The step is but short from Swift, Temple, Marlborough, to Cobbett, Wellington, Palmerston (another of the Temples), whose grave is the newest in Westminster Abbey. Two or three lives stretch over great changes in thought and history. Many men and things very notable in their day are well-nigh or wholly forgotten, even in so short a period of time. A Book with genius in it has the best chance of survival. If Sir William Temple could by possibility have guessed that Moor Park—that his own name—would have a meaning in men's ears after two centuries solely on account of his rough Irish amanuensis !

RAMBLE THE FIFTH.

EXETER AND ELSEWHERE.

THE long narrow steep High Street of Exeter, with its lofty old houses hung to-day with flags of every size and colour, almost realises one's notion of a city of the middle ages *en fête*. The ghost of a fourteenth-century citizen would not perhaps see much change at first glance, though by-and-by he must begin to peer with wonder at the omnibuses and plate-glass shop-windows. The men's coats and hats would look dull and queer (a 'wide-awake' might pass muster), but I don't know that the costumes of the comely Devon damsels who brighten the street with their white or blue skirts and tiny floral hats atop a mountain of chestnut or brown or golden hair, would, supposing him a ghost of some experience in his day, cause much astonishment. Women, in fact, were women in the fourteenth century (whatever they may become in the twentieth), fashions changed in his time as they change in ours, and Master Ghost might probably recollect some phases of robe and coiffure not much unlike that of the Cynthia of the minute.

East and west, or nearly, runs the street for a mile and a half, rising narrow and very steep from the river, ascending more gradually past the projecting curved front (1593) of the Guildhall, widening above and branching into the country, bye-streets and narrow courts going off on either hand; and one of these latter, on the right going up, bringing you briefly into the Cathedral Close, where through

sparse elm trees of moderate size, peeps forth the antique
bulk of grey stone, west porch rough with worn sculptures
under the great west window, row of wide and close-set
northern windows alike in size, unlike each from each in its
rich 'geometric' tracery, and two square low massy
Norman towers, long ago pierced as transepts, standing
midway the edifice. The Close is mainly of non-ecclesiastic
appearance, 'dis-established'-looking, bordered with hotels,
a bank, and common dwelling-houses. But the worst is a
new church, a big church, incredibly ugly, built cheek by
jowl alongside that venerable west front. Words cannot
express the disgust inspired by this pretentious monstrosity,
its lumbering spire browbeating the solemn and ancient
beauty of the cathedral. And what can be the good of it?
Here is a most beautiful church in perfect order, furnished
with all due appliances, already six times too big for any
possible congregation; in which three or four separate
sermons might be preached simultaneously, if that could be
thought desirable; and beside this, almost touching it, you
build up another church of the same worship, a costly and
pretentious building, odiously unsightly in itself, and most
damaging to its neighbour's beauty.

What avails it to protest against the great guild of
uglifiers who are busily at work on the surface of this poor
old earth, destroying or disfiguring whatsoever beautiful
thing they come near, setting up their abominations everywhere, to the injury of present and future mankind? Little
I fear; yet there is some small satisfaction in speaking one's
mind, and giving such people to know what certain others,
however few, think of their works—of any work helping to
permanently uglify the world. Such an evil may be sometimes absolutely unavoidable, like shaving a sick man's head
or cutting his leg off, but the necessity ought to be clear and
real, not, as so often, a pretended need generated in a com-
post of stupidity, weak desire of novelty, and some kind of

low self-interest. Once more suffer this to be repeated, since men are continually forgetting it : the world is not ours absolutely, or any part of it; but only ours *in trust.* We have ' a user,' as the lawyers say, and that without prejudice to all others, born or to be born. Pray, how can mortal do, in a common way, worse turn to mankind than by permanently lessening the world's beauty, in landscape, in architecture, in dress, in (what is sure to go with the rest) manners, tastes, sympathies? An evil governor, or the writer of a clever vile book, perhaps does worse, but that is not in a common way. To those who would care nothing, or rather prefer it, if the whole world were a model sewage-farm (deodorised at best), with towns of new bricken streets and stuccoed villas, churches and railway stations at proper intervals, as per contract, I have nothing to say, save to wish them Australia or Central America all to themselves, to build and live in after their own hearts, export boundless wool and preserved beef, and become richer, fatter, and stupider year by year.

The interior of the Cathedral, chiefly thirteenth and fourteenth-century work, is at once rich in effect and simple in plan ; rows of clustered pillars supporting pointed arches, rows of wide windows of varied tracery, long line of vaulted roof, groined and bossed, all symmetrically beautiful, a lovely *coup d'œil* from the west door—but with one huge blot, the lumbering bulk of the organ, like a gigantic chest of drawers, heaved up on the screen midway. Why is this organ *unlike* a peacock? Because it delights the ear and tortures the eye. It ought to be transplanted to-morrow to one of the transepts. On the stone screen is painted a row of curious scripture-pieces, well preserved and harmonious in colour, six from the Old Testament, and seven from the New. The east window is bad perpendicular, but filled in with ancient stained glass of fine subdued colour ; the west window a geometric rose, but with petals of glaring modern

glass. In the Lady-Chapel ('the ladies' chapel,' I heard
a visitor call it, so far is the famous word on its way to
popular oblivion) and side-chapels, are many tombs, some
of them lately painted and gilded in true upholsterer fashion.
The Chapter House, a stately vaulted room, contains a
library of old books, and there I saw and handled the
original 'Doom Book' for Devon and Cornwall, its
parchment leaves and black and red writing quite fresh to
this day. Some clever fellow among the suffering Saxons
invented the sensational name of *Domesday Book* for these
reports, a phrase absurdly kept still in serious use; for
'Doom Book' means neither more nor less than 'valua-
tion book,'—'doom,' what is *deemed*—in this case what is
deemed the value of people's landed properties throughout
England.

Southwards from Exeter Cathedral to the river, straggles
a network of narrow slums, crossed by the wider South
Street; and over these crowded alleys the steep lower part
of the High Street goes on arches, from which the downlook,
especially at night, is picturesque enough. Here and there
a quaint old house rewards the adventurous explorer; and
the 'White Hart' in South Street, with its courtyard and
galleries, is a charming bit of the Past, while its flowers
and bright bar give good promise of present comfort.[1]
Beyond the Exe, an easy-flowing stream of some thirty
yards wide, is a suburb, not legally part of the city, and
above this rise the rich hills of grove and cornfield, by which
Exeter is well-nigh encompassed; seawards only, along the
river's right shore, goes a stretch of flat pasture land, here
and there embanked from the tide. The good old city combines the characters of an inland and a seaport place. From
most points of view the wide-sweeping circle of rich slopes
is unbroken, and the great trees stand tall and straight, or
mass their foliage 'in heavy peacefulness,' without any

[1] Burnt down a few years after.

sign of conflict with sea-gales. Yet the salt tide is not far off; sailors and yachtsmen, cockles and fresh herrings, walk familiarly through her streets; by help of a short canal the ocean-furrowing keels lie alongside her wharves; and but a little way down, the river opens widely to ebb and flood, and all the incidents of sea-side life.

Near as it is, the breath of the sea is not much felt in Exeter, unless perhaps when southerly or south-easterly winds are blowing. The air in the close streets during those sunshiny autumnal days felt very heavy and stagnant, and was mingled morning and evening with a fog from the river. The roads and lanes, too, as usual in Devon, are thickly shut in with trees and hedgerows. Lover of antiquity, I must own that the new and comparatively broad Queen Street, leading towards the railway station, is doubtless a very good thing for the public health.

Between this and the High Street is a large mound or small hill, crowned with a public walk under lofty elms, called Northernhay (*hedge*, no doubt) and the red-sandstone ruins of the ancient castle of Rougemont. These red stones of Red Hill were laid by the men of William Duke of Normandy and Conqueror of England, when Exeter had sullenly surrendered, after a fierce and bloody siege of eighteen days. You can enter the castle-yard through a postern, climb to its battlement and overlook the city, and descend to the High Street by the corner of a lofty gateway, now wrapt in ivy, and shaded by a huge walnut-tree.

> ' Richmond!—when last I was at Exeter,
> The mayor in courtesy showed me the castle,
> And called it—Rouge-mont : at which name I started ;
> Because a bard of Ireland told me once
> I should not live long after I saw Richmond.' [1]

In this castle-yard stands the County Assize Court, guarded by a statue of Earl Fortescue, thick-haired (or

[1] *King Richard III.*, iv. 2.

wigged ?), whiskered, aquiline, robed and gartered. He was
' Lord Lieutenant of Devon,' died 1861, and is here praised
for a ' noble and generous character,' and ' unwearied diligence in the discharge of public duty ;' conveying but little
to a stranger's mind.

On the grass plot of Northernhay are two other modern
statues, sightly enough : Thomas Dyke Ackland (1861), a
handsome man standing cloaked, motto ' *Præsenti tibi
maturos largimur honores :*' and John Dinham, old man in
chair, with large book open on his lap, the inscription speaking of ' Piety, integrity, charity,' etc. I confess I never
heard of John Dinham before, and would fain have had
some particulars. A man's monument should carry on it
a biography, brief, accurate, and pregnant, addressed to all
comers. The motto here was a text from the Bible—' The
book of the law shall not depart out of thy mouth, but thou
shalt meditate thereon day and night, and then thou shalt
make thy way prosperous, and then thou shalt have good
success.' What kind of prosperity and success did the
citizens of Exeter suppose to be meant in this sentence ?
Something very tangible, I suspect, of a kind which by no
means ' passeth all understanding.' A wealthy, diligent,
shrewd, respectable, and also benevolent man, is a good solid
figure of great worth in his place. I was satisfied, if not
exhilarated, to see this memorial, which I took to belong
to some such person, but somehow misliked its motto.

Each of these three statues, in white marble, stands on a
British pedestal of gray granite. The British pedestal, in
which a noble simplicity is no doubt aimed at, is bare and
rectangular, with meagre mouldings—a thing ill-proportioned
in every part, thoroughly uncomfortable and mean. A
harsh, spiky railing round the Ackland pedestal enhances
its ungainly appearance. Now there is no reason on earth
why sculptors, if they know how, should not put their
statues on pedestals of varied design, each, whether simple

or rich, being decorative and delightful. Even a plain, four-cornered block of stone may be well or ill-proportioned in relation to that which it supports, and to the general surroundings. It is true the sculptor does not always design the pedestal; but he always ought to do so.

Besides Northernhay there is a Southernhay, with good houses and shady trees, and also a Bonhay and a Shilhay in the suburbs.

If you wish to see what the country round Exeter is like, go up the long narrow High Street, leaving the Castle-mound on your left hand, and the Cathedral-close on your right, and so along the wider street of St. Sidwell (properly Sativola, an obscure saint with an ugly church of Georgian architecture), till the road forks. Take the left-hand road, and again, at a turnpike, the left hand, and after a mile uphill a slope is reached, looking northward across the valley of the Exe, and a wide landscape of wonderful richness; great hill-sides one behind another, loaded, when I saw them, with yellow harvest, dark with luxuriant groves and copses, the warm red ploughed fields here and there adding to the ripeness of the picture; in front a white mansion (Sir Stafford Northcote's) in its woody park rising from the river; granges and farmhouses scattered or clustered amid foliage; the proud and wealthy vale stretching far away, crowned by a range of hills almost mountainous; and, as we look, a running flag of white vapour shows where the North Devon railway has found its winding course.

Retracing our steps to Exeter, we see the elms of Northernhay, a solid, straight-topped, and conspicuous grove, the two square towers of the Cathedral scarcely rising above the surrounding roofs; then down a steep hill and up a moderate ascent, and here we stand again in the High Street, bustling with human mortals and hung with brilliant flags.

But why these flags? Because the old city is in these

days entertaining a distinguished guest, the British Association for the Advancement of Science, and on corners and doorposts you see mysterious printed placards, 'Section A,' 'Section D,' and so on. Exeter is overflowing with learned men and pretty girls, hearty wholesome-looking Devon lasses, well grown, with complexions that seem nourished on rosy apples and clotted cream, who can turn science itself into a gala. The meeting was a lively one. Theology in the shape of three clergymen pitted itself against Darwinism; but the arguments are no longer interesting. The fact is, Science is impregnable within its own limits, outside of them powerless.

Does the Man of Science in investigating, elucidating and formulating the phenomena of the material world necessarily tamper with essential religion, with our sense of duty and purity, and truth, our feelings of love, joy, and wonder and adoration, our passionate longing for the Spiritual Best and Highest? Just as much as a grammarian's inquiry into the components of language ought to affect the influence of Shakespeare's or of Goethe's mind on mine. When the Man of Science as such meddles with religion or poetry or art, he is most decidedly going *ultra crepidam.* To reduce every statement to a mathematic form would be the ideal perfection of Science.

So we leave this topic, and step on a sunshiny morning into a railway carriage that speeds us along the right shore of the Exe (*Uisge,* the Keltic for water; Exeter, if in Ireland, would be named something like *Cahirisky,* say 'Water-fort,'—'Water-city'), quickly broadening from river to estuary, opening to sands, to merry sea-waves, and showing Exmouth town on its headland opposite, with a little crowd of masts below. The crags and pyramids of red sandstone, the bathers sporting in the bright sea, the old village-green of Dawlish and the new villas above it, are come and gone; so is the estuary of the Teign among grovy hills, with long wooden bridge and vessels at anchor : and here is Torquay, famous Torquay—lovely scenery, Italian climate, William of Orange, Napoleon in the *Bellerophon*, etcetera,—transformed from a name into a reality.

A friend of mine (the Magician), an unimpeachable authority on such things, told me that, some thirty years ago, Torquay was the most beautiful place in England. Its wide-sweeping bay and richly wooded shores, crags garlanded with foliage and flowers from wave-washed basis to summit in the blue sky, rocky creeks that, while you sat musing, filled silently with the crystal green of the rising tide ; its old-fashioned cottages under shady rows of elms, peaceful neighbouring farmhouses and inland meadows, old field-paths and honeysuckle lanes,—these A. T. recalled with a regretful delight in contrast with the Torquay of our own day, the rows of brick and stucco, felled trees, rocks blasted away, gaunt wide roads, cockney shops and churches, sun-baked esplanades and piers, the once clear tide polluted with torrents of feculence, so that bathing (as a medical man there told me) can hardly be ventured on.

'Vast improvements on the whole,' says and thinks the practical man, whose name is Legion; 'investment of capital,—increase of business and employment — national prosperity—greatest happiness even (if you like to bring that in) of the greatest number.' Well, the world must change, certainly, and in its changes some old and precious things must go. We must lose something, but we gain a great deal more, you say. How? in happiness? It seems to me, I confess, though a very expensive, not a very happy generation, this of ours. I doubt if it really enjoys its stucco and its gravelled esplanades. Are they necessary to its pleasure or even to its comfort, or are they rather the vulgar inventions of scheming builders, contractors and engineers, and huckstering tradespeople, like the large shop-fronts and staring placards of the period? Moreover, — change is inevitable, often reasonable : admitted. But the changes that have overrun and disfigured many of the fairest spots in England during the last twenty years, were they all inevitable, allowable, and reasonable? merely the natural result (whether pleasant or otherwise) of the course of prevalent ideas and manners? or, on the contrary, were they in very many instances as much opposed to practical common sense and common honesty as to the sense of beauty and venerableness? Is it not the notorious fact that most of these new-built pleasure-towns are, in commercial phrase, thoroughly *rotten* places, insolvent, staggering on from season to season under a burden of debt incurred in making roads and rails, piers, villas, terraces, crescents, which *were not really wanted*—in crowding into five years the proper work of fifty? Over and over again you find, on a little inquiry, that a great part of the splendid new town—the brilliant fashionable watering-place, is mortgaged to cunning builders and lawyers lying perdue. The names on the shops and lodging-houses seldom indicate a real owner-ship. Small wonder if these unhappy creatures seize the stranger with voracity, suck his blood without mercy. And the showy houses are often ill built, soon begin to lose their one virtue of a smug tidiness, and fall into premature decay almost before they arrive at their teens. Three-fourths of them were not wanted, are 'bad investments,' and likely to grow worse; meanwhile they disfigure the world, and transmit, not improvements and conveniences, but eyesores and obstacles to the coming generations, who will certainly prefer to follow their own tastes, and be little grateful for these tawdry piles of ill burnt brick and bad mortar. In short, from the mere business point of view, these 'vast improvements' mostly rest on a basis of greed, gambling, and unveracity :—

> The earth hath bubbles as the water has,
> And these are of them.

8

Would they might vanish 'as breath into the wind;' but
unhappily they are ulcers, and will leave permanent scars on
the fair face of nature.

A steamer, coasting the bay, put me ashore at Babbicombe, where I plunged ecstatically into the translucent
water of a sea-cove walled with lofty rocks, and swimming
round a corner faced the beautiful sunny shadowy coast
sweeping off towards Lyme Regis, red crags, crested with
green slopes and woods, every steep rock and crevice hung
with foliage and broidered with creeping verdure; the little
strand of Babbicombe, half-mooned-shaped and white as
the moon, receiving kiss after kiss from the purple sea; and
over all a pure blue sky.

One great blot there was, one eyesore, a conspicuous
headland hacked and torn away by quarrymen; and at
Anstey's Cove, across the hill, I found another headland
undergoing the same treatment by the same wealthy lord-
of-the-soil. To say the least, one would rather not make
money precisely thus; one would rather not shake the hand
of the man who could do it.

A walk over the hills brought me to a verge looking down
into Anstey's Cove, where the red cliffs and tumbled fragments, crested and seamed with bright green sward, the
firm sands, purple sea, sunny blue sky, seemed familiar as
my birth-place, by reason of a little picture of the place by
George Boyce on my wall at home. I was able at last to
satisfy my curiosity as to the end of the headland, which
lay outside the picture; but I missed the man on horseback
from the road, forgetting for an instant that he must have
passed a long while ago.

An elderly man and his pretty little grand-daughter were
at the choice view-point where a block of stone lies on the
bank by way of seat. They seemed to take little or no
notice of the prospect; were come to meet the child's
mother who had gone down to the beach on some errand.

The man lived only a mile or two away, but had not been here for I think he said ten years before to-day. He was a mason and had speculated in house-building, not to his gain, I understood; but some one else whom he named, some contractor, had 'made a lot of money,' and on this he would have talked for hours. His eyes were turned inwards and downwards; to his entrails as Swedenborg would have said. This is the state of vast numbers around us, and held to be the right state for them too. These are some of the men, with their 200*l.* capital, their greediness and stupidity, who build Cockneyville-super-mare on every fair coast, with the co-operation of speculators, loan-societies, building-companies, cunning lawyers, quack-architects, gambling contractors, and swindling money-brokers. The little local men commonly lose their venture. There are some more rows of tawdry stucco, for the *beau monde* and its imitators, while the fashion lasts, to lounge and flirt and yawn away a part of its time in; while quieter folk, instead of a homely lodging, must pay three or four times as much for French varnish and gilt curtain rings, with a hundred times worse food and attendance than of old, and no kindness or gratitude.

After a delightful spell of solitary freedom in the midst of beautiful scenery, I joined a swarm of masters and scholars in science, and we all made together for Kent's Hole, a rather ugly slimy cavern burrowing and branching into the limestone bowels of a grovy hill. From hot sun and dusty hedgerows we stepped into an icy gloom dim-lit with numerous candles stuck against the dripping walls, on gluey stalagmites and heaps of quarried rubbish; heard a geologic lecture, then wandered off through narrow passages, and peeped into dark holes, and out again to the hot air and cheerful daylight world. In these unsunned recesses under the slow incrustations of many thousand years, are found bones of elephants, rhinoceroses, cave-bears, and

8—2

other monsters, and less deeply imbedded, tokens of the presence of human creatures like ourselves, bone needles, flint tools, and even some bones and skulls.

Several men, I think three or four, dig and pick daily in this cavern, at the cost of the British Association, and under the superintendence of Mr. Pengelly of Torquay, who has now collected herefrom over 50,000 various bones, and kept account of the situation and depth where each was found. Mr. Pengelly is a brisk and ruddy old-bone-man, with merry blue-gray eyes.

I don't wonder that students of physical science are commonly long-lived, healthy, and cheerful. Their field of study, whatever the department may be, is practically boundless. They advance into it with sure and deliberate steps, adding particular experience to experience, and at the same time gaining a wider interest in the general universe ; while the pursuit in itself is amusing and full of expectation, and employs the senses along with the intellect.

In the carriage for Exeter I fell in talk with a gentleman whose special study is entozoa, those queer little creatures that live and breed inside the bodies of beasts, birds, and fishes, and our own too, inhabiting the blood, muscles, liver, brain, etc., and there making out life in their own fashion, without, in the majority of cases, it would seem, the least inconvenience to their landlord. Each of us lodges crowds of these, and it is very rarely that one turns troublesome; they are by far more peaceable than an ordinary Irish tenantry. My scientific friend tells me that his experienced eyes never fail to see some entozoa in *every* dish of animal food that comes to table, and often a great many. 'When there are a great many, what do you do?' 'Eat 'em, if the meat be properly cooked. The odds are millions to one that no harm will come of it.' Sometimes when he encounters an extra-large Distoma, or Spiroptera, or Cysticercus, he sets it aside on his plate, and not long ago totally refused a dish of mutton, because it swarmed with Echinococci ; for if a creature from the body of a sheep, cow, pig, be transferred *alive* into yours or mine, the consequences might be serious. Such appearances at the dinner-table might make some people uncomfortable, but my friend proved no exception to the rule as to men of science, being a merry, fresh-complexioned man whose food clearly agreed with him.

The universality of entozootic life makes one cease to care much about it. But trichinosis is a real and dreadful disease for all that, like hydrophobia ; and though one may see no risk in eating a rasher or patting a dog, there are certain precautions fit to be observed. My microscopical friend does not think the little beasts in the pig more dangerous than others ; but ham, sausages, etc., are often eaten with slight cooking, whence come evils.

Science, it would seem, is in hopes of being able to trace all the steps between an Entozoon and a Goethe, but long before it arrives at Goethe's soul (pass me the old-fashioned phrase) science will find its instruments fail it, I imagine.

I am far from thinking, however, that our leaders in science wish to teach that there is nothing but matter ; or that they suppose it possible for themselves, or for any man, to comprehend all phenomena physical and mental, or to know the innermost nature of any single thing. They say, as I take it, there are certain exact methods called scientific, of investigating any given subject ; to some subjects these methods are found to be more applicable, to others less ; we will strictly apply these methods as far as we are able to every subject that presents itself. As soon as we clearly perceive them to be inapplicable in any case (a perception which is an important element in the pursuit of truth) we will cease our attempts in that particular direction. On the

other hand, so long as our methods of investigation show a
real hold upon any subject and a fruitful relation to it, we
will employ them with the utmost simplicity and fearless-
ness,—truth (which is multiform and yet one) being safely
left to protect her own interests.

This, *au fond*, is probably the attitude of the best scientific
minds of our time. And yet there are, perhaps, some real
dangers connected with the vastly increased activity of
scientific investigation. First, a successful investigator is
under the temptation of building up theories, top-heavy for
the basis on which they are raised; of forgetting that the
most learned of men is still but a young pupil in the great
school of nature. Secondly, one set or combination of facts
may be so put forward as that they shall for a time take up
a disproportionate share of attention, and throw out of
balance many minds of thinking men, thus affecting, in-
juriously, the general health of public thought. Thirdly,
the tone of scientific authority itself may be less modest
(keeping within its proper limits) and less reverent than it
might be in presence of the wonders and mysteries (so
unfathomed, so unfathomable) of the universe, and man's
life therein. The Man of Science—I mean the *Master* in
Science—should be exact, fearless, and profoundly reverent.
Reverence, you may tell me, is a moral not an intellectual
quality, but I own that to me it appears that moral and
intellectual qualities are inseparable, and that a masterly
insight into nature is only possible to the reverent spirit.
True Masters, indeed, are always rare; but we have usually
plenty of clever people, and a fair supply of able ones, and
some of these are no more unwilling to wear the robe of
ephemeral mastership, than the multitude is unwilling to
confer it.

From Exeter to Moreton-Hampstead, on the eastern edge
of Dartmoor, is no more than twelve miles as the bird flies,

but hills intervene, and our railway took us three times the distance round about, winding at last among deep vales. Moreton (Moor-town), a gray old village, sent us on in a gig to Chagford, a smaller and grayer old village, with rude stone cottages straggling up-hill, and a few new brick houses of the meanest ugliness. To east and north rise woody hills, and westward the bare slopes and crest of Dartmoor, cheerful to-day in the sunshine, but in bad weather gloomy, dreary, and desolate. In summer, we are told, folk say, 'Chaggiford, and what d'ye think o't?' in winter, 'Chaggiford—Good Lord!' Climbing Featherbed Lane, the dry course of a mountain stream, its rocks bordered with ferns, shaded with hazel and holly, we emerged a-top on the heather, and made for Castor Rock, one of those huge heaps of gray granite which dominate like ancient castles the broad expanses of Dartmoor, its slopes and ridges of heather, and its huge morasses whence flow a dozen rivers to all points of the compass.

It was sultry in the vale, but not on Castor Rock. A strong and steady southerly breeze swept over purple heath and green fern-brake, blowing health and freshness into our blood. Broad sunny lights and shadows rested on the wide-spread loneliness. Far below we could see, winding through the waste, an avenue or double row of rude stones, whose origin and purpose are lost in antiquity, and in a seam fledged with coppice the infant Teign was leaping, invisible, though not inaudible, from pool to pool. A large and pure contentment infused itself into our souls, and we found nothing better for the time than to lie on Castor Rock, drinking in the solitude, the antique mystery, and the autumnal glory of the vast moorland. Descending, we failed not, as sworn hydrophilists, to visit the Teign, where tall trees, mossy rocks, crystal pools brimmed with green shadows, drew us into a mood of more gay and lyrical delight. On our drive back to Moreton we heard some anecdotes from a clergyman of the neighbourhood, of the people's belief, at this day, in pixies, witches, and supernatural cures. 'Seventh son of a seventh son,' is a not uncommon inscription, he said, on a herb-doctor's signboard, and the herb-doctor's patients are mainly treated by 'charms' of various kinds.

It was nightfall when I quitted the train at Totnes station, and walked off alone along a dark bit of road under the stars, to enter a strange town,—a special delight; turned a corner into the long, narrow, roughly-paved High Street; downhill, to the poetic sign of The Seven Stars, a large, old-fashioned hostel, with garden to the river; then, after choosing bedroom, out again for the never-to-be-omitted-when-possible immediate and rapid survey, by any sort of light, of the place not seen before since I was born.

Uphill goes the steep, narrow street, crossed, half-way up, by a deep arch bearing a house; then the houses on each side jut over the side-path supported on stumpy stone pillars; then I zig-zag to the left, still upwards, and by-and-by come to the last house, and the last lamp, throwing its gleam on the hedge-rows and trees of a solitary country road. This last house is an old and sizable one, with mullioned windows, one of which is lighted, and on the blind falls a shadow from within of a woman sewing. The slight and placid movements of this figure, at once so shadowy and so real, so close at hand and so remote, are suggestive of rural contentment, a life of security and quietude. Yet how different from this the facts may be!

Inexhaustibly interesting to the imagination is any old edifice; and the nearest to my own sympathies, the most touching, is neither church nor castle, but a dwelling-house, not a grand one, but such as generations of the stay-at-home sort of people have been born in, have lived in, and died in; every particle of its wood and stone, as it were,

imbued with human life. No vast antiquity is needed; a
hundred years does as well as a thousand; long dates only
confuse and baffle the imagination.   Enough if the house be
evidently *before our time*, if men before us have lived and
died there.   Death, the great mystery, is the dignifier of
Human Life.   Where Death has been, as formerly where
lightning struck, the ground is sacred.

Next morning I mounted to the castle-keep of Judael de
Totnais, through a wildly-tangled shrubbery, and from the
mouldered battlements looked over Totnes's gray slate roofs
and gables, and the silvery Dart winding amongst wooded
hills.   Opposite, stood the tall, square, red sandstone tower
of the old church, buttressed to the top, and with a secondary
round turret running up from ground to sky near the centre
of its north face, an unusual and picturesque feature.   Then
hied I to the churchyard, and beside it, in a rough back
lane, saw an old low building, with an old low porch; the
old key was in the old iron-guarded door, and I entered,
without question asked, the old Guildhall of the old town.
Over the bench hung a board painted with the arms of
Edward VI., supported by lion and wyvern, 'Anno Domini,
1553,' with motto, 'Du et mond Droyit.'   The latticed
windows looked into an orchard whose apples almost touched
the panes.   It was a little hall with a little dark gallery at
one end, for the mediæval public, and under this the barred
loopholes for the mediæval prisoners to peep through.   But
it is still in use, as testified by two modern cards on the
walls: 'This side, Plaintiff and Plaintiff's witnesses;'
'This side, Defendant and Defendant's witnesses.'   On
the Defendants' side I found, roughly cut on the wood panel,
'R. P., 1633,' but could not guess in what cause he appeared.

No pleasanter change in travel from more or less fatiguing
exercise, than the rest in motion of a river steamboat, sliding
from reach to reach of some easy-flowing stream, like that

which bore us seven miles from the woody slopes of Totnes to the steeper hills of Dartmouth's almost land-locked harbour, and again, from broader to narrower reaches, back again to Totnes. Then, bidding adieu to The Seven Stars, off started the Rambler once more on his favourite vehicle, sometimes called *Irish tandem*—namely, one foot before another; striking off by field, park, meadow, and millpond for a certain hamlet obscurely lurking somewhere among the swelling hills and deep lanes—Dean Prior, the church and vicarage of old Robin Herrick.

Devonshire Lanes—Herrick's Poetry—Dean Prior—Sketch of the Poet's
Life—Herrick and Martial.

I STARTED on foot from Totnes in search of a hamlet
hidden among rounded hills of corn and coppice, and
shady Devonshire lanes, deep, steep, solitary; often showing, where the tangled hedges opened at some gate, a wide
and rich prospect over harvest fields and red ploughed lands.
Long and sultry was the pilgrimage, the way often taken at
haphazard, sometimes mistaken, in lack of people or houses;
but at last the scent grew hot, when, after climbing an endless lane, I found myself descending t'other side the hill
with Dartmoor's uplands before me, dim in afternoon sunlight; and, at foot, the square church tower of Dean Prior,
of which Robert Herrick was a long while vicar, two centuries ago. Many a time he certainly trudged up and down
this steep old lane—now lamenting his banishment from
London, now humming a lyric fancy newly sprung somehow
in that queer gross-fine brain of his.

> More discontents I never had
>   Since I was born, than here;
> Where I have been, and still am sad,
>   In this dull Devonshire.
> Yet justly too, I must confesse,
>   I ne'r invented such
> Ennobled numbers for the presse
>   Than [As?] where I loath'd so much.

Saying these lines to a tune of their own making, I went down the long lane, its wide borders all a-tangle with leaves and flowers, mint, meadowsweet, golden fleabane, blackhead, hemp-agrimony, and red campion, countless green tufts of hartstongue, male fern, and bracken, and a few late foxglove-bells. In front, at every step rose higher the bare purply slopes of Dartmoor, ridge over ridge, putting on, from this point of view and in this light, the aspect of a solemn mountain region.

I was not prepared to find so grave a charm of landscape in Herrick's Devonshire, and it has left no trace in his verses, which carry the impression (I mean the best of them) of a quiet, sleepy, remote ruralism among flowery meadows, hay and corn-fields and old farm-houses, its winter season cheered with great wood fires, flowing cups, and old-world games.

Of the larger aspects of nature and life, Herrick had no apprehension—at least, no habitual apprehension; if he caught a glimpse of these it was by effort and against his will. His flower-pieces have a flower-like delicacy and sweetness, as in the unfading little song—

> Gather ye rosebuds while ye may,
>   Old Time is still a-flying,
> And this same flow'r that blooms to-day
>   To-morrow will be dying, etc.

Or this—

> Faire Daffodills, we weep to see
>   You haste away so soone;
> As yet the early rising sun
>   Has not attain'd his noone.
>   Stay, stay,
>   Until the hasting day
>   Has run
>   But to the even-song;
> And having pray'd together, we
>   Will goe with you along, etc.

Only, daffodils are by no means among the evanescent flowers. His pages are full of roses, violets, primroses, asphodels, breathing a natural freshness :—

> I sing of brooks, of blossoms, birds, and bowers,
> Of April, May, of June, of July-flowers ;
> I sing of May-poles, hock-carts, wassails, wakes,
> Of bridegrooms, brides, and of their bridal-cakes.

In his style is a quality of elegant naivety, grown rare of late in English poetry. The French cultivate and excel in this. Our Thomas Hood has it. In his ' Matins, or Morning Prayer,' old Robin sings :—

> First wash thy heart in innocence, then bring
> Pure hands, pure habits, pure, pure everything.

How simple without flatness are such lines as these :—

> Here down my wearied limbs I'll lay ;
> My pilgrim's staffe, my weed of gray,
> My palmer's hat, my scallop-shell,
> My cross, and cord, and all farewell.
> For having now my journey done,
> Just at the setting of the sun,
> Here have I found a chamber fit,
> God and good friends be thankt for it,
> Where if I can a lodger be
> A little while from tramplers free,
> At my uprising next I shall,
> If not requite, yet thank ye all, etc.

He abounds in happy turns of phrase, which sometimes carry a very pleasant tinge of humour. A quaint gravity sits well upon him, as in the lines ' Thus I, Passe by, And die,' etc., or these—' Give me a cell, to dwell, Where no foot hath a path,' etc. Of delicate sense of metre, the most specially poetic of natural gifts (using the word poetic in its strict meaning), he has a larger share, perhaps, than any other English poet of his rank. As good in its manner

as the pensive gaiety of 'Gather ye rosebuds while ye
may,' is the jollity of

> The May-pole is up,
> Now give me the cup;
> I'll drink to the garlands around it;
> But first unto those
> Whose hands did compose
> The glory of flowers that crown'd it.

And the best of his longer pieces (yet not long), 'Corinna
going a-Maying,' winds delightfully throughout its course.
Verse, like wine, acquires a special fine flavour by age. But
to imitate this in new verse is like fabricating mock old-wine,
and such concoctions are scarcely palatable or wholesome,
though they often take the public taste for a while.

I hardly know why Herrick seems interesting beyond
other poets of a similar rank. There was not 'much in'
the man, and there is not much in his verses: and perhaps
that's just it. The endurance of his little writings gives
strong testimony to the value of art. His subject-matter is
neither new nor remarkable. There is no interest of narrative or of characterisation; very slight connection with the
times he lived in, or with any set of opinions, national,
social, or individual. That which has saved the verses and
name of the obscure Devonshire vicar is simply and solely
ars poetica. The material is nothing, the treatment everything. If good verse can preserve even trivialities, how
potent a balsam is good verse, and how fit to entrust fine
things to!

What does appear of the man himself disposes one to a
mood of good-humoured slightly contemptuous toleration—
usually a rather agreeable mood. We can't look up to him;
he is frail, faulty, sometimes rather scandalous, often absurd; but he confesses as much himself, and gives the
world in general that sort of easy lazy toleration which he
would fain receive. A Pagan he habitually is, though
varnished with another creed. The ideas of home and

fireside, of pleasure, of death, even (despite his parsonhood) of marriage, of prayer, of funeral-rites, present themselves to his mind in the same light, and commonly under the same forms as they did to Horace or Martial. It seems more than mere adoption of classic phraseology and imagery, like that of Milton in 'Lycidas;' it was his way of seeing things :—

> So when you and I are made
> A fable, song, or fleeting shade;
> All love, all liking, all delight,
> Lie drown'd with us in endlesse night, etc.

This is the felicity he truly aims at:

> I'll feare no earthly powers,
> But care for crowns of flowers.

Anything for a quiet life:

> The Gods are easie, and condemne
> All such as are not soft like them.

He loves good cheer, and is convinced that

> Cold and hunger never yet
> Co'd a noble verse beget.

In his 'Farewell to Sack,' 'Welcome to Sack,' and elsewhere, are some admirable Bacchanalianisms. An easy-going, light-hearted man, he is not given to look below the surface of things. He has no narrative or dramatic power. His views of human life are general, coloured with perception of beauty, with gaiety and desire, with sense of the shortness of life. His attempts at individualising take the form of the rudest ill-drawn caricature. His amorous verse is frankly sensuous and outward. His Julia, Electra, Corinna, are names for the bodily sweetness of womanhood. There is just a modicum of sentimentality, itself superficial, or, as it were, subcutaneous. We find here no chivalrous strain like Lovelace's 'Tell me not, sweet;' no ingenious comfort in neglect like Wither's 'Shall I, wasting in despair;' no

heap of glittering clevernesses as in Donne's pages (with here
and there a wonderful bit of old coloured-glass, as it were,
worth keeping even as a fragment) ; no exaltation of mental
and disparagement of external qualities as in Carew's ' He
that loves a rosie cheek.' Herrick sings of Electra's petticoat,
of Julia's bosom, of bright eyes, trim ankles, fragrant
breath.   He is not, or very seldom, prurient, only pagan,
bodily, external.   There is not the slightest hint of those
modern schools—the sceptical, the scofling, or the diabolic.
His tone, too, entirely differs from the witty, ingenious im-
morality of the next generation, Rochester, Sedley, and
other Merry-Monarchy men.   Herrick's collected poems were
published in 1648, when the author was about fifty-seven.

But here is Dean Prior.   What is it?   Church and churchyard on one side the road, vicarage on the other ; three
or four cottages, a brook, a farmyard, some solitary country
lanes ; visible inhabitants, a man and a boy, to whom, afterwards, enter an old woman.   The vicarage, though it has a
gray old-fashioned look, is not of Herrick's time—a disappointment ; 'tis perhaps of Anne's reign, or one of the
earlier Georges.   But it probably stands on the site of
the older edifice.   The present vicar was unluckily from
home, and the old woman who showed the church knew
nothing beyond parish matters of her own day.   The church,
old, but restored throughout, is now a trim ordinary edifice
of stone, with a west tower.   Inside you find three aisles
(it is not a small church), and on the wall of the north aisle
a brass plate, about 36 inches by 20, surrounded by a deep
frame of white stone or marble, cut into Renaissance scrollwork, like what you see on title-pages of the fifteenth and
sixteenth centuries.   The inscription runs: ' In this Churchyard lie the remains of ROBERT HERRICK, Author of the
Hesperides, and Other Poems, Of an   ancient family in
Leicestershire, and born in the year 1591.   He was educated
at St. John's College and Trinity Hall, Cambridge, Pre-

sented to this Living by King Charles I. in the year 1629,
Ejected during the Commonwealth, and reinstated soon
after the Restoration. This Tablet was erected to his
Memory by his Kinsman, William Percy Herrick, of Beau
Manor Park, Leicestershire, A.D. 1857.

> Our mortall parts may wrapt in scare-clothes lye,
> Great spirits never with their bodies die.
>
> *Hesperides.*
>
> Virtus Omnia Nobilitat.'

The churchyard has many old graves, among which the
poet's lies perdue.

Dean *is* a lonesome place, the old dame admits; so much
so, it appears, that servants can hardly be got to live at the
vicarage. Think what it must have been 200 years ago.
No wonder if the lively young scamp who had left
Cambridge in debt, and lived a gay life in London till both
purse and credit were quite exhausted; getting somehow
ordained, as a *pis-aller*, and then presented to a living by
his friends' influence (for such appears to be something like
what the few known facts amount to); no wonder that this
jovial, clever, petted, insolent, amatory poet turned parson,
finding himself stuck in the Devonshire clay, four days'
journey from town, should sometimes grumble at his fate.
He was about thirty-eight years old when he came to Dean,
and remained there some twenty years, till Cromwell turned
him out. It was in 1648, the last year of King Charles
(and which that monarch spent mostly at Carisbrooke), that
Herrick's volume appeared, 'to be sold at the Crown and
Marygold in St. Paul's Churchyard.' It is dedicated 'to
the Most Illustrious and Most Hopefull Prince, Charles,
Prince of Wales.' The political allusions are not many;
all on the loyal side, of course. It is manifest that he had
no notion of the dangerous condition of the king's affairs.
Nor indeed had the king himself, even up to that day in
January when he so unwillingly appeared in Westminster

Hall, and at first 'laughed' when the charges against him were read. 1648 was an odd year for the publication in London of a book of light lyrics, mingled with compliments to royalty.

See, this brook among the hazel-bushes is that very Dean-bourne to which friend Robin bade farewell in no very affectionate strain. Never could he wish to see it again, 'were thy streames silver, or thy rocks all gold.'

> Rockie thou art ; and rockie we discover
> Thy men, and rockie are thy wayes all over.
> O men, O manners ; now, and ever knowne
> To be a rockie generation !
> A people currish, churlish as the seas,
> And rude almost as rudest salvages !

On his 'Returne to London' he writes :

> From the dull confines of the drooping west,
> To see the day spring in the fruitful east,
> Ravisht in spirit, I come, nay more, I flie
> To thee, blest place of my nativitie !
>
> .　.　.　.　.　.
>
> London my home is : though by hard fate sent
> Into a long and irksome banishment.

Yet, by degrees, as old age crept on, and after experience, probably, of how much worse it is to have no home than a dull one, he became reconciled to his rural life, and has left many pleasant pictures of it.

> Sweet country life, to such unknown
> Whose lives are others', not their own.

His 'Grange, or Private Wealth,' is delightfully quaint in which, as often elsewhere, he praises

> A maid, my Prew, by good luck sent
> To save
> That little, Fates me gave or lent.

When Charles II. was 'restored,' Herrick came back to Dean, now a man of near seventy years of age, and there he lived peaceably some fourteen years longer, and laid down his bones in the dull quiet churchyard through which he had passed so many thousand times from vicarage to church, and from church to vicarage.

The Poet did not entirely forget his cassock. In deference thereto, he appended to his 'Hesperides' a set of quasi-religious poems, under the title of 'Noble Numbers,' but most of these are evidently no less artificial than that one which is so arranged as to print in the figure of a cross. The best pieces, probably, in this division, are 'A True Lent' and the 'Litanie,' which has a serious naivety that is touching, though even here peeps out evidence that it is mainly the poet's *fancy* that is engaged. This is quaintly natural :

> When the priest his last hath pray'd,
> And I nod to what is said,
> 'Cause my speech is now decay'd,
>   Sweet Spirit, comfort me !

but this runs into the comic :

> When the artless doctor sees
> No one hope, but of his fees,
> And his skill runs on the lees,
>   Sweet Spirit, comfort me !

The true and habitual meditative glances of the man were turned to the shortness of life; his philosophy was the wisdom of gathering rosebuds while you may. Moments of graver mood no doubt he also had, and he expresses here and there the sense of hurt or rather ruffled conscience in one whose love of pleasure is stronger than his will. He stumbles and hurts his shin, recovers himself, walks carefully a few steps, grows careless, and trips again, never quite falls, but goes on his way stumbling and resolving not to stumble so much.

A fat, sly, droll, good-humoured, lazy, smutty old parson was Robin Herrick, thick-necked, double-chinned, with a twinkle of humour in his eyes, fond of eating, drinking, and singing, part man-of-the-world, part homely and simple almost to childishness. He doesn't hate anybody, blames nothing but what teases him, longs for a quiet life, has no opinions, and is ready to conform to anything. He reads little, looks into a few favourite Latin poets, cares very slightly for contemporary literature, saving the verses of two or three friends of his, and especially 'Saint Ben' (whose minor poems are a good deal like Robin's). There is no Saint Will in his calendar. Will, unhappily, though clever, was not an 'educated' man, like *nous autres ;* and this undoubtedly was the general feeling as to *him* among the lettered class.

A century after the old vicar's funeral, it would have seemed that his verses (though not without some recognition in their own day) were no less lost in silence and oblivion than his bones. But they possessed an unsuspected vitality. Somebody rediscovered them, and made known the fact in the 'Gentleman's Magazine' in 1796 and 1797 ; the 'Quarterly Review' followed suit, with due deliberation, in 1810. By that time a selection from Herrick's poems had appeared, edited by Dr. Nott. In 1823 a collective edition was published at Edinburgh, another by Pickering in 1846; 'Selections' by Murray in 1839; 'Works' (but not complete) by H. G. Clarke & Co. in 1844; 'Works' by Reeves & Turner, edited by E. Walford, 1859—from which my quotations are made. Lastly, a complete edition, including several pieces hitherto uncollected, was published in 1869 by J. Russell Smith, edited by W. C. Hazlitt.

Whether or not it is necessary or desirable to resuscitate *all* the writings of such a writer as our old friend, is a question of no small importance. His Floralia, so to speak, are accompanied by a great deal of licence. He sets before his guests roast partridge, apricot tart, and clotted cream, but alas ! with these, rotten fish, and even dirt-pies. He is not only often sensual, but not seldom coarse and even filthy, in imitation for the most part of classical models. He has gleaned and translated from Anacreon and from Horace, but most I think from Martial. For example, ' What kind of Mistresse he would have ' (329), has its parallel in the Roman poet's ' Qualem, Flacco, velim quæris, nolimve puellam,' etc.; as have these lines—

> Numbers ne'er tickle, or but lightly please,
> Unlesse they have some wanton carriages : (p. 414).

in Martial's ' Ad Cornelium ' (i. 36).

' On a Perfumed Lady ' (155) conveys the ' non bene olet, qui semper bene olet.' Herrick's epitaphs much resemble that pretty one on Erotion,

> Hic festinata requiescit Erotion umbra (x. 61).

> Fat be my hinde ; unlearned be my wife ;
> Peacefull my night ; my day devoid of strife (420)

is a translation of

> Sit mihi verna satur : sit non doctissima conjux ;
> Sit nox cum somno : sit sine lite dies (ii. 90) ;

and so is

> When the rose reigns, and locks with ointment shine
> Let rigid Cato read these lines of mine.

of

> Cum regnat rosa, cum madent capilli,
> Tunc me vel rigidi legant Catones (x. 19).

' To my ill Reader,' agrees with ' Ad Fidentinum ' (i. 39).

He often echoes Martial's ' Possum nil ego sobrius,' and his

> Lassenturque rosis tempora sutilibus,
> Jam vicina jubent nos vivere Mausolea,

as well as imitates the old writer's confidence in his verses, immortality—

> Casibus hic nullis, nullis delebilis annis.

Herrick's

> Let others to the printing presse run fast ;
> Since after death comes glory, Ile not haste (p. 450)

is Martial's

> Vos tamen O nostri ne festinate libelli :
> Si post fata venit gloria, non propero. (v. 10)

and so on.

In a crowd of short epigrams, if he fails to match the un-parallelled foulness of Domitian's flatterer, he outdoes the occasional pointlessness of his prototype :—

UPON EELES. Epig.

> Eeles winds and turnes, and cheats and steales : yet Eeles
> Driving these sharking trades, is out of heels.

UPON PENNIE.

> Brown bread Tom Pennie eates, and must of right,
> Because his stock will not hold out of white.

UPON MUDGE.

> Mudge every morning to the postern comes,
> His teeth all out, to rinse and wash his gummes.

UPON CROOT.

> One silver spoon shines in the house of Croot,
> Who cannot buie or steale a second to't.

Flatness in this degree becomes funny, but it seems scarcely worth while to go on making luxurious reprints of matter like this. The question as to foul parts, unhappily too many, is more serious. Surely, mere filthy words, devoid of either literary or antiquarian value—these, at least, need not be carefully resuscitated, be kept alive and in circulation, because the writer of them also wrote things worthy of preservation. Even in the case of ancient writers, and giving full weight to the venerableness of antiquity, should we really lose much by losing the intolerably disgusting passages of Catullus and Martial? At least let

these literary coprolites (but not deodorised by time) rest as
far as possible among the shadows of learned shelves. Are
they thus treated? Here is a subject which has received
less consideration than perhaps it deserves. Look at certain volumes of Bohn's 'Classical Library,' which has an
immense circulation in England and America. Any bookseller will sell them; any boy may have them as *cribs.*
They translate literally into English all but the perfectly
intolerable passages; of these they give the original text in
large type (so that they can be turned to one after another
at a moment's notice), accompanied by a French or Italian
translation, or both, and also in many cases by a veiled
English version. Martial, with his worst passages imbedded in a jungle of close Latin pages, is bad enough.
Martial, with all the worst passages set forth in distinctive
type, and all the filthiest phrases of the Latin tongue sup-
plemented by French or Italian equivalents, or both, is a
public offence. Nothing more charming in their way than
this poet's pieces on the villa of Julius Martial (iv. 64), or
those addressed to the same Julius, ending

> Summum nec metuas diem, nec optes (x. 47),

or those on his own 'rus in urbe,' where a cucumber hasn't
room to lie straight (xi. 18); nothing happier than many of
his lines and phrases: yet there is in him a deep vein of
blackguardism, a very different thing from sensuality. I
believe him when he says he invented vile things deliberately to make his books sell.

Strange, to find in his pages those solemn words (inscribed
on a clock in Exeter Cathedral, and on the Temple sun-dial),
'Pereunt et Imputantur.' But the phrase, I should think,
is not applied in precisely Martial's meaning—'If you and
I,' he says to his friend Julius (v. 20), 'were really to
enjoy our lives, we should quit the halls of patrons and rich
people, and the cares of public life, and drive, walk, read,

bathe, converse at leisure. But now neither of us can live
in his own way, and sees his good days fly and vanish '—

> Nunc vivit sibi neuter, heu. bonosque
> Soles effugere atque abire sentit ;
> Qui nobis pereunt. et imputantur ;
> Quisquam vivere cum sciat, moratur ?

'Should any one that knows how to live (i.e., pleasantly)
put off doing so?' By 'imputantur' he seems to have
merely meant 'are reckoned up' in our assigned number.
Certainly the expectation of any reckoning in a deeper sense
for his foul and deliberate treasons against human dignity
might well have made the Spaniard shiver. If there be any
right or wrong in these matters, he and such as he are
damnably wrong.

Several other volumes of 'Bohn's Library' are almost if
not quite as bad. Nor is the indecency committed in a
merely stolid and business-like manner; prurient leers and
winks are not wanting in the notes. In the Plague of
London, letters were sent to obnoxious people enclosing rags
from a plague sore. These pages, steeped in foulest mental
contagion, fly over all the world, and especially into the
hands of the young. As regards the relation of the sexes,
Latin poetry is the most degraded in all literature. And
now our girls are learning Latin. Some think all this of no
consequence, but 'Rank thoughts of youth full easily run
wild.'

> Dociles imitandis
> Turpibus ac pravis omnes sumus. [1]

External prudishness (England is notably prudish) and inner
coarseness make a very bad combination.

Herrick is nothing like so bad as Martial, or as Herrick
would himself have been perhaps as a poet of the Roman
Empire; still there is much of his writing that were best
allowed to fall into oblivion. The graceful fancy and lyric

[1] Juvenal, xiv. 40.

sweetness of his best verses will long preserve them in men's memory.

So, Dean Prior, adieu!—Robert Herrick, thy name echoes pleasantly after all, and I drink this cup of cider, in default of sack, to thy half-disreputable shade. How unlike to thy contemporary brother-poet and brother-clergyman, the almost too-respectable vicar of Fuggleston, near Salisbury,— George Herbert!

> Various the tones, the skills, the instruments ;
> One Spirit of Music at the heart of all.

I had several questions to ask at Dean, but found no one to put them to. It was Saturday evening; it was some four miles to Brent station, with just time to catch the last train for Exeter; I caught it by the tip of the tail, as it were, and was whisked away by that Fiery Dragon of our period.

RAMBLE THE SEVENTH.

BIDEFORD AND CLOVELLY.

Exeter Again—A Cathedral Service—Bideford—Westward Ho!—
Bathing—Clovelly.

THE tall-housed Exeter High Street, with its blazing
shops and Saturday-night bustle, has a metropolitan
air as I pass up. It was only yesterday morning that I
passed down ; and a crowd of new images meanwhile have
taken lodgment in the mystic chambers of my brain, and
swarms of thoughts have been busy.

At the Guildhall is the police station, and with a constable's leave you can enter the spacious and stately old
Gothic hall, dimly lit with gas throughout the night, see its
lofty window with the emblazoned date ‘1464,’ and the
full-length pictures of Henrietta, daughter of Charles I., of
Monk, Duke of Albemarle, of King George II., of Chief
Justice Pratt, the first two by Lely, the second two by
Hudson, with several more. At one end is an old gallery,
at the other the magistrate's bench.

Next morning I renewed and deepened my mind-picture
of the beautiful Cathedral, and heard a Sunday afternoon
choral service, worship without words or nearly, waves of
solemn harmony, like the billows in a great sea-cavern,
rolling down those vaulted aisles ; and also a sermon, which
was as remarkable for earnest eloquence as cathedral sermons usually are. Modern Thought, that pushed itself in
last week, is gone again, like a ship that touched at some
enchanted island, and all is tranquil as of old.

Last week there were sermons on 'Science and Religion,' even here ; but the disturbers are gone. The lotos reigns in its old territory. The robed procession moved along the aisle, between ancient carven pillars and coloured windows, like a moving picture.

The congregation assembled in the nave, and nearly filled it. A cathedral is certainly a great resource on a British Sunday, and the sermon keeps it from appearing too pleasant —a set-off against the music and architecture. Surely an easy and most valuable reform in the Church of England would be the total abolition of sermons in connection with the ordinary service. Let there be sermons, lectures, expositions, discourses of whatever kind, ordinary or special, at times and in ways thereto appointed, close following a service of prayer and praise if you will ; but enable us to join in such a service by itself, O bishops and archbishops! and earn the gratitude of millions of distressed laymen, nay, I doubt not, of hundreds and of thousands of the clergy also. Pulpit-incubus! vile impersonation of solemn ineptitude, of heartless and brainless routine, pretending to be an oracle, a prophet, an angel, how many souls hast thou numb'd— coming upon them perhaps all secretly a-tremble with mystic joy of praise and prayer, social at once and profoundly personal. What unsuspected evils—but hold, Patricius, wilt thou thyself begin to preach, and without a licence of any sort? Certainly, however, this too, is an evil under the sun, and I hope I shall live to see the end of it.

My thoughts wandered over hill and vale to the lonely church of Dean Prior. The old vicar in his 'Hesperides' ventured to address one little piece ' To Jos. Lo. Bishop of Exeter : '

Whom sho'd I feare to write to, if I can
Stand before you, my learn'd Diocesan ?

for none of my poems, says he, are 'so bad but you may

pardon them.' I suppose the classicality excused a great
deal; and indeed Herrick most likely would never have
thought of soiling his pages as he has done, save through
the childish superstition (only just dying out) of imitating
classic models, not merely in style, but in matter. He
made no independent reflections on the subject. It was
easy and in a sense creditable to follow a classic lead, even
into the mire. In our day the Vicar of Dean would probably have been a contributor to 'Good Words,' perhaps
a canon of the cathedral, and consumed his share of
' sack,' or else port, in a fitting and undemonstrative
manner. What would he have said to Darwin and Huxley? Not much, I fancy, one way or another. He would
have eaten his lotos and been thankful.

One of my old landscape-longings was Bideford Bay, and
though but a day and a half remained of my holiday, I
resolved to snatch a taste of that North Devon coast which
Charles Kingsley's pen and John Hook's pencil are so fond
of. With a passing glimpse at neat-looking Barnstaple, set
snugly in tall trees by its river-brink, I reached Bideford
—By-th'-Ford—after sunset; and having pitched camp,
established a fresh basis, founded a new little home for a
day in the civil inn by the water-side, set off along the quay
and up and down the steep lanes of the old town; then
crossed the famous bridge, and walked left way beyond the
houses, to look back from a hillock on the broad dim river,
and the lamps that marked the bridge, the quay, and the
irregular cluster of buildings rising from the water.

Next morning showed me the broad tidal stream, sweeping
merrily round its grovy hills and corn-slopes, the sunshine dancing on its mingled currents. A silver salmon
leapt up and disappeared with a splash. Two or three
small vessels sailed in and came to anchor. Rowing-boats
crossed. Windlasses rattled on the quay. The first omni-

bus went off to the railway. Shops opened in lazy rural
fashion. Whatever life belonged to little Bideford was
awake and stirring. Bright morning, open window, cheerful prospect, breakfast, beginning with fresh salmon cutlet
and ending with clotted cream and preserve, the offerings of
Devonshire river, dairy, and garden—these (with temper
and mood to taste them—how needful the postulate!) make
no unpleasant combination. I enjoyed it, and the main
relish was the expectation of new scenes, of realising
places hitherto but names, and converting them into solid
memories.

Our memory is ourself—' that immortal storehouse of the
mind.' True, it may be said that material objects are little
or nothing *in themselves;* but the framework, the body of
this world is material, and all its phenomena are abundantly
significant in their varied relations to us. Moreover, even
the wine of abstract thought is often presented to us in the
cup of external circumstance, and if that be of Cellini's gold
the draught is more precious. A happy hour is good to
remember, and can reflect its brightness upon dark seasons.
I am in gloom: so have I been ere now, and said, 'joy is
no more,' yet after all came the free and happy hour, and I
perceived that the clouds had been in me—of my own
making most likely—not in life. With health of body and
soul (merely that!) nothing could daunt or depress for a
moment. Yet I know that the dark hours are fateful, they
too are precious.

'All this about a good breakfast!' Well, that was a
part of the matter—but only a very little part, a touch of oil
to the machinery.

The morning's survey of Bideford added not much to the
night's impressions. The ancient bridge has been widened
by two side paths, supported on iron brackets, which, with
the iron balustrade, give it the air of a railway bridge. The
Bridge Hall, where the trustees meet, re-edified in 1758,

was done up in 1859; but the old tapestries remain. The old Guildhall has been destroyed; and the old church, too, except its tower. I peeped into the new church, spick and span Puginesque with gaudy glass, and found morning service going forward, with a single worshipper. Bideford shops are rustic and backward; the one newsroom discoverable was very poor and rude. As to my waterside inn, it was civil, comfortable, and cheap.

Two or three miles below Bideford is the bar, and the double river loses itself in the wide bay. On the right juts out a distant headland; on the left run the long and level rabbit-burrows, faced with a barricade of shingles, and at the angle where the hilly south shore trends to Clovelly and Hartland Point stands the cluster of new houses—a big hotel and two or three score of bathing-villas—named 'Westward Ho!' from Mr. Kingsley's novel. 'Kingsley Terrace' and 'Kingsley Hotel' are also to be seen, an embodied fame. Pleasant traces from the said novel remained in my own memory: the author has a certain glow and *entraînement* irresistible to youthful readers. I like the name 'Westward Ho' so far as it is a compliment to Charles Kingsley; but, unluckily, as a topographical designation, it is a monument of bad taste. 'Hoe' is a common word in Devon, meaning 'Height' (*Haut*), but in the title of the novel, borrowed from an old play, 'Ho!' is an interjection, and the temptation to follow up Martinhoe and Morthoe with a Westward Ho! ought to have been resisted. The new name is a kind of bad pun.

From Westward Ho! (since it must be so), I followed the south coast of the bay, on the edge of its clay and pebble escarpment, rough green hills one after another shutting out the inland prospect; on the other hand a rough, rocky shore, summer waves rising, rolling in, breaking without tumult, and a blue sea-line stretched from the dim northern horn of the curve to its nearer southern limit, where the coast became almost precipitously steep, and was seen, though some seven miles off, to be clothed in rich verdure from top to base. Something in the distance that might be taken for the broken steps of a gigantic stair, at one point climbed from the shore and lost itself among the foliage, and this was the famous old fishing village of Clovelly—a rich name to ear and fancy. Meanwhile the bare green hills, and rocky shore beset with solitary surges, the wide blue bay with its guardian headlands, reminded me strongly of another bay by which I often rambled—that of Donegal in the north-west of Ireland. The two bays are much of a size, the Torridge with its bar and sandbanks stands for the Erne ; nor are the town and bridge of Bideford altogether unlike, at least in position, their ragged Irish cousins at Ballyshannon. Moreover, Lundy Island answers curiously to Innismurray. The scenery of the English bay, as a whole, is much richer, in its foliaged shores and inland glimpses ; that of the Irish is wilder and grander, watched by blue mountain ranges and the great ocean cliff of Slieve-League,

> Six hundred yards in air aloft, six hundred in the deep.

It struck me, too, that I had noticed some curious resemblances in the speech of North Devon to the somewhat peculiar accent of English which is found in part of Donegal, and speculated whether a colony from this bay might not have settled on that other. Of some such thing as this having happened in Elizabeth's time I seem to have heard, but cannot for the present trace it out. The 'say' for sea, 'tay' for tea, and so on, now supposed to mark an Irish tongue, are ordinary Devonian.

In Hibernian English are many old forms of English, and many provincial forms, and along with these a strong Keltic admixture of words (some translated, some not), phrases, and grammatical constructions : to these add mistakes and awkwardnesses in the use of a foreign tongue, and you have a strange compound, deserving perhaps a closer examination than it has yet received. An English-speaking Irish peasant, while expressing the same meaning, would shape almost any sentence whatever differently from a Londoner of a similar degree of intelligence and education.

At Portledge the rocks yielded to a space of sand, over which I gladly ran, in Adam's dress, into the embrace of the folding waves. The afternoon sun sparkled on the wide sea ; two merry fishing boats danced past under sail. As the embrace of Earth invigorated the old giant, so doth the sea renew her sons. First, the sense of *individuality* when you stand in the face of earth, sea, and sky, without one husk or lending, defenceless, undesignated. Rags or robes, purse and credentials, if you had them, are gone. Next, the ' reverential fear,' the profound awe of committing your helpless self to the terrible and too often treacherous potency. A little prayer is never out of place. Then the thrilling flash of will—the self-abandonment—the victorious recovery, the triumph over a new element—and the glow bodily and mental of one's emergence, not soon fading even when the livery of servitude, the trammels that remind us of ' man's fall,' are resumed.

Leaving the shore, whose huddled rocks offer little convenience to the foot, and winding up a glen or ' mouth' to the high road, I push on quickly for Clovelly, full of expectation. The long plain road between hedges was adorned and made important by my condition of expectancy, and therefore I recall it clearly. I was on the edge of realising a place often thought about, never seen.

The sun had almost set when I turned, on the right hand, through a gate and into a dark avenue of trees, winding downwards till the sea came through its branches, and

running round one headland after another ; the purple bay
on my right through foliage, and the great bank of trees on
the left. At every turn I hoped to see Clovelly, but it was
some three miles long, this winding way terraced among the
slanting woods, and the golden clouds had sunk from
western heaven, and a dark purple dome overhung the
darker ocean, when two or three glimmering lights far below
beckoned to me from cottages near the little harbour.
Venturing a bye-path, it led me to a small opening in the
woods. The trees, heap after heap, were piled into the
stars. At my feet, between precipitous banks, a very steep
and narrow glen dropped sheer to the sea, losing itself in
foliage, and among the foliage were actually roofs and
chimneys, cottages one below another, holding on somehow
to the dangerous slope. Far down, the unseen surf was
heard gently breaking on the beach, and the dim sea rose
in front like a mighty and mysterious wall. I had been
regretting the lack of daylight, but now felt glad to be
entering Clovelly thus. Everything looked very remote and
old-world, very quiet, very beautiful. A sense of soothing
solitude, of largeness in the lofty woods and wide ocean, of
pathos in the cluster of ancient cottages, and the little
street, like a ladder, into which I was about to step down, a
stranger seeking supper and bed ; and these feelings were
harmonised and deepened by the dusky twilight sky, lit with
some faint stars.

I was afraid of finding Clovelly, famous in picture, spoilt,
but it has as yet escaped the hand of 'improvement:' no
villas here, no railway, nor even a coach ; the street is still
only two to three yards wide ; the inn, while clean, is
properly old-fashioned and rustical. I regret to add that I
found a pert and careless handmaiden and a heavy bill.
'There was a *very* nice lass at the inn,' I heard next day,
'but she's married, and now it's the landlord's niece, and
she's too proud for her place.' There are lodgings, I under-

stood, where they would be glad to harbour you even for a single night.

'Clovelly Street' is a very long flight of flag-stone steps descending between two irregular rows of cottages, in one place passing under an archway house, and then dropping more steeply than ever to the little harbour, whose pier, built in Richard I.'s reign, puts its arm of gray stone round a little fleet of herring-smacks. The steep and lofty sea-bank is smothered in woods, from shingle-beach to sky. In my bedroom, to which I ascended by many stairs, I found a second door, opening on—the garden, and to this garden one did not descend but ascend, and above it were still other gardens, and above these a dark mass of trees. So like a cluster of shore-side nests is this ancient fishing-hamlet.

Next morning, bright, breezy and gay, I made some acquaintance with the villagers. A girl was scrubbing a doorstep, and her skirt (not a fashionable train) reached quite across the street. Under the archway sat a shoe-maker at work with open door, and showed all the readiness of his craft for conversation. He must have quite a variety of visitors, and takes intellectual toll of all strangers. 'Crazy Kate's House' on the beach, well known to photo-graphers, has no right, he told me, to any such name, which has merely been stuck upon it by some idle tourist. From an old man who had lived here all his days, I learned that there is no doctor in or near Clovelly, 'he couldn't get a livin'.' He himself 'had never touched a dose of medi-cine.' 'Was Clovelly much altered since his youth?' 'Oh, yes, very much! the street was new-paved from top to bottom, and two new houses built nigh the foot of the hill.' An elderly woman who takes care of the Methodist Chapel (there are many Methodists among the nine hundred Clovellians) praised the beauty of the Clovelly children, their regularity at school, and the pride their mothers had in keeping them tidy. Mr. Hook, Mr. Naish, and other painters, were well known to the general population, and inquired after as friends.

Half-way down the street is a sea-captain's house with a china bowl in the window, embellished with a ship under sail, and the legend, 'Success to the Mary Jane of Bideford,' and here is a favourite lodging for artists, and to all appearance a comfortable. The captain was at sea when I called, but passes the winter at home. It seemed it might be a good sort of life, with its alternation of adventure with deep home-repose.

But I must say good-bye, for my part, to the beautiful old sea-hamlet. A cart bound for Bideford market helped me along the miles of road, first winding up a long hill; one of my fellow-travellers being a girl with a touch of fashion in her dress, a Clovelly maiden, now at service in London ('a very black place,' she said), and sent home for a month to revive the faded roses in her cheeks. Three weeks were gone and had done her much good; in another she must return to the Great Smoke—'A pity,' remarked an old woman beside us, 'to miss the first of the herrin'.'

But London sucks in people and things from every corner of the land. As courtly and intellectual centre, Herrick's wishes pointed to it from Dean Prior, and these attractions still belong to it; but its more widely-felt power nowadays is from mere magnitude, the mass of money and human needs packed within a fifty-mile circuit. Thither gravitate coarse things and fine, are sucked in and absorbed, some to their natural uses, many to waste and destruction.

I came into Clovelly at nine yesterday evening, and leave it at eight this morning: I seem to have lived there about two years.

In gliding out of Devon into Dorset the landscape grows evener and simpler. I leave behind me a peaceful region of rich swelling hills, loaded with corn and woodland, and deep fertile valleys, with a coast, north and south, of verdured

cliff and leafy glen, and 'bowery hollows crown'd with
summer sea;' old towns and old farmhouses; an easy-
going, good-natured population of stalwart men and comely
lasses; a state of life not yet broken up, though not unaf-
fected by the brute power of monstrous London, that
Mountain of Loadstone.

RAMBLE THE EIGHTH.

UP THE VALE OF BLACKMORE.

Wimborne—River Stour—Blandford—Sam Cowell—Popular Songs— Sturminster Newton—Barnes's Poems—The Dorset Dialect—The Peasantry.

IN the spring-time 'longen folk to gone on pilgrimages,' and in that season also I turn often to the poetry shelves of my little library. So, stepping into Dorset for a two-day walk, I had for a companion a little volume of poems; and many recollected snatches of verse, and thoughts about poetry and poets, mingled with the vernal delights of those 'woods and pastures new,' and clear flowing waters.

The map of Dorset seems peculiarly crowded with *double-worded* names, many of them quaint and enticing. Cerne Abbas, Bere Regis, Melcombe Horsey, Milborne St. Andrew, Winterborne St. Martin's, Sturminster Marshal, Owre Moyne, Winfrith Newburgh, Iwerne Courtnay, Froom St. Quintin, Toller Fratrum, Wooton Glanville, Mintern Magna, Blanford Forum and a host beside. Here am I at the railway station of Wimborne Minster, viewing with expectation the two beautiful towers which dominate the little town. A long and crooked street, noway remarkable (yet it is always a peculiar pleasure to *walk* into a new place—you thus take possession of it), led me to the churchyard, where the pollard-lindens parallel to the street, with boughs interwoven overhead and forming a green arcade, yielded

149

glimpses through their thin foliage of the central tower of red sandstone, broad and short, with crooked pinnacles at the four corners; its rich look enhanced by a growth of ivy rooted high up on the south face, embroidering with verdure the interlaced arches of the stonework. There was once a spire, which fell 250 years ago. The gray-coloured west tower is taller, and of perpendicular gothic. A little girl nursing a baby and two or three other children loitered in the light-leafy linden arcade; the street was full of spring sunshine and empty of people; one wondered why the shops were kept open. It was the middle of the day, the townsfolk at dinner, the boys in Queen Elizabeth's grammar school at their lessons.

I found the north door of the Minster open, and entered; the verger was showing the church to some rural acquaintances, and I followed a little way off, evading the vexations of a formal guidance. The oldest parts of the Church are some 800 years old. Steps over a pillared crypt ascend to the choir, and there lie, hand-in-hand, the well-carved alabaster figures of a Duke and Duchess of Somerset, who left this earth 450 years ago. His helmet, hanging above upon a nail, does more towards making the vanished man real. He died some years after Joan of Arc was burned, and while the Duke of York was Regent of France. The lid of the tomb was raised not many years ago, and this verger looking in saw the two coffins apparently perfect, and some cords, supposed the cords by which they had been lowered. He showed in the wall aside the altar, the *piscina*, a thing not used by the present owners of this costly building. They have lately, however, got all the Minster repaired and re-embellished, by means of a public subscription, and not merely or mainly on archæologic claims, but in great part on religious.

Our nobles of to-day wear no helmets; our clergy dip their fingers in no *piscina*; but we still have dukes and huge domains, bishops and great churches. We are living strangely in the end of a long period, among names and things gray with the crust of antiquity, delightful from an antiquarian point of view, and retaining, some of them, an aroma of that romance, a tinge of that picturesqueness, infused without conscious effort into men's doings in certain by-gone times. No wonder that these names and things, and the thoughts connected with them, should be dear and venerable to many minds. Modern life, public and private, in its typical forms, is neither romantic nor picturesque. Those who love the ideal in man's life (body and spirit) are not well at home in this present time ; they belong more to the Past and to the Future.

At the other end of the church an old clock-face of large size on the wall inside, marked with twenty-four hours, showed correctly the passing hour of the new spring day by means of a gilt sun travelling round the circle. A ball represents the moon and her changes. The ancient carven font below was not dry like the *piscina*, but besprinkled from the baptism of two babes that morning ; and the brazen water-jug, replaced on its old shelf, stood ready to continue its share in the mysterious office for children yet unborn.

To get out of any building, however beautiful or interesting, into the open air and free world, is to me a pleasant escape. Narrow streets hem in the Minster. I first reached the market-place, an irregular open ; and then, through bye-lanes, a pretty field-path on the west side of the town, where, amidst broad meadows, guarded north and south by heavily-wooded slopes, winds the tranquil Stour, with deep pools, where, looking into the transparent water, I could see some of the inhabitants, little pike at feed, who know nothing of Wimbourne, or Dorset, or the South Western Railway, but have their own towns and districts and lines of travelling. Two young ladies came along the path from the town, sat down on the grassy margin close to an island or promontory shaded with tall green withies, and began to read unknown mysterious books; it was poetry I felt sure, and finer than any I have yet seen in print. Yet could I have looked over their shoulder it would doubtless have changed into . . . The damsels themselves seemed, in that sunny spring meadow by the clear river, more than semi-celestial; yet already their features have mingled irrecoverably with the cloudy past. I too had my companion book, the third series of Barnes's 'Poems in the Dorset Dialect;' and the little river, winding down from the Vale of Blackmore to meet the waters of the Avon in Christchurch Harbour, flows also through the book; wherefore every sunbeam in the real stream was brightened, and every shadow enriched. Strolling northward, I struck a road which went by a mill among trees and hedges, on a clear brook or *bourne*, the Wim, hurrying to join the Stour: and so returned to the town, the little market-place with the two old church-towers rising behind it making a picture as one approached. At the inn were good refreshments and a civil landlady.

The right-hand window of the railway-carriage showed the meadows, groves, and hamlets of Stour Vale and Brad-bury Rings (supposed an ancient British fortress) conspicuous on a hill some miles away; and so brought me to Blandford Forum — otherwise called, descending from classic to vernacular, Market Blandford. Entering on foot by back streets, I stood to admire a not large yet important-looking old square house of dark red brick, ivied, and shaded with tall trees growing in a little court-yard. The bricken chimneys are of rich design, apparently octagonal, with a slender detached pillar at each angle, and a double cornice a-top. These chimneys I saw afterwards, overtopping other roofs, and found them as pleasurable as a fine piece of land-scape. This old house is the Mayor's, two children tell me, and he has often been mayor. Is he a properly quaint old gentleman, I wondered—with an old library, old pictures, old furniture, old-fashioned hospitality; loving his native town and townsfolk, full of fatherly care of all their interests, lapt round in his age with honour and affection? Might he not possibly send out an old servitor to greet the stranger, observed gazing at his picturesque dwelling with intelligent and respectful interest, and invite him—even me, Patricius Walker—to an inspection of the interior curiosities, and a glass of old port wine? The old house took no notice of me : I have already left it behind, and turned into the High Street, which has a very different aspect.

The town of Blandford Forum was burnt down, all but a few houses (of which the above-mentioned was one) on the 4th of June 1731, and rebuilt mainly by a general public subscription. The High Street, therefore, with its solid bricken houses, and large lumpish church with urns on the cornice, square steeple, and heavy portico, is like a street in Hogarth's pictures. Blandford, thus built at a stroke, has more of a *town* look than most other places in this part of England. Wimborne, Fordingbridge, Ringwood, are like large villages; and even Salisbury in great part has a village look — the appearance probably of all our towns under the first class, some centuries ago. The 'Crown,' a stately inn, and comfortable withal, fronting the west end of the High Street, commands a view of Lord Portman's rich park, a broad meadow bounded by the curving Stour, with lofty bank of trees beyond. This Bryanston Park has given name to a London square, not far from which are its cousins of Portman, Dorset, and Blandford.

An uphill street led me northward out of the town and by a cemetery, and I turned down a little rustic lane, where I had never been before and would most likely never be again (a singular delight—I know not why). There were orchards, and a wooded vale to the westward, and a gentle cloudy

twilight coming on. Then I returned to supper at the
'Crown,' in a room adorned with engraved portraits of famous
musicians—composers, singers, instrumentalists, including
one of a Hungarian violin-player with autograph, a gift from
the original. What does this mean? I learn from the
conversable waitress, that mine host of the 'Crown' is himself
a professional musician of no small note; is even now at
Weymouth, taking part in a public concert. Having
alluded to my stroll as far as the cemetery, I am asked,
Did I see Sam Cowell's grave? 'No: who was Sam
Cowell?' The celebrated comic singer,—yes, to be sure,—
and how came he to lay his bones at Blandford? The
little story was not without interest. Among the many
curious branches of industry which are to be found in the
metropolis, is the production of those slang songs which are
so great an attraction in the Music-halls, 'coal-holes,'
'cider-cellars,' and other night-resorts of London. As the
old ones get stale, new are put forward in their stead, jingling the topic of the hour in a quasi-comic fashion of their
own, and hitching into rhyme the latest inventions of
cockney jargon and buffoonery. Now and again one of
them makes 'a tremendous hit,' the Great So-and-So is
re-engaged for another month, and soon you may hear the
children in every rural hamlet throughout the kingdom
yelling the new slang ditty, redolent of gas and sewerage.
The hayfield borrows its lyrics from the Haymarket, and on
the sea-shore, if you hear a sailor sing, or a fisherman
whistle, ten to one it is some melody of the Strand, W.C.
Often the singers who bring these into vogue are the con-
coctors also; and to be successful in their line they must
of course possess special gifts; the notabilities are generally
skilful and telling, and sometimes show remarkable neat-
ness and agility of vocalisation, along with some real power
of comic expression, which could hardly be worse applied,
for the words are always trashy and frequently base. A

few years ago, the favourite name in the bills of the music-halls and on the covers of comic song-books was perhaps that of Sam Cowell. I have before me a ' Comic Songster,' price twopence, with several of his famous ditties, one being ' The Ratcatcher's Daughter,' of which here is a verse :

> They both agreed to married be
>   Upon next Easter Sunday,
> But ratcatcher's daughter she had a dream,
>   That she wouldn't be alive on Monday.
> She vent vunce more to buy some sprats,
>   And she tumbled into the vater ;
> And down to the bottom, all kiver'd with mud,
>   Vent the putty little ratcatcher's daughter.

Spoken :—Considering the state of the Thames at the present moment, what mustn't she have swallow'd !

> Doodle dee, etc.

Her lover, a man who sold ' lilyvite sand,' said ' Blow me if I live long arter ! '

> So he cut 'is throat vith a pane of glass,
>   And stabbed 'is donkey arter ;
> So 'ere is an end of Lily-vite Sand,
>   Donkey and ratcatcher's daughter !
> Doodle dee, etc.

. . . .

Spoken :—Well, ladies and gentlemen, arter the two bodies was resusticated, they buried them both in one seminary, and the epigram which they writ upon the tombstone went as follows :

> Doodle dee ! doodle dum !
> Di dum doodle da !

Let us shut up our song-book. Pain, murder, death and the grave, are very favourite ingredients in all these ' Comic Songsters.' But humorists of higher rank, the clever Barham and the true poet Hood, for example, are by no means guiltless in this respect.

Sam Cowell had constant engagements, and was well paid. What more ? A common story—' unbounded applause,' unwholesome living, drink, broken health. Said our host of the 'Crown' one day (being up in London, and knowing all these celebrities): 'You're not looking well, Sam; come down to Blandford, and we'll set you right again.' Some months after which, a ghostly pale man arrived at the 'Crown' in the railway omnibus, and this was the celebrated Mr. Cowell. The waiter and chambermaids regarded him with curiosity; the stablemen talked of him over their beer; his arrival made more or less sensation throughout the town. He was very ill; grew worse and worse; consumed a bottle of brandy per diem, when he could get it; and was sometimes noisy. At length the 'Crown's' hospitality being worn out, though not the host's kindness, a lodging was taken in the town, and the sick man's wife brought from London. He was carried downstairs in an arm-chair; and next and lastly, before many days, his body was laid in the cemetery, among these Dorset fields and orchards. A little subscription was made for his wife and children, and a stone placed over his grave. Some well-meaning people had administered ghostly consolation of the usual kind to the poor Grotesque, and his last words were, ' Safe ! safe ! ' On his tomb is engraved, ' Here lies all that is mortal of Sam Cowell. Born April 5, 1819. Died March 11, 1864 ;' with the words of a text—Hebrews vii. 25.

During the last seven years or so the most popular English songs, as well as I can remember, have been these : ' The Ratcatcher's Daughter,' ' The Perfect Cure,' ' Bob Ridley,' ' I'm a Young Man from the Country,' ' The Whole Hog or none,' ' Paddle your own Canoe,' ' Polly Perkins of Paddington Green,' ' A Motto for every Man,' ' Slap Bang,' ' Jessie at the Railway Bar,' ' Champagne Charley,' ' After the Opera is Over,' ' Not for Joseph.' This last has, like most of them, a catching bar or two in the tune ; the words set forth the same subject as ' The Young Man from the Country,' and many other ditties—a countryman in town who is too shrewd to be taken in, e.g.:

> Then a fellow near whisper'd in my ear—
> 'I would the bargain soon close if
> I'd got the cash, but haven't, so buy it for yourself;'
> I in reply said, 'Not for Joseph!'

The sixth and eighth in our list are vulgar-economic (a class by itself); while 'Champagne Charlie,' 'Slap Bang,' and 'After the Opera,' are songs of Haymarket life, as inane as they are ugly—unless, as a particle of salt, they may be thought to involve some coarse satire on the 'Young Man about Town.'

The country is the natural birthplace of lyric poetry; the dwellers in the Big Smoke ought to be solaced with sweet songs of wholesome life and nature, and not the country contaminated by the ugly selfishness and vulgar satire of the city. Town will have its slang and its sarcasm, no doubt; but the preponderance now of ugly town elements in the popular songs of the kingdom is one of the unpromising signs of the times. 'Popular song' and 'slang song' are almost convertible expressions; and the slang, too, is mean and witless. Looking into any old song-book, I fancy that I perceive a degeneracy in our own day. The standard of taste thirty years ago was not very noble; but compared with that of the present time it seems sentimental, romantic, poetic. The influence of modern London upon English thought, character, and society—here is a fruitful subject for reflection. It can hardly be denied that ill effects are more discernible than good; and, with the Popular Song, many things have become less sweet and wholesome than they used to be in more tranquil and deliberate times.

Next morning I went by rail to Sturminster Newton, an old village with an old church, crooked lanes, small rustic shops, civil people (who looked at the one stranger with a natural curiosity), and its bye-nooks sheltering snug embowered houses, with flower-gardens and climbing roses.

Passing out at the top of the street, I followed a country road; on my left hand, fields sloping to the Stour, and a rich view under showery clouds of the vale with its river winding along. Taking shelter from a dash of rain in a poor but neat enough cottage, where an old woman and a girl were sewing leather gloves—a common employment in the district—I asked the old dame about Duncliffe Hill, showing her the woodcut of it in Mr. Barnes's volume, and trying to awaken some interest in 'Poems in the Dorset Dialect.' But it was impossible for her to conceive that a printed book of which she had never heard before could hold anything to concern her.

My next shelter was under a hedge, where I turned over the leaves of my pocket companion. The verses were much unlike those of the 'Comic Songster.' Rural pictures, fresh and pure, their minute touches harmonised into a general tone, and their apparently artless simplicity concealing no slight mastery of execution ; the ways of life (sweetened by love and neighbourliness) among fields and flowers and wholesome country labours — the neat cottage, the home vale, the winding brook and bridge, the field-path to the church, the tidy wife and dear children ; dashes of country fun interspersed; a sense of rustling leaves, flowing waters, lowing cattle, tinkling sheep-bells ; with this a gentle humanity towards all creatures, and an old-fashioned, homely piety—these delightful impressions were renewed as I turned over the pages of the little book, pausing here and there at sight of some special favourite—' Echo,' or ' The Snowy Night,' or ' Zummer Winds,' or—

THE RWOSE IN THE DARK.

In zummer, leäte at evenèn-tide,
  I zot to spend a moonless hour
'Ithin the window, wi' the zide
  A-bound wi' rwoses out in flow'r,
Bezide the bow'r, vorsook o' birds,
An' listen'd to my true-love's words.

A-risèn to her comely height,
  She push'd the swingèn cäsement round ;
And I could hear, beyond my zight
  The win'-blown beech-tree softly sound,
On higher ground, a-swayèn slow
On drough my happy hour below.

An' tho' the darkness then did hide
  The dewy rwose's blushèn bloom,
He still did cast sweet aïr inside
  To Jeäne, a-chattèn in the room :
And tho' the gloom did hide her feäce,
Her words did bind me to the pleäce.

An' there, while she, wi' runnèn tongue,
  Did talk unzeen 'ithin the hall,
I thought her like the rwose that flung
  His sweetness vrom his darken'd ball,
'Ithout the wall ; an' sweet's the zight
Ov her bright feäce, by mornèn light.

But the general effect of Mr. Barnes's poetry is still more delightful than the impression, however charming, made by any of the poems taken separately. It is like the content-ment remaining after a long and pleasant day of rambling by rustic ways through a country of groves and green flowery pastures, and clear brooks and happy cottages, where the wayfarer is regaled with home-made bread and sweet milk, and perhaps a leaf of strawberries or a plate of red-cheeked apples. To some palates such simple diet and narrow scenes would be unsatisfactory, and few of us would choose to be confined to them; but there are many, surely, to whom a day so spent would yield large store of sweet and whole-some memories. Human nature is portrayed by our Dorset bard mainly with reference to the domestic affections in humble life—virtuous courtship, happy marriage, parent-hood and childhood, filial piety, family bereavements, with the village church always in the background of the picture, and sometimes in the foreground. The author (whose father and grandfather were farmers in this rich, soft, secluded Vale of Blackmore, where I sit reading his book) came to be, first, a schoolmaster ; then, in mature life, a clergyman of the Church of England ; and is now vicar of the small parish of Winterbourne-Came, in his native county (close to Dorchester), dwelling in an appropriate cottage vicarage, with his little old church hid in lofty elms a mile away, among the green slopes of Came Park. A simple, cheerful, wholesome and happy life is unmistakably reflected in his poetry ; the childhood in the farmhouse, the manhood aiming at and at last attaining the quiet rural parsonage. With his love and practice of poetry he combines a considerable research in philology, and prides himself, no doubt justly, on using his native Dorset dialect with thorough accuracy and purity.

'To write,' he says, in the preface to this third collection of poems, 'in what some may deem a fast out-wearing speech-form, may seem as idle as the writing of one's name in snow of a spring day. I cannot help it. It is my mother-tongue, and is to my mind the only true speech of the life that I draw.'

Whatever difference of opinion there may fairly be as to the propriety of clothing in a provincial dialect such thoughts and images as belong to general literature and are perfectly expressible in modern English, few if any will deny the fitness and success with which Mr. Barnes has used the Dorset forms of speech in treating purely rustic subjects, like 'Not goo hwome to-night,' 'The Humstrum,' 'Don't ceäre,' 'What Dick and I done.' 'Christmas Invitation,' 'The Farmer's woldest Dacter,' and especially in dialogues, such as 'The Waggon a-stooded,' 'A bit o' sly Coortèn,' 'Shodon Feair,' 'The best Man in the Vield,' 'A Witch,' and many more. For my own part, I am thankful for all these poems, just as they stand. In even those which are substantially least rural, come verses and phrases that have a new and delightful flavour ; and we feel that, as the poet tells us, this is his natural mode of speech, in which he was born and bred, the ready instrument of his heart and tongue.

The Dorset dialect, according to our author himself, 'has come down by independent descent from the Saxon dialect, which our forefathers, who founded the kingdom of Wessex in Britain, brought from the south of Denmark;'[1] it is 'a broad and bold shape of the English language, as the Doric was of the Greek,' 'rich in humour, strong in raillery and hyperbole,' 'purer, and in some cases richer, than the dialect which is chosen as the national speech;' 'it retains many words of Saxon origin, for which the English substitutes others of Latin, Greek, or French derivation,' and 'it has distinctive words for many things which book-English can hardly distinguish but by periphrasis.' As an example of niceties owned by the Dorset, take *theas* and *thik;* these pronouns are not mere equivalents of *this* and *that* (which are also used), the former being applicable 'only to individual nouns, not to quantities of matter;' so that if one Dorset man heard another mention 'theas cloth' and 'thik glass,' he would know that a table-cloth and a drinking glass, or some such distinct things, were meant; but 'this cloth' and 'that glass' would convey the notion of a quantity of cloth, as in a bale, a quantity of glass, as in sheet or in broken pieces. To make use of such phrases as 'theas milk,' 'thik water,' is a common blunder of imitators of the dialect, which 'is spoken in its greatest purity in the villages and hamlets of the secluded and beautiful vale of Blackmore.'

Our poet has written from what he knows and feels. As to style, his verse has the essential quality of melodiousness, and many Dorset names come in with a sweetness that scarcely Val d'Arno could outvie—Lindenore and Paladore, Meldonley and Alderburnham. His manner of description is minute; we see the mossy thatch, the shining grass-blades,

[1] Dissertation, in *Poems of Rural Life*, 2nd edition, 1848.

the bubbles on the stream, the gypsy's shaggy-coated horse
and the carter's sleek-haired team, 'the cows below the
shady tree, wi' leafy bough a-swâyèn,' the girls' bonnets
'a lined wi' blue, and sashes tied behind,' grammer's gown
pulled through her pocket-hole to keep it from the dirt, 'a
gown wi' girt flowers like hollyhocks.' A thousand truthful
touches bring his rustic scenes and people before our eyes.

Some of those critics who prove, if nothing else, their
own narrow limitations by disparaging one style in art to
the exaltation of another, or perhaps all others, can easily
make objections here, complaining of elaboration of detail,
triviality, want of breadth and loftiness; too much of this,
too little of that. But ought the works of all artists to be
alike? Do we wish to have every picture in a gallery done
in one particular style? If the great principles of art, you
say, are invariable, an infinite variety is possible and
desirable in the application of them. What an artist ought
to do is that which he finds himself fitted to do and
delighted in doing. Nor does this imply neglect of work,
lazy and careless handling: it implies real work, the closest,
watchfullest, and most thorough execution of which the man
is able; 'labour of love' is the effective kind of labour in
the world of art.

To every true-born artist (in words, musical tones, forms,
colours) working in this spirit, the right attitude of the
public and of the critics is one of respect. It is not that any
artist whosoever is to be regarded as above criticism, but
that we should always keep in mind that the true principles
and rules of the critics can be derived from no other source
than the genius of the executive artists. Abstract criticism
on art is an absurdity. The true artist proves that beautiful
things, otherwise impossible, can be done, by doing them;
the intelligent critic may then, if he will, and so far as he
can (thoroughly he never can), point out the how and the
why, and thus do service of its kind, helping us all to know

good work when we see it. The artist, whatsoever his medium of expression or his rank among others, is a miracle-worker, literally inspired from heaven, able to be an enricher and exalter of human life, and to deserve the gratitude of mankind. Happy are they whose power of enjoyment sympathises with good art of many different styles, with Van Eyck and Rembrandt, with Holbein and Titian, with Hogarth and Reynolds and Turner, with Greek Architecture and Gothic, with Pheidias and Cellini, with Bach, Mozart Handel, Beethoven, Rossini, and the old harp and bagpipe tunes, with Æschylus and Theocritus, with Dante and Béranger, with Homer and Burns, with Spenser and Shakespeare and the Border Ballads.

To return to our Dorset friend—his little volume (the third of a series of three) was a pleasant pocket-companion up the soft, wide, woody-hilled, brook-watered Vale of Blackmore, with many a quiet gray village and village-church, and many a snug old farmhouse in its ' home ground,' with garden and orchard, and rook-nested elms. I have compared a reading of these poems to a fine day's walk through such a district as this, and in each one sees mostly the pleasant side of things. Tinges of gentle melancholy are not wanting ; we see aged cottagers at their doors, and glance at the inscriptions in rural graveyards ; but the ugly pain and disappointment, the sins and struggles of life, lie out of ken. All the better for the delight of our day's walk, and perhaps for our pleasure in the book also ; yet—yet—one can't help sometimes glancing or perhaps even prying into the actual daily life that underlies these fair pictures. If the peasantry hereabouts, old and young (thought I), have so warm and intelligent a love for the Church and her clergy and her ceremonies as the poet indicates, and so pure a tone of morals, they must be much unlike any English peasantry that I have any acquaintance with ; but this reflection was partly of a speculative kind, and one that I did not wish to pursue. Presently I come to a swing-gate, across a charming shady fieldpath, leading towards the church and vicarage of Marnhull, on which gate is some pencil-writing, decidedly unfit for publication, smacking of the slums of Drury Lane, wofully out of keeping with an innocent idyllic scene. And here let me recall another little incident which occurred to me later in this same county of Dorset, some twenty miles farther south. Taking shelter from heavy rain in a rather poor cottage, I found an elderly man and woman, two grown-up daughters, and two children. ' Were these grandchildren?' 'Yes.' Each daughter owned one. ' Did they all live in that cottage?' 'Yes.' 'The daughters' husbands too?' 'They've a-got no husbands.' 'What! both widows, and so young?' 'Na! th'ant never bin married.' The questioner was the only person who showed any embarrassment at this answer; and I learned subsequently that there was nothing uncommon in the situation.

From Marnhull Church and its noble yew-tree, I descended the other side of the hill, and finding a stone-breaker sitting at work on a heap of stones by the road-side, put some questions to him as to the localities. He was not old, but poor and sickly-looking, and answered in a slow, confused manner, for which he begged my pardon, saying that his head was wrong sometimes. I found he was subject to epilepsy, and had had a fit that day. He used to live a good way off, with his brother, but his brother married, and then there was no room for him. He came to this neighbourhood, and sometimes got a little work on a farm, sometimes on the roads. Some days he was not able to do any work. He got no parish relief, because this was not his parish. He had a place to sleep in at a cottage. This poor man uttered no tone of complaint, showed no desire to talk of his miseries, nor even any recognition of them as such: he had no expectation of anything in the world, not even of a chance sixpence; he answered my questions, one by one, neither willingly nor unwillingly, but with a certain effort, sometimes looking vaguely at me without the least curiosity, and all the while chopped slowly and mechanically with his hammer. It was another bit of harsh reality.

My lyrical, idyllic, artistic mood was rebuked and abashed. From the bitter weed of that poor man's condition, I tried to extract some drops of medicine for my own discontents. The mood was abashed indeed, but not shamed; and so it gradually recovered itself, as I walked on by bowery roads and green paths, over hill and dale, with the Stour, now a rushy, willowy brook, twisting hither and thither in the meadows, through the villages of Stour Provost (pausing to admire an ancient house smothered in ivy), and East Stour; till Duncliffe Hill, 'the traveller's mark,' rose on my right hand, and a wide rich prospect, extending into Wiltshire, opened in front. Again seeking shelter from a sudden shower, I tried to interest the people of the cottage in my volume of Dorset poems, and read a comic piece to them, but to little purpose; the goodwife at first thought my object was commercial, but finding I did not want to sell the book, she knew not what to think, and retired into herself.

At Gillingham, a long straggling street, I dined, and stepped into the train for Salisbury.

RAMBLE THE NINTH.

Salisbury—Old Sarum—Stonehenge—Wilton House—Bemerton—George Herbert's Life and Poems—His brother, Lord Herbert.

ARRIVED at Salisbury, I left my bag at an inn, made straight for the Close, turned a corner, and there, from greensward carpet, behind a light veil of budding elm boughs, the gracious old warm-gray Cathedral (with its long centre-line, two transepts, lancet-windows, lofty tower and spire) sprang light, perfect, musical. Evening sunshine glowed upon the grass and on the elm-tops, where high-church rooks were cawing by their nests, and on the warm old red-brick domiciles of the dignified clergy ranged round the sacred precinct, and spread lights and shadows over the great edifice, without disturbing its harmonious unity. More solemn buildings I have seen, more stately, more fantastic, more rich ; none so elegant.

The verger who showed me round the interior next morning had the air of mild superiority and gentle dogmatism which characterises the higher specimens of his order, and delivered his routine information with a very creditable air of impromptu. The building is all of one period, and in one style (called 'Early English'), say 1220-50, except part of the tower and the spire, which were added some years later. The vast weight of these has pushed askew some of the sustaining pillars and arches. The great interior has a bare

and cold aspect ; but the chapter-house, with its quaint bas-
reliefs from Scripture, is newly done up in bright colours.
Under the shadow of his cathedral, on its west side, stands
the Bishop's palace in its pleasure-grounds, and the gray
pile, with cloisters and chapter-house, takes new aspects of
beauty rising between and above the flower-shrubs and
foliage.

Apart from this its jewel, the city of Salisbury is not to be
ranked as a striking place ; yet it is quietly pleasant and
interesting. It stands on a flat among trees, chiefly elms,
with low sloping green hills on every side, between which
wind the clear waters of the Avon and its tributaries, irri-
gating bright green pastures, full of sheep. The quiet, homely
streets, with here and there an ancient gable-front, or gateway, have rather a village than a city aspect. There are
two or three old churches, of ' perpendicular ' gothic, and
an old market-cross with buttressed arches, the whole in
shape like an imperial crown. Nearly every street shows
you a green hill or grove at its end, and here and there
comes a glimpse of fresh-flowing waters, with a mill, a
bridge, a group of willows or poplars. Footpaths lead
through gardens and cottages into the open country ; and at
every turn you see once more the tapering stem and spire
with bands of stone diaper-work and airy cross. I recollected
Mr. Pecksniff, who is said to have lived hereabouts, and his
views of Salisbury Cathedral ' from the north-east, north-
west, south-south-east,' etc. ; and now, being at Salisbury,
I perceived that the author of ' Martin Chuzzlewit ' had
never been there up to the time of his writing that novel ;
at least, the topography of the book (if it matters) is so far
entirely wrong.

In the wide market-square, whereto flows the produce of
many a Wiltshire and Hampshire farm (the market, long an
important one, has been much increased by the railways)
stands the Court House, and in front of this the statue of

Sidney Herbert—black, bareheaded, gigantic, in frock-coat and trousers, on a hideous light-gray granite pedestal of the modern British pattern, rectangular, with ill-proportioned cornice, lumpish and scraggy at once. Why are such things done? Who likes them? Could we not, in the matter of pedestals, at least follow some good model? The garish, many-coloured tomb in the Cathedral to a late major of volunteers aims at richness, as the Herbert monument at simplicity, and with no better success.

I cannot help fancying that Wilts is a county of more gentle and kindly manners than its neighbour Hants. High people and low, at the railway and the inn, shopkeepers, children, rustics, all were good-natured and obliging. I well remember, in my first days in Hampshire, how rude and insolent I thought most of the people. The South Wilts accent, too, sounded quiet and mild, and without that self-asserting drawl of 'Ya-a-as!' and 'Nau-au-o!' From the talk of the children in any place one can soonest catch the flavour of the local speech.

Famous Old Sarum surpassed my expectations. I looked for a bare green mount, with half-obliterated entrenchments, a 'rath' on large scale, scarce distinguishable from the surrounding fields; but the great terraced hill is a marked and grand object in the landscape; beautiful, too, in the unbroken sweeping curves of its grassy mounds, and the grovy crest of its inner foss—a dell of coppice wood mixed with larger trees. The outer foss you find to be huge and deep, a narrow vale between two steep grassy slopes; and from this to the inner circle stretches a broad, green, level space. Here and there, too, remains in its old place some fragment of flint-built wall; but the largest is so undermined by the picking of visitors and idlers that to all appearance it may tumble any day. A little modern masonry applied in time would preserve it. In the central space the grass is heaved and sunk in little mounds and hollows, where lie buried the foundations and low fragments of the castle, and of that ancient church whose proud successor in the valley lifts in view its lofty head; one day, sooner or later, to come into the same condition.

Sarum, *Sorbiodunum*, Latinised form of a Keltic name, is usually translated, 'The Dry Fortress;' but another, and perhaps better interpretation, is 'Service-tree Fort.' At all events, the wild service-tree, or sorb, still buds in the new spring sunshine on this hill—the stronghold in turn of Ancient Briton, Roman, Saxon, and the modern Borough-monger—for, as everyone knows, till some thirty years ago, two members represented in Parliament the blackbirds and field mice who had long been the only inhabitants of this green city.

The words of another living poet (of firm worth, but unshowy, and whose voice is for the present drowned by the street-cries of pseudo-poetry and pseudo-criticism) came into my mind:

> I have stood on Old Sarum: the sun,
> With a pensive regard from the west,
> Lit the beech-tops low down in the ditch of the Dun,
> Lit the service-trees high on its crest:
> But the walls of the Roman were shrunk
> Into morsels of ruin around,
> And palace of monarch and minster of monk,
> Were effaced from the grassy-foss'd ground.
> Like bubbles on ocean they melt,
> O Wilts, on thy long rolling plain;
> And at last but the works of the hand of the Celt,
> And the sweet hand of Nature remain.[1]

Quitting with reluctance the lonely city, I walk north-ward by a long path from field to field, which leads me to the edge of a steep green slope, and see shining through the vale below a pure silvery river, called by the commonest of

[1] *Lays of the Western Gael*, etc., by Samuel Ferguson. Bell and Daldy, 1865.

all Keltic names for flowing water—'Avon.' I am now some thirty miles west of the Stour, but the two rivers mingle under the old Norman tower of Christchurch. Below, as in a picture-map, the green Vale shows its villages and farmhouses, warm-brown, amid orchards and home-groves, its mills and willows and little islands, under the varying sky of spring. From river pastures and sloping hills comes the sound of the sheepbells, saying their name in German, *glocke! glocke! glocke!* Then I drop into the valley, issuing, at last, upon huge solitary fields, the beginning of the Wiltshire Downs. I am approaching Stonehenge, one of those things that in childhood we hope to see before we die, like Niagara, Switzerland, Rome, the Pyramids, a volcano, etc. At Amesbury (mere straggling village now, whatever it may have been) I found shelter in the inn, where two great men once on a time got no milk to their tea (see 'English Traits'), and set off again between and through heavy spring showers: but these, I think, have some electric and vitalising quality; autumnal or wintry rain is an enemy to meet, but vernal rain (if one is in health) exhilarates. The road to my object was disappointingly trim and civil, leading past a park with big white mansion, on the site of the ancient abbey; and other enclosed ground. A mile or two further on, I found a man, who proved to be on duty. He was placed there by the lord of the soil to look after 'the *Stones*' (that is their local title) and to see that the expected holiday visitors (for it was Easter Monday) did not carry them away—bits at least, as they were too prone to do. 'And how far to the Stones?' 'You'll see 'em when you turn the corner.' Sure enough there they were : but not, alas !

A cirque
' Of Druid-stones upon a forlorn moor.

New macadamised roads cross the long slope of the Down, a newish farmhouse crowns the ridge, a new and formal grove of fir-trees intrudes its wedge below. At the Stones I found only one visitor, essaying a pencil sketch from under his umbrella. He had long desired to see Stonehenge, he told me, had come down from London on purpose by an excursion train, and was going back early the next morning. He was a plain little man, apparently of the mechanic class, and disclosed no other interesting qualities; but his having made this holiday-journey alone and with such an object was interesting, and I misliked the rain more for his sake than my own.

I was not particularly impressed in any way by the famous Stones. Similar things I had seen elsewhere, smaller, but not a whit less charged with antiuqe mystery. There was no new sensation here, and the immense notoriety of the place made one feel, as sometimes happens, rather sulky and captious. As to wondering at the size, that is childish. Even the Great Pyramid considered as a bulk of building is a thing of which any commanded swarm of men are capable, with the aid of a few common tools and mechanical appliances. That man can impart *beauty* to his work—beauty from the same Divine source that fills every atom and veinlet of the universe with enchantment—here, it seems to me, is something worthy of wonder and awe. If the sudden sight of Salisbury Cathedral sends a thrill through one's body and soul (as through mine it did) it is not because so many cut stones have been laboriously lifted into the sky. A sentence of Shakespeare, a strain of Mozart, carries the same effect—a celestial thrill, from the recognition of Beauty. The Great Pyramid has acquired respectability, and even solemnity from its vast age; it is but a stupid brutal bulk after all, and must weigh like a nightmare on the spirit of the gazer.

Forgive me, Old Druidic Circle! (if such thine origin)— think me not unfeeling. Fain would I wander again and often, by sun and moon, among thy tall, gray stones, where they stand in rude pillars and portals, or lie confused upon the sward—at some fit hour perhaps to receive a vibration from the uncouth and solitary presence.

The walk back to Salisbury, by path and road, and margin of willowy Avon, was wet and long. Next day I saw Wilton House, without much result; the housekeeper showed a large mansion, with pictures and busts far too many to look at, a great room with Vandyke portraits, and windows viewing the lawns and groves of a handsome park. Such places make one sad; all the appliances of life in perfection and over-abundance, to such little purpose, great parks and pleasure-grounds and palaces kept up at huge cost, for the owners to yawn in and run away from. Not far off rises the gaudy New-Anglican church, built a few years or months too soon, for it represents a phase of opinion (or pseudo-opinion) out of which the founders by-and-by took their departure.

On my road back to Salisbury was a more interesting church, a little old ivied building, about the size of a cottage, with steep roof and small leaded panes; and a plain old little rustic interior. This was Bemerton, George Herbert's chapel of ease, and familiar house of prayer; and they brought me the key from the parsonage across the road, which was his parsonage. This little old church, or chapel, is now shut up, but will not, let us hope, be destroyed.

Barnes's poems are full of natural rustic piety, Herbert's reflective and didactic. A simple attachment to Mother Church appears unobtrusively in the Dorset vicar's poetry —a spire peeping in a rural landscape. Our Wiltshire priest is loftily clerical. This clericalism, while it deprives Herbert of the wider influence which belongs to wider poetry, attaches to him a certain special class of admirers; and some of his wise thoughts and terse admonitions are not easily forgotten by any reader; for, as he himself says, 'A verse may find him who a sermon flies.'

My own thoughts certainly run a good deal on poetry and poets, especially in spring-time. Many people, as I now know very well, think this a frivolous subject ; perhaps they are right. All I can say is, that I took to it very early in life (in infancy, I may say), out of pure love, and it still retains my affection. 'The holy incantation of a verse' comes often into my mind ; many a verse, fitting many a mood, soothing or heightening it. I can remember, in a thousand cases, the *ipsissima verba* of the poets, which carry their own music, and waft besides an aroma of delightful associations. Many of the objects that occupy men, even the grave and dignified, seem to me, on the other hand (I must own it), frivolous enough. Not that I have not often had qualms about poetry, whether it were not a delusion ; but I have always come back to faith in it, and a firmer faith. George Herbert was no mighty man, yet his thoughts and moods, being embalmed in musical words, do still live. Many are in my own and other memories ; and whoso needs his book has but to ask for it in a shop. He had really in him a touch of the Poet ; and the good old Shopkeeper and Angler who wrote his life had also some sprinkle of that preservative spice which we name Genius.

I saw in Salisbury yesterday in a second-hand bookseller's a good copy of another writer's folio, also connected with this place ; it contained the 'Arcadia,' 'Defence of Poesie,' and 'Sonnets.' The *preux chevalier*, good at sword and pen, being at Wilton (but not in this present house, which Inigo Jones built), wrote his romance of 'Arcadia' to please his sister, wife of Herbert, Earl of Pembroke, and to fill up some of the hours of an exilement from Court. When Sir Philip Sidney, years later, and then only thirty-two years old, was fatally wounded at Zutphen, Edward Herbert, afterwards Lord Herbert of Cherbury, was a child of three years, whose brother George did not come into the world until seven years after this.

Of George Herbert, no important yet not an insignificant or uninteresting human being, I have a clear little picture in my head, which has formed itself since I saw his parsonage and chapel. Men and events, I confess, are to me vague and shadowy, scarce half-believed, until I can *place* them distinctly. At Paris, Napoleon the First became real to me; at Weimar, Goethe.

The younger son of a high old family, always of delicate health, shy and studious, but lofty and hot-tempered, George Herbert was brought up and guarded with the most anxious care (even after he had attained to manhood) by a pious and prudent mother, his father having died when the boy was but four years old. He was born in Montgomery Castle, in 1593, and spent his childhood ' in sweet content ' under the watchful eyes of his mother and the tuition of a chaplain. When about twelve years old he went to Westminster school, ' commended to the care ' of Dr. Neale, Dean of Westminster, and by him to Mr. Ireland, the head master; and by his ' pretty behaviour ' there seemed plainly to be ' marked out for piety.' The words between inverted commas I cull from good Izaak Walton. About his sixteenth year, being a king's scholar, he was elected to Trinity College, Cambridge; and his mother procured Dr. Neville, Master of Trinity, to take the youth ' into his particular care, and provide him a tutor.' She had before this time accompanied her eldest son Edward (afterwards Lord Herbert of Cherbury) to Oxford, and there taken up her abode during four years, ' to see and converse with him daily,' and so, by the methods of love and good example, prevent his falling into vice or ill company, in which she happily succeeded. In his first year at Cambridge we find George writing to his mother, ' my poor abilities in poetry shall be all and ever consecrated to God's glory,' he finding the heathenism and lightness of the poets of the day very contrary to his mind. He encloses two sonnets :

> My God, where is that ancient heat towards thee
>   Wherewith whole shoals of martyrs once did burn,
> Besides their other flames ? Doth Poetry
>   Wear Venus' livery ? only serve her turn ?
> Why are not sonnets made of thee ? and lays
>   Upon thine altar burnt ? cannot thy love
> Heighten a spirit to sound out thy praise
>   As well as any she ? Cannot thy dove
> Outstrip their Cupid easily in flight ? . . .

The second sonnet ends thus :

> Why should I women's eyes for crystal take ?
>   Such poor invention burns in their low mind
> Whose fire is wild, and doth not upward go
>   To praise, and on thee, Lord, some ink bestow.
>   Open the bones, and you shall nothing find
> In the best face but filth ; when, Lord, in thee
> The beauty lies in the discovery.

These verses of the boy show in an unusual degree all the characteristics of his maturer writings : a decided talent for writing in verse, some imagery, a certain subtlety and vivacity of thought, a tendency to conceits ; and the whole pervaded by a genuine piety, but of that sort which feeds itself with disdain of all mere natural beauty and pleasantness, valuing them only as matter for a sermon or a hymn.

In the same letter George speaks of his ' late ague ; ' and he seems to have spent the most part of his life under sufferings from one or another kind of sickness. In person he was ' inclining towards tallness,' ' very straight,' and ' lean to an extremity.' He was a strict student, and in 1615, being then in his twenty-second year, became M.A. and fellow of his college. ' The greatest diversion from his study was the practice of music, in which he became a great master.' If his friendly biographer can find in him any error, it is that ' he kept himself too much retired, and at too great a distance with all his inferiors ; and his clothes seemed to prove that he put too great a value on his parts and parentage.' And here I must add a touch to the portrait, from his brother's autobiography : [1] ' He (George) was not exempt from passion and choler, being infirmities to which all our race is subject ; but, that excepted, without reproach in his actions.' This tendency, however, we may be sure, was well controlled and subdued, and only lived in him in later life as a warm, religious, and virtuous vehemency. In 1619, aged twenty-six, he was chosen Orator of the University, and held that office for eight years with high credit. He was not insensible, as his letters prove, to the glory of it, nor was the salary of 30*l.* a year unacceptable. Though of high family his allowance was not large, and in an interesting letter to Sir John Danvers, his mother's second husband, written in 1617, more than a year after gaining his fellowship, he writes : ' I want books extremely,' especially books of divinity, and wishes to raise a sum on security. ' " What becomes of your annuity ? " Sir, if there be any truth in me, I find it little enough to keep me in health. You know I was sick last vacation, neither am I yet recovered ; so that I am fain ever and anon to buy somewhat tending towards my health, for infirmities are both painful and costly. . . . I am scarce able with much ado to make one half-year's allowance shake hands with the other.'

The Orator's first great opportunity was in writing a letter of thanks to King James (*Serenissime Domine noster, Jacobe invictissime !*) when that learned monarch enriched the University with a copy of his invaluable book entitled ' Basilicon Doron.' Our orator finished off thus :

> Quid Vaticanam Bodleianamque objicis, Hospes ?
> Unicus est nobis Bibliotheca Liber.
>
> Talk of the Vatican, Bodleian,—stuff !
> Here in one Book we've library enough.

[1] *Life of Edward Lord Herbert of Cherbury*, written by himself. London, 1770 ; p. 12.

'This letter was writ in such excellent Latin, was so full of conceits, and all expressions so suited to the genius of the king' that he made inquiries regarding the Cambridge Orator and began to notice him; whence George conceived great hopes of court favour, and trimmed his sails accordingly. After this, Herbert engaged in some pen-combats with one Andrew Melville (a good honest man, it appears) minister of the Scotch Church, and rector of St. Andrews, who 'had scattered many malicious and bitter verses against our liturgy, our ceremonies, and our church-government.' Melville being summoned to a friendly conference of clergy at Hampton Court, so much offended the king, that he was deprived of his rectorship and shut up in the Tower of London, 'where (saith Izaak) he remained very angry for three years.' There were short methods in that day of dealing with too troublesome controversialists. Herbert wrote *ex officio* Latin epigrams against Melville, but not very bitterly. Among the memorials of this part of his life we have a very long letter of George's, written from Cambridge to his mother, then lying in sickness; from beginning to end a sermon-like composition and much too proper.

When King James came a-hunting to Newmarket, he often visited Cambridge, 'where his entertainment was comedies suited to his pleasant humour; and where Mr. George Herbert [though theoretically regarding all these things as dust and ashes] was to welcome him with gratulations and the applauses of an orator.' He was rewarded with a sinecure of 120*l.* a year, the prebend of Layton Ecclesia in the diocese of Lincoln, the same which Queen Elizabeth had formerly conferred on Sir Philip Sidney; and being thus richer, 'he enjoyed his genteel humour for clothes and courtlike company, and seldom looked toward Cambridge unless the king were there, but then he never failed.' He had often desired to leave the University, but continued,

at his cautious and careful mother's wish. Finding the
parish church of Layton Ecclesia in a ruinous condition, the
conscientious prebendary (though warned by his mother,
'George, it is not for your weak body and empty purse to
undertake to build churches') re-edified it, with the help of
subscriptions from his kinsmen and friends. His mother,
who, after twelve years' widowhood had married a brother
of the Earl of Danby, died in 1627. In 1629 George, suffering from ague, removed to the house of his brother, Sir
Henry Herbert, at Woodford in Essex, where (according to
Walton) he cured himself of that disease by eating *salt meat*
only, but brought on 'a supposed consumption;' and therefore he moved again to Dauntsey in Wiltshire, the house of
Lord Danby. Here his health and spirits improved; and
he declared his resolution both to marry and to enter the
priesthood.

He was now about thirty-six years of age. Having
resolved to marry, he had not long or far to seek for a wife.
Mr. Charles Danvers of Bainton, Wilts, a near kinsman of
Lord Danby, and an old and attached friend of George Herbert,
had 'often publicly declared a desire that Mr. Herbert
would marry any of his nine daughters—for he had so many
—but rather his daughter Jane than any other, because
Jane was his beloved daughter.' When George came to
Dauntsey, Mr. Danvers was dead; but George and Jane
met, and each having heard much commendation of the
other, they agreed without many words, and were married
'the third day after this first interview.' The true friends
to both parties who brought them together 'understood
Mr. Herbert's and her temper of mind, and also their
estates,' so well before their interview that the suddenness
was justifiable by the strictest rules of prudence. Their
short union was a happy one; their 'mutual content and
love and joy did receive a daily augmentation, by such daily
obligingness to each other as still added such new affluences

to the former fulness of these divine souls, as was only improvable in heaven where they now enjoy it.'

About three months after this marriage the living of Bemerton became vacant, and was offered to Mr. Herbert. He, dreading the responsibility, now that it came close to him, considered on it for a month, fasting and praying often, and sometimes almost resolving to give up both priesthood and living. In the midst of these spiritual conflicts, Mr. Woodnot, an old friend, coming to visit Mr. Herbert, they went together to Wilton House, King Charles and the Court being then at Wilton or Salisbury. Mr. Herbert thanked his kinsman the Earl of Pembroke for the offer of the living, at the same time declining it; but Dr. Laud, Bishop of London, who was with the Court, came and reasoned with George on the subject, and did ' so convince Mr. Herbert that the refusal of it was a sin, that a tailor was sent for to come speedily from Salisbury to Wilton to take measure, and make him canonical clothes against the next day; which the tailor did: and Mr. Herbert being so habited ' was immediately inducted (he was already a deacon) into the living of Bemerton and Fugglestone. When at his induction he was shut into the church, ' being left there alone to toll the bell, as the law requires him,' he remained so long that Mr. Woodnot looked in at a window and ' saw him lie down prostrate on the ground before the altar.' He was setting himself rules of life (as he afterwards told his friend) and vowing that he would labour to keep them. That same night he said to Mr. Woodnot, ' I now look upon my aspiring thoughts, and think myself more happy than if I had attained what I then so ambitiously thirsted for.'

When King James looked so favourably on him, Herbert is thought to have aspired to be made a Secretary of State. He accepted at last the humble position of a country clergyman, not without effort, and carried all through a certain

self-consciousness in his humility and piety, which nevertheless were very genuine.   Having 'changed his sword
and silk clothes into a canonical coat,' and thus returned to
his wife at Bainton, he said to her, ' You are now a minister's wife, and must now so far forget your father's house as
not to claim a precedence of any of your parishioners,' etc.,
to which she cheerfully agreed.   Going over one day to
Bemerton about repairs of the church, the new rector met
a poor old woman who began to tell him her troubles, as
poor old women do, but through fear and shortness of breath
her speech failed her, whereupon Mr. Herbert 'was so
humble that he took her by the hand, and said, "Speak,
good mother; be not afraid to speak to me;"' etc., and
gave her both counsel and money.   Telling this to his wife
when he went home, Mrs. Herbert 'was so affected' that
she sent the poor old woman a pair of blankets with a kind
message.   All which was very kind and pretty, but scarcely
enough to account for the rapturous manner in which it is
narrated by friend Izaak, who remarks : 'Thus worthy, and
like David's blessed man, thus lowly, was Mr. George
Herbert in his own eyes, and thus lovely in the eyes of
others.'

The rector repaired the parish church (which is not called
Bemerton, but Fugglestone, and stands near Wilton), and
almost rebuilt the parsonage at his own charge.   He also
improved the little chapel of ease of Bemerton (which I
visited), just across the road from his parsonage; and in
this appeared twice every day at church prayers, 'strictly
at the canonical hours of ten and four,' with his wife and
three nieces (the daughters of a deceased sister) and his
whole household.

I wish I knew what Mrs. Herbert was like : I can see the
tall, thin, straight figure of the rector, with a long, mild,
serious face, somewhat pale and hollow-cheeked; and hear
his grave tones, with a cough now and again, 'which makes

me sorry.' ' If he were at any time too zealous in his sermons,' it was in reproving those worshippers, and those
ministers too, who did their part in the divine service in an
indecorous or hasty manner; and he took great pains to
expound the meaning and value of all the appointed forms
and ceremonies and set times of the Church. ' His constant public prayers did never make him to neglect his own
private devotions,' nor family prayers, which were always
a set form, and not long, ending with the collect of the day.

Yet Mr. Herbert in these matters came much short of his
friend and correspondent, Mr. Farrer, of Little Glidden,
near Huntingdon (ex-fellow of Clare Hall, Cambridge), who,
besides all possible Church prayers, fasts, vigils, etc., etc.,
had an oratory in his house in which praying and reading
or singing of psalms was kept up *continuously,* day and
night, for many years, the members of his family keeping
watch and watch; and ' in *this continued serving of God,*
the Psalter or whole Book of Psalms was in every four
and twenty hours sung or read over, from the first to
the last verse.'[1] This Mr. Farrer, sometimes called the
' Protestant Monk,' died in 1639.

Mr. Herbert's chief recreation was music; he composed
many hymns and anthems, and sung them to his lute or
viol. He usually attended twice a week the cathedral service at Salisbury, and afterwards went to a private music-
meeting in the city, at which he was one of the performers.
One day, in his walk to Salisbury, the rector saw a poor
man's horse fallen under his load, and helped the man to
unload, lift, and reload his beast: ' at his coming to his
musical friends at Salisbury, they began to wonder that
Mr. George Herbert, which used to be so trim and neat,
came into that company so soiled and discomposed; but he
told them the occasion.' One of them seeming to think that
the rector ' had disparaged himself by so dirty an employ-

[1] Walton.

ment,' Mr. Herbert made a proper and somewhat elaborate little speech (unless Izaak has made it for him), saying that certainly it was not pleasant to do; but that he felt he had acted conscientiously; the thought of it ' would prove music to him at midnight,' and he praised God for the opportunity—'and now let us tune our instruments:' an anecdote which has a certain comic colour not intended by good Mr. Walton. Both he and his wife were very bountiful to their poor parishioners; and when a friend advised him to be more frugal, he made a speech (according to Izaak) ending thus: ' Sir, my wife hath a competent maintenance secured to her after my death; and therefore this my resolution shall, by God's grace, remain unalterable.'

In fact, as to the external conditions of life, Mr. Herbert had an easy time of it all through, though at one period he found his allowance hardly enough to admit of his purchasing all the books of theology which he desired. This easy and secure life, from birth to death, a contemplative introspective habit of mind ('he would often say he had too thoughtful a wit'), a sickly body, and a temperament that inclined him in all things, both physical and mental, to orderliness, punctuality, and primness, go far to explain his character and the form into which his religious aspirations were moulded. In addition, he had that melodious faculty which expressed itself both in music proper and in verse, and which makes him interesting.

Nothing, I think, can be more erroneous than to look on poetical writings as mainly fantastic and trivial. They delight us by their happy and melodious forms; but we are also attracted by their *sincerity*. In the works of a true poet, be his rank what it may, you find an expression— freer than he could elsewhere venture—of how he was impressed by life. In verse the poet (a choice kind of man) declares his best self: if you know how to look, you will find the essence of his love, his faith, his hope and fear, his strength and weakness. Herbert, in his prose 'Country Parson,' cannot write one free sentence, nor even in a letter to his friend or his mother; he is sophisticate to the marrow. In his poems, precisian as he still is, a larger wisdom shines out here and there; 'the glory of the sum of things' declares itself; he rises at moments out of formal into universal religion.

The good rector held his parish less than three years. The seeds of early death were in him. One usually thinks of George Herbert as an elderly man, from his grave look and reputation; but he was only forty when he died. When much weakened by consumption he continued to read prayers twice a day in the chapel close to his parsonage; but at last was persuaded by his wife to allow his curate to take that duty, he himself attending as a hearer as long as he could. About a month before his death he was visited by a clergyman, one Mr. Duncon, bringing a brotherly religious message from Mr. Farrer, of Glidden Hall. Mr. Herbert lay on a pallet, weak and faint, and asked Mr. Duncon to pray with him, in 'the prayers of my mother, the Church of England: no other prayers are equal to them;' and Mr. Duncon 'saw majesty and humility so reconciled in his looks and behaviour,' as begot 'an awful reverence.'

His old and dear friend Mr. Woodnot came from London to Bemerton, and never left him till the end. On the Sunday before his death he rose suddenly from his couch, called for one of his instruments, and having tuned it, played and sang a pious verse. 'Thus,' says Walton, 'he sang on earth such hymns and anthems as the angels, and he, and Mr. Farrer, now sing in heaven.' On the day of his death, his wife and nieces 'weeping to an extremity,' he entreated them to withdraw to the next room and there pray for him. After murmuring some pious words he breathed his last, 'without any apparent disturbance;' and

Mr. Woodnot and the curate, Mr. Bostock, closed his eyes.

The quaint biographer remarks: ' If Andrew Melville ' —he who was in the Tower for three years very angry— ' died before him, then George Herbert died without an enemy.'

Izaak Walton, London tradesman, fond of reading, and his holiday amusement angling, had for his wife's brother a clergyman, who rose to be Bishop of London. Izaak's social dignity thus came to him through the Church; and his mind, loving literature, ran also continually on Church men and matters. After retiring from business he wrote ' The Complete Angler,' and the lives of Wotton, Donne, Hooker, Sanderson, and Herbert, and won himself a place on the bookshelf.

As to George Herbert's writings: he left behind him ' The Country Parson; or, Priest to the Temple,' containing his own rules, which at his death came in manuscript into the hands of his friend Mr. Woodnot; and poems, under the itle of ' The Temple,' which, being on his death-bed, he sent in manuscript to Mr. Farrer to be made public or not, according to that friend's opinion. In his college days he had written some Greek and Latin poems, not remarkable.

The first words of ' The Country Parson ' plainly indicate the author's point of view. ' A pastor is the deputy of Christ; ' and a few sentences down we find, ' Christ . . . . constituted deputies in his place, and these are priests.' In the divine services he *bears the sins* of the congregation. He ' exacts of them all possible reverence ' and observance of the forms of worship. Those who do not attend church, or habitually come late, must be ' presented.' He must fast on Fridays. He is to give much to the poor, but chiefly to those who can say the Creed, etc. The church is to be carefully kept, and at times ' perfumed with

incense.' He must persuade the sick or otherwise afflicted
' to particular confession, labouring to make them understand the great good use of this ancient and pious ordinance,
and how necessary it is in some cases.' 'Those he meets
on the way he blesseth audibly.' 'The Country Parson is
in God's stead to his Parish, and dischargeth God what he
can of his promises. Wherefore there is nothing done,
either well or ill, whereof he is not the rewarder or
punisher.' 'He exacts of all the doctrine of the Catechism;' 'that which nature is towards philosophy, the
Catechism is towards divinity.' 'The Country Parson
being to administer the Sacraments, is at a stand with himself—how or what behaviour to assume for so holy things.
Especially at Communion times he is in great confusion [or
perturbation] as being not only to receive God, but to break
and administer him.' The Churchwardens are 'to present
[i.e. lodge an information against] all who receive not thrice
a year;' and also 'to levy penalties for negligence in
resorting to church,' etc. 'The Country Parson desires to
be All to his Parish; and not only a Pastor, but a Lawyer
also, and a Physician. Therefore he endures not that any of
his flock should go to law; but in any controversy, that they
should resort to him as their Judge.' 'If there be any of
his flock sick, he is their Physician, or at least his wife.' If
he or his wife have not the skill he is to maintain relations
with some practitioner, who is to act with and under the
parson. 'If there be any of his parish that hold strange
doctrines,' he 'useth all possible diligence to reduce them
to the common faith.' 'It is necessary that all Christians
should pray twice a day every day of the week, and four times
on Sunday, if they be well. This is so necessary and
essential to a Christian that he cannot without this maintain
himself in a Christian state.' Prayers beyond this are
' additionary;' and the Parson, in this and other matters,
is to point out the distinction between 'necessary' and

'additionary' duties. 'Neither have the Ministers power of blessing only, but also of cursing.'

Our excerpts sufficiently indicate the idea in Mr. Herbert's mind of a country parson's right position and duties in the world. That such notions are based on erroneous principles, and are impossible to carry into practice, it seems needless to point out. Yet we see that the vicar of Bemerton does to this day by no means lack successors in this line of thinking. With all this are mingled in his book many wise and subtle thoughts, and a continual inculcation of holiness of life, love and humility, as the parson's best weapons—weapons wherewith Mr. Herbert himself was nobly armed.

And now let us turn to his poetry, without which his memory would have but a slight interest. George Herbert's little book is alive after two centuries. He wrote the verses from and for himself. They are religious musings. No human figures or incidents appear in them; there is but himself and his God. The world of nature only serves to illustrate his spiritual relations. He has a 'heart in pilgrimage,' and his life is a prayer; all day long he feels the great Presence—'If I but lift mine eyes, my suit is made.' When—such as all men must have—he has times of forgetfulness, or unfaith, he flies back into contrition:

> But as I raved, and grew more fierce and wild
>   At every word,
> Methought I heard one calling 'Child !'
>   And I replied, ' My Lord!'

Many are his acknowledgments of sin; not expressed with fear of punishment (he never speaks of hell in the vulgar sense, and he says that 'devils are our sins in perspective'), but with deep awe and humble contrition, and a pleading that he may not be deprived of his

Father's love and care. Here is a very tender little religious poem :

LOVE.

Love bade me welcome ; yet my soul drew back,
    Guiltie of dust and sinne.
But quick-ey'd Love, observing me grow slack
    From my first entrance in,
Drew nearer to me ; sweetly questioning
    If I lack'd anything.

'A guest,' I answered, 'worthy to be here—'
    Love said, ' You shall be he.'
'I the unkinde, ungratefull ? Ah, my deare,
    I cannot look on thee.'
Love took my hand, and smiling did reply,
    'Who made the eyes but I ?'

'Truth, Lord, but I have marr'd them : let my shame
    Go where it doth deserve.'
'And know you not,' sayes Love, ' who bore the blame ?'
    ' My deare, then I will serve.'
'You must sit down,' sayes Love, 'and taste my meat :'
    So I did sit and eat.

Herbert has many a beautiful verse and stanza of universal religion, strains of meditation, aspiration, or holy tranquillity ; but his piety and poetry have clothed themselves for the most part in those special dogmatic forms by which he set so much store.   He often runs into quaint conceits and oddities ; yet in his purer and simpler moods he sometimes attains an unusual happiness of expression, at once easy and terse :

What skills it, if a bag of stones or gold
    About thy neck do drown thee ? raise thy head
Take starres for money ; starres not to be told
    By any art, yet to be purchaséd.

Scorn no man's love, though of a mean degree ;
    Love is a present for a mighty king.

There are frequent touches of practical wisdom, such as these :

> When thou dost purpose aught within thy power
> Be sure to doe it, though it be but small ;
> Constancie knits the bones, and makes us stowre,—
>
>   .   .   .   .
>
> Who breaks his own bond, forfeiteth himself.

> Envie not greatnesse : for thou mak'st thereby
>   Thyself the worse, and so the distance greater.
> Be not thy own worm.   Yet such jealousie
>   As hurts not others, but may make thee better,
> Is a good spurre.

> Look not on pleasures as they come but go.

His verses bloom out here and there in true and delicate beauties, like little flowers among grass :

> I made a posy while the day ran by :
>
>   .   .   .   .
>
> But Time did beckon to the flowers, and they
> By noon most cunningly did steal away,
>   And wither'd in my hand.

> I know the ways of pleasure, the sweet strains,
>   The lullings and the relishes of it ;
> The propositions of hot blood and brains ;
>   What mirth and music mean ; what love and wit
> Have done these twentie hundred years and more.

> Sweet day, so cool, so calm, so bright,
>   The bridal of the earth and skie :
> The dew shall weep thy fall to-night ;
>   For thou must die.

But the three other verses of this poem are very inferior, save this one line :

> Sweet Spring, full of sweet days and roses.

Among the best pieces are the allegorical—as ' Peace ' (' Sweet Peace, where dost thou dwell ? '), and the

'Pilgrimage,'—reminding one of Bunyan; and the moral-
meditative poems, as 'Constancie,' 'Employment,' 'Man'
('Man is one world and hath another to attend him'),
'Mortification' ('How soon doth man decay'), 'Miserie,'
'Providence.'

Altogether, George Herbert's character, views, life, and
writings are easy to understand. Of kind nature, shy
temperament, and sickly body, refined fancy, meditative
mind, and tender conscience, receiving careful and seclusive
training—domestic and scholastic; timidly conservative in
all his ideas, seeing everything through the medium of his
Church, and hearing (most characteristically) 'church bells
beyond the stars,' such was the vicar of Bemerton. We
seem to have seen the tall thin consumptive man, in his
black skull-cap, mildly grave and ceremonious, scarce middle-
aged, yet old-looking; to have heard him reading the Church
prayers in a hollow solemn tone, or repeating a few of his
own verses in the parsonage garden, or playing some little
sacred air upon his lute, by a window commanding a distant
view of the spire of Salisbury Cathedral. There were
doubtless few dry eyes among those parishioners who followed
the coffin to the parish church of Fugglestone, when George
Herbert's body was laid under the altar.

Mr. Herbert had no children. 'His virtuous wife' (says
Izaak) 'continued his disconsolate widow about six years,
bemoaning herself and complaining that she had lost the
delight of her eyes,' etc. 'Thus she continued mourning
till time and conversation had so moderated her sorrows
that she became the happy wife of Sir Robert Cook, of
Highnam, in the county of Gloucester, knight.' . . .
'Mrs. Herbert was the wife of Sir Robert eight years, and
lived his widow about fifteen; all which time she took a
pleasure in mentioning and commending the excellencies of
Mr. George Herbert.' This, however, one can imagine to
have now and then become tiresome. 'Lady Cook had

preserved many of Mr. Herbert's private writings, which she intended to make public, but they and Highnam House were burnt together by the late rebels.'

George's eldest brother (Lord Herbert) says, in his autobiography, that 'about Salisbury where he [George] lived beneficed *for many years* he was little less than sainted.' The time was only about four years, and this mistake perhaps indicates that there was no very close intimacy.

Edward, Lord Herbert, equally or still better guarded by his careful mother, lived a very different life from George. He married at sixteen, had several children, was a chivalrous soldier, a learned student, a gallant courtier, a wise ambassador, fought duels, travelled and saw courts and varieties of life, and wrote philosophical treatises that drew the attention of the literati of Europe. Yet, different as they were, a family character is very perceptible in the brothers.

In the small quarto edition of the autobiography (from Horace Walpole's press) is a large portrait of Edward, Lord Herbert, lying meditative by a brook in a wood, a man in the background holding his horse; he is in full dress of James I.'s time, and by him lies a shield inscribed ' Magicâ Sympathiæ' (' By the magic of sympathy '), and emblazoned with a heart in flames. His notions of herbs, cures, and other natural things, were like George's.

Edward was a theist (which is not the same as atheist), believing in God, in right and wrong as shown by the conscience, and in a future life. His treatise ' De Veritate,' in defence of natural religion, excited much attention and some attacks. His two Latin poems—' Vita ' and ' De Vitâ Cœlesti Conjectura '—are in substance the most impressive modern Latin poems I have ever met. He seems to have cared little for English literature, and speaks slightingly of his brother George's English writings.

From Salisbury I sped back south-eastward, after two pleasant spring days, full of fancies and thoughts.

AT CANTERBURY.

I CARRIED a couple of American friends the other day to one of the most interesting parts of London, especially to natives of the new country, and yet a *terra incognita* to many thoroughbred cockneys: namely, certain old places on either side of London Bridge; and first to that ancient church, Saint Saviour's, with its tombs of Fletcher, Massinger, and Gower.

From the fine old church, dishonoured by modern hands both in what has been done and what left undone, it is but a step to the Borough High Street, with its row of ancient inn-yards, all much alike in plan—a gateway leading into a wider space overhung with wooden galleries. There are the 'George,' the 'White Hart,' the 'Queen's Head,' which is the trimmest; but the most famous and the one we have come to see is 'The Talbot,' formerly, as the sign tells us, 'The Tabard'—the herald's coat having given way to the

mastiff probably through mere corruption of the sound of
the word.

> Befell that, in that season [April] on a day,
> In Southwark at The Tabard as I lay,
> Ready to wenden on my pilgrimage
> To Canterbury with full devout courage,
> At night was come into that hostelrie
> Well nine and twenty in a company
> Of sundry folk, by aventure i-fall
> In fellowship, and pilgrims were they all
> That toward Canterbury wolden ride.
> The chambers and the stables weren wide,
> And well we weren eased atté best.
> And shortly, when the sunné was to rest,'
> So had I spoken with them everyone
> That I was of their fellowship anon.

How pleasant and fresh sound the old, old lines! And
now see a new April day, and pilgrims, from a land that
even Poet Chaucer never dreamed of, come to look, for his
sake, at the old Inn!

I had heard a rumour that it was pulled down, and
approached the gateway with some touch of anxiety, and,
going through, saw with relief, the tavern on the right hand,
the old balconies and tottering roofs on the left, the stables
at the end, all remaining exactly as I first saw them, a
young poetic pilgrim, some five-and-twenty years ago.
Perhaps nothing in the present edifices can be proved to
be of Chaucer's time; but parts of them are several centuries old, and the inn in all probability holds the same site
and the same general plan as in the reign of Edward III.
Indeed, as far as I can see, we are not forbidden to suppose
that portions may still be here of the very 'Tabard' of
Chaucer.

The yard was full of the clatter and litter of a carrier's
inn, and half blocked up with huge carts and elephantine
horses. The balconied part rests upon stout oaken pillars,
which show no sign of decay; but from the empty and

neglected state of the rooms one infers that the old edifice
is awaiting the harlequin stroke of this motley Nineteenth
Century of ours. A big, carter-like man, who was lounging
against one of the pillars, handed me the key—'You can go
up and take a look round.' There was nothing to see in
the nest of little chambers—made, most of them, by parti-
tions out of one large room, the very room, as some enthusi-
asts declare, in which the thirty pilgrims met—nothing save
the squalid desolation of a long-forsaken house of the
humbler sort. It was odd to find so much waste space
within a bow-shot of London Bridge, and things can
scarcely stay so much longer. When the 'Talbot-Tabard'—
up to this moment remaining the same that it has always
been within the limits of living memory (only more grimy,
perhaps, than it was a generation or two back, and these
empty rooms were then occupied)—shall be really pulled
down, London will certainly be the poorer by an object of
interest to readers of English poetry.[1]

Yet, after all, the supper at which Harry Bailey presided
was never aught but a dream-supper, the lively picture of a
company which no room ever held. Doubtless the 'Tabard'
was a usual starting-place for Canterbury pilgrims; but
those pilgrims for whose sake we still seek the dirty inn-
yard in the Boro' are but children of a poet's brain. Out
of true material indeed he shaped them; but his the
shaping and the bringing of them together, twenty-nine
representative figures from the England of Edward III.
Many million men and women have passed and left no
discoverable trace, while these fine puppets remain.

But one feels sure that Chaucer did come to the 'Tabard,'
and see the humours of the place. Our American friends,
too, have an immense appetite for every 'famous thing
of eld,' and are the reverse of sceptical or captious. No
folk so charming to go about with in the Old World. Besides

---

[1] It has since been utterly demolished.

their habitual *bonhommie*, frankness, and obligingness, their
curiosity and appreciation open the eyes of a native to
many things not seen because always seen. 'Chaucer's
Tabard,' that is enough; and whether the old balcony is of
the time of Edward or Elizabeth, or the Second Charles,
matters little,—it is crusted with antiquity and perfumed
with poetic associations. Let us also take the wise part
of making the most of our 'Tabard.' After all, though the
great fire of Southwark, in 1676, most likely burned part of
the ancient inn, it may have spared part. Would any such
balcony have been newly put up at that time of day?

I fancy Chaucer sleeping here, and constructing—he, the
English 'maker'—out of the dream-stuff of which the real
pilgrims whom he met were composed, his own company of
more durable phantoms. And thus remain alive for us to
this day the honourable Knight, the gay young Squire, the
sturdy Yeoman, the gentle Prioress (who had a nun and
three priests with her), the lusty fat Monk, the merry Friar,
the grave Merchant, the learned Clerk, the discreet Sergeant
of Law, the dinner-loving Franklin, the Haberdasher, the
Carpenter, the Weaver, the Dyer, the Tapisser, the Cook,
the Shipman ('with many a tempest had his beard been
shake'), the Doctor of Physic, the naughty Widow from
Bath, the poor and pious Parson, the sturdy Miller, the
Ploughman, the Manciple, the Pardoner, the Reeve, 'a
slender, choleric man,' and the Summoner, with 'fire-red
cherūbyne's face.'

They all met at supper, with abundant victuals and strong
wine, the host of the inn, Harry Bailey, at the head, no
doubt, of the table. He was a large man, a seemly, and
a manly, bold of his speech and merry, but also wise and
well-taught.

Supper done, he makes a speech to his guests, in style at
once familiar and respectful, proposing to accompany their
party to Canterbury at his own cost, and to act as their

guide, and further that, to make the journey pleasanter, each pilgrim shall agree to tell two stories going, and two more on the way back; the best story-teller to sit free at another general supper here at the 'Tabard' when all is finished.

This was accepted; and next morning, 'when that day began to spring,' they all arose, and being gathered in a flock, rode forth at an easy pace, the miller playing them out of town with his bagpipe; and when they reached the watering place of St. Thomas (at the second milestone, 'tis said, on the road to Canterbury), the host made them all draw cuts, and it fell to the Knight to tell the first tale—

> Whilom, as olde stories tellen us,
> There was a duke that highte Theseus;

who wedded the Queen Hippolyta,

> And brought her home with him in his countré
> With much glorie and great solemnité,
> And eke her young sister Emelye.
> And thus with victorie and with melodie
> Let I this noble Duke to Athens ride.

So will we let the pilgrims ride forward. But that return-supper, ordered five centuries ago, has not yet been eaten; indeed, the company never arrived at Canterbury, however near they came, and are still—men, and women, and horses, in all their fourteenth century array—somewhere on the road, ever riding forward and telling their tales in turn.

Nay, this were to wrap the bright procession in too dark a cloud of fancy! Rather let us hold for certain that they knelt at the shrine of 'the holy blissful martyr,' rode prosperously back to London, telling many a fine tale on the homeward journey, and sat down to a noble supper at the 'Tabard,' at which all drank to the best storyteller, by decision of their manly host and fellow pilgrim Harry

Bailey. Who that best was, and what the stories told on the return, we shall never know; inasmuch as the quiet pilgrim, rather short and fat, with mild, grave face—which, however, had somewhat 'elvish' in it—and who usually looked upon the ground, as though he would 'find a hare,' laid down his pen too soon, and no other man could repeat the sayings and doings of the company.

The sum of all the accounts of Chaucer's early life is simple and complete as the O of Giotto. Nothing is known of Chaucer's early life. We cannot learn where or when he was born, or anything authentic as to his family or education. The name originally is French (spelt Chaucier, Chaussier, and other ways), and means shoemaker, or perhaps breeches-maker. It is guessed that he was born in London, about the year 1328. There are rumours, all baseless, of his having been a member of the University of Cambridge, of Oxford, of the Inner Temple, and beaten a friar in Fleet Street. That he somehow received a high cultivation, and came into Court favour, is certain; and he appears to have gone to France with Edward the Third's army, in 1359, and to have been made prisoner; but he got safe back to England, and within a few years took to his wife Philippa, daughter of Sir Payne Roet, and maid of honour to the Queen. Another daughter of Sir Payne, Katherine by name, was of the retinue of Blanche, Duchess of Lancaster, first wife of John of Gaunt. Katherine married Sir Hugh Swinford, a Lincolnshire knight, became a widow, returned to John of Gaunt's household as governess to his children; he having meanwhile lost his Duchess Blanche, and married a Duchess Constance. After a time, this Duchess also died, and then John of Gaunt married the governess, his old friend Katherine; and thus Poet Chaucer, of no family, became closely connected by marriage with the Royalty of England.

He and his wife enjoyed various gifts and pensions; and

Chaucer was frequently employed in the King's service, on diplomatic missions ; for in those days kings thought a good brain a useful commodity, and were glad to find work for it. In Italy, at the same time, the learned Petrarch was busy in state affairs.

But neither Chaucer nor Petrarch had a public and its publishers to depend upon, and little foresaw, with all their wit, into what a glorious thing Literature was one day to develop itself. If they could have been told prophetically of the books, magazines, newspapers, etc., that would be produced in London alone, in a single twelvemonth, the 'capital invested' therein (this phrase *would* have been a puzzle), and the revenues accruing, it would certainly for a moment have surprised them. While on a mission in Lombardy, Chaucer is thought to have met Petrarch, that 'learned clerk,' at Padua ; and perhaps he did ; but there is no proof of it.

Chaucer filled, moreover, for a number of years the office of Comptroller of Customs for the Port of London, and was returned to Parliament in 1386, as knight of the shire for Kent ; the feeble Second Richard, aged 19, being King. Richard wished to govern through a clique of his personal favourites. Parliament met in October, 1386, and impeached the King's ministers. At the end of a month of violent disputes, the King dissolved Parliament, and Chaucer, as one of the obnoxious members, and a connection and supporter of the Duke of Lancaster (who was in opposition), was dismissed from the Customs' service. This at least is the residuum of probability from a mixture of various statements. It has often been stated that, to avoid the enmity of the Government, Chaucer retired to the Continent, and on coming back to England was imprisoned for three years in the Tower. There is no real ground for any such statement ; but it does seem certain that the Poet in his old age was ill-off for money, and in 1398 the King granted him a protection from arrest. Next year Bolingbroke (son of John of Gaunt, Chaucer's friend and connection by marriage), took the crown, and immediately granted Chaucer a pension of 26*l.* 13*s.* 4*d.* a year.

On Christmas Eve, 1399, the Poet, some seventy years of age, and now, let us hope, at ease from duns, went into a house situated in the garden of 'the Chapel of the Blessed Mary' (where Henry the Seventh's Chapel now stands), which house he took from the Abbot and monks of Westminster, on a lease of 53 years, at 2*l.* 13*s.* 4*d.* a year. But he occupied it only ten months. He died October 25, 1400, and his body was laid in the adjacent Abbey.

Soon after this visit to the 'Tabard,' I enjoyed my first sight of the famous old city of St. Augustine and Thomas à Becket. At a curve of the railway the three towers of the Cathedral rush into view not far off; and here is Canterbury Cathedral.

Why, I wonder, are all the railway stations in this part of England—the rich and flowery Kent—so mean and uncared for? The 'London, Chatham and Dover' has a blight upon it, which perhaps extends to the station-masters, and they are too dispirited to plant mignonette or train a rose-bush. The aspect of the stations on the London and Hastings line (to take one in the same part of England) is very different.

Here is part of the gray city wall, with green hawthorns growing out of the bastions, and tall elm-trees rising within. That grassy mound at one angle bears the odd name of 'Dane John'—corruption probably of *donjon*, which, by the way, is the same as *dungeon*, and means a strong place. The word is Keltic, and gives name to several places in Ireland, including Dangan in Meath, the Duke of Wellington's birthplace.

And now we turn into the High Street—long, level,

narrowish, slightly bending, with many old gables and projecting windows; the houses not lofty; the general aspect rural and quiet. Up a narrow bye-way on the right is caught an exciting glimpse of a huge stone gateway covered with time-worn sculpture; while in front, closing the street, stands the old West Gate of the city—a massive fortalice, through whose low-browed arch is seen the suburb of St. Dunstan. Over the battlements rises to view a grovy hill, part of the sloping ridge that shelters the shallow vale of Canterbury on the west.

The 'London, Chatham and Dover' brought us in behind time in due course—about half an hour—and it was too late to get into the Cathedral; nevertheless, I hastened to that fine old gateway up Mercery Lane. At the left-hand corner of the lane was once a famous pilgrims' inn, in which, if you like, you can fancy Chaucer's company putting up. The Cathedral-yard is not a striking one. The south porch (the principal one in all Saxon-English churches) is finely proportioned; but, ah me! how the *restaurateur* has been at work! What raw and coarse recutting of the sculpture work! What mean little new statues! Not mean because little: in good sculpture, figures the size of a penny doll may be as grand in their sort as the Parthenon.

More of these statues are swarming in the lower niches of the west towers—'by Phyffers,' says Murray. 'And who is the sculptor Phyffers?' I asked a virger ('rod-carrier,'—the spelling adopted here being perhaps the etymological Dean Alford's doing). 'I don't know, sir, more than he lives in the Walworth Road, London, and whoever subscribes 25*l.* can have a statue put up.' Not, I suppose, one to himself. Surely, statues ought not to be cheap? They ought to represent somebody worth recollecting. Nowadays they are springing up, little and big, like mushrooms, or rather toad-stools. However, these statues *are* dear—dear at the money.

ERASMUS. 201

Among the latest of Phyffers' performances are Erasmus
and Dean Alford, side by side. Erasmus's claim to stand
here in cheap stone is in kind no better than I may myself
boast of by-and-by. He made a ramble to the Cathedral
about 350 years ago, and wrote some account of it in his
'Colloquia Familiaria,' under the title, 'Peregrinatio
Religionis ergo.' Ogygius, devout believer in holy things,
describes to his friend Menedemus three pilgrimages he
has made—one to St. James of Compostella, who
gives his devotees a scallop-shell, 'because he has plenty
of them from the neighbouring sea,' and who of late
has had fewer visitors 'by reason of this new opinion
that is spreading abroad in the world;' another pilgrimage to the shrine of St. Mary at Walsingham, where
he saw, among other relics, a vial of the Blessed Virgin's
milk. After this, Ogygius went to Canterbury, 'one of
the most religious pilgrimages in the world.' 'There are
two monasteries in it,' he says, 'almost contiguous, and
both of Benedictines, St. Augustine's being the elder.
But the church sacred to the divine Thomas—*divo Thomæ*
—lifts itself to heaven with such majesty that even from a
distance it strikes the gazers with religious awe. With its
splendour it dims the neighbouring lights, and throws
into obscurity that anciently thrice-renowned place of St.
Augustine. There are two great towers, saluting from afar
all comers, and sounding with a wondrous boom of brazen
bells through all the neighbouring regions far and wide.'

This passage seems to describe the Cathedral before the
great central tower, that beautiful model of the perpendicular style, was raised above the roof, or at least before
it was finished. Professor Willis and others date this erec-
tion 1495; but the original authorities cited only say that it
was raised by Prior Goldstone II. and two other ecclesias-
tics. Goldstone became prior in 1495, but this does not
prove the tower to have been raised in that year, and

indeed it could scarcely have been one year's work. Now
Erasmus came to England in 1497, and then began his
personal acquaintance with John Colet. (See Colet's letter
dated Oxford in 'Eras. Op. Omn. Lugd. Bat.' 1703, Epist. XI.)
This Colet, afterwards famous Dean of St. Paul's and
founder of the school, was the very *Gratianus Pullus*, or
Gratian Dark, who visited Canterbury along with Erasmus;
each being then—if I am right as to the time—about thirty
years of age.

That *Gratianus* is Colet is beyond question. Witness
Erasmus himself, who in his 'Modus Orandi Deum' speaks
again of the relics shown at Canterbury, adding, 'To John
Colet, who was with me, these things gave much offence;
but I thought it best to endure them till an opportunity
should come to amend them quietly.' And elsewhere he
says of Colet, ' non nisi *pullis* vestibus utebatur, cum illic
vulgo sacerdotes et theologi vestiuntur purpura '—he wore
nothing but black or dark robes, instead of the usual scarlet.

But later in the Colloquy, Warham is named as Archbishop, whose rule began not till 1503. Probably Erasmus
paid several or many visits to Canterbury during that
wandering, poor-scholar life of his, and puts no exact description of its appearance at any particular date into the
mouth of Ogygius in this ' Colloquium,' which was not
completed till 1524 (witness the date of Virgin Mary's letter
quoted therein). But I think it likely that he first saw the
Cathedral before the great central tower had lifted its
beautiful lines of stone into the sunshine and rainclouds
of Kent.

Let us go on with the Colloquy, which I translate in
abbreviated manner, for the English version of Nathan
Bailey, φιλολογος (1725), has the garlic flavour (so to speak)
common to Sir Roger L'Estrange, Mr. Thomas Brown, and
other such writers of that time. Among many similar
wants (discreditably many), our literature has no good

translation of any of the works of Erasmus. A translated selection of the 'Epistolæ,' well done, with brief elucidations, would be valuable as well as amusing.

'In the south porch' (proceeds Ogygius) 'stand three armed men sculptured in stone, who with their impious hands murdered the most holy man; their names added, Tusci, Fusci, Berri ' [possibly meaning, it is guessed, Tracy, Fitz Urse, Brito.]. 'Why this honour to such men?' (asks Menedemus). 'They have the same kind of honour done to them as is done to Judas, Pilate, Caiaphas; and they are set there as a warning. For their crime drove them raging mad, and they recovered their senses only by the solicited favour of most holy Thomas.' 'O the perpetual clemency of martyrs!' 'When you enter, a certain spacious majesty unfolds itself; and to this part everyone has free access.' 'Is there nothing to be seen, then?' 'Only the massiveness of the fabric and some books fastened to the pillars, the Gospel of Nicodemus among them [a spurious gospel: they ought to have known better, hints the satirist], and also a sepulchre of I know not whom. Iron gratings prevent ingress to the choir, but allow of a view of the whole extent of it. You mount to this by many steps, under which a kind of vault admits to the north side, where they show a little wooden altar sacred to the Blessed Virgin, only notable as a monument of antiquity condemning the luxury of these times. Here the pious man is said to have uttered his last farewell to the Virgin when death was imminent. On the altar is the point of a sword, wherewith was pierced the skull-top of that best prelate. We religiously kissed the sacred rust of the sword for love of the martyr. Thence we went to the crypt, which hath its mystagogues. And first we were shown the perforated skull of the martyr, covered with silver save the top of the cranium, which is left bare to be kissed. At the same is shown a leaden plate (*lamina*) with the name *Thomæ Acrensis* insculpt upon it.'

[*Corpus* understood? Such plates were placed inside coffins. It is not settled what *Acrensis* was meant to say; some think ' of Acre,' *i.e.*, born there, and that his mother was a Saracen. One ingenious guesser sees in *Acrensis* the Latin equivalent of à Bec, of the beak, or point; à Becket being diminutive.] 'Here, also, hang up in darkness the hair-shirts, girdles, breeches, with which he used to subdue the flesh; enough to make one shudder; and condemnatory truly of the softness and delicate living we now indulge in.' 'And the monks, too, perhaps.' 'That I will neither assert nor contradict; 'tis no affair of mine.' 'You say right.'

'We now returned to the choir, where various reposi-tories were opened, and O! what a quantity of bones they brought forth—skulls, jaws, teeth, hands, fingers, whole arms—all of which, having first adored, we earnestly kissed. There would have been no end to it, I think, but for the indiscreet interruption made by one of my companions, an Englishman, by name Gratianus Pullus, and a man of learning and piety, but not so well affected toward this part of religion as I could wish.' 'I opine he was a Wicliflite.' 'I think not; but he may have read his books. This gen-tleman, when an arm was brought forth with some bloody flesh still sticking to it [this seems incredible!] shuddered at the notion of kissing it, and showed his disgust in his countenance. Whereupon the mystagogue shut up all his things. After this we saw the altar and its ornaments, the wealth of which would beggar Midas and Crœsus; and in the sacristy a wonderful pomp of silken vestments and golden candlesticks. There also we saw the foot of divine Thomas plated with silver; and a coarse gown of silk, without ornament, and a handkerchief retaining marks of sweat and blood. These were shown by special favour, because I was somewhat acquainted with the most reverend Archbishop William Warham, and had from him three words of recommendation.' 'I have heard he was a man of singular humanity.' 'He was humanity itself: of such learning, such sincerity of manner, and piety of life, that no gift of a perfect prelate was wanting in him.'

'Behind the high altar we ascended as into another church, and here saw the whole face of the best of men set in gold with many gems. Here Gratian got entirely out of the good graces of our attendant by suggesting that St. Thomas, in his lifetime so kind to the poor, would be better pleased to see all this wealth applied to charitable uses rather than in a vain show. The mystagogue frowned, pouted out his lips, and looked with the eyes of a Gorgon; and I doubt not would have spat upon us and turned us out of the church, but that he knew we were recommended by the archbishop. I partly pacified him with gentle words, saying that Gratian spoke not seriously, but had a jesting way with him, and I also gave him a little money.'

' I entirely approve your piety. Still it sometimes comes into my own mind that it is a very wrong thing to expend such vast sums in the building, adorning and enriching of churches. I would have the sacred vestments and vessels of a proper dignity, and the structure of the edifice majestic; but to what purpose so many fonts and candelabra and golden images? Why this immense expense for organs, as they are called? Why this musical whinnying [*musicus hinnitus*—I fear Erasmus was not a lover of music], got up at such cost, when meanwhile our brothers and sisters, Christ's living temples, are pining with hunger and thirst?' To this Ogygius in reply agrees that moderation in these costlinesses is desirable, but thinks at the same time it is better for kings and great folks to spend their money on churches than in gambling or in war, and says he would rather of the two see a church luxurious than bare and mean.

Then he goes on to tell how the Prior came, and showed them the shrine itself of the martyrs. They did not see the bones, which is not permitted, nor could it be done without a ladder; but the outer wooden case being lifted up by pulleys, gave the inner shrine to view. 'The basest material in it was gold. Every part beamed, glittered, and flashed with precious stones, the hugest and rarest, some of them bigger than a goose-egg. Some of the monks stood round in attitudes of the deepest veneration; and when the cover was lifted we all adored. The Prior touched with a white rod the jewels one by one, telling its name in French, the value, and the donor; the chief ones being the gifts of monarchs.'

'Hence the Prior carried us back into a crypt, and showed us by candle-light a wonderfully rich altar of the Virgin, guarded with iron bars; then again to the sacristy, where was brought out a box covered with black leather, and placed on the table; it was opened, and all present fell on their knees and adored.' 'What was in it?' 'Torn pieces of linen, many of them bearing marks of having been used to blow the nose with. Others, they told us, were used by the pious man to wipe the perspiration from his face and neck. Here again Gratian got out of favour. The Prior, knowing something of him as an Englishman of reputation and of no little authority, kindly offered to bestow upon him one of these bits of rag as a most valuable gift. But Gratian, far from being grateful, took it fastidiously on the point of one of his fingers, and laid it down, making a contemptuous movement of his lips, as though he said "Phew!"' 'I was both ashamed and alarmed by this; but the Prior, who is no stupid man, pretended not to notice it, and after giving us a glass of wine, kindly dismissed us; and we went back to London.'

This touch about the Prior is delicious, and his urbane omission to take notice contrasts well with the anger of the inferior exhibitor of relics. The whole account is very curious, especially considering the point of time to which it refers.

Erasmus little thought there was a boy then in England whose breath would by-and-by scatter these relics to the four winds. Yet the world moves slowly. Here, in the year 1872, stands this great edifice, not on the terms on which some rare shell is preserved in a museum, but as though it were still the habitation of the deepest and dearest thoughts of living England. Erasmus's prior of 300 years ago is very like Emerson's bishop (see ' English Traits ').—' If a bishop meets an intelligent gentleman and reads fatal interrogatories in his eyes, he has no resource but to take wine with him.' Have we got no further, after all the satirists and reformers ? Civility costs nothing, it is said—nothing, that is, to him that shows it ; but it often costs the world very dear.

It is not likely that friend Desiderius could possibly have foreseen that his own statue would ever decorate a niche of the famous edifice in right of his having written (an odd claim surely !) the sub-sarcastic account of his visit to the Cathedral which we have just been reading. But in our day some one has given 25*l.*, and there stands Erasmus (a small copy of the Rotterdam statue) beside King Ethelbert and Dean Alford, carved by Phidias of the Walworth Road.

Is it possible that Patricius Walker may one day find an ecclesiastical pedestal somewhere ? One might take this Erasmus statue, if it meant anything, to have affinity to the Prior's glass of wine—one other example of how civil the Church is to everybody. But in truth it means nothing ; men have long since ceased to care about these things as questions of truth and error, right and wrong. The dilettantism of archæology, and the more serious affairs hinted in the phrase ' loaves and fishes,' are now the only two living interests connected with these old monuments.

The raw statues and scraped south porch disheartened me ; the uniform west towers (one rebuilt) are just tolerable, rather pleasing, not beautiful, and the whole aspect of the

Cathedral yard was disappointing. There was a cold sky, too, and a chilly wind blowing, and I felt lonely and tired, and as if I had no business at Canterbury. Still there was an enticement in the Norman transepts and towers of Andrew and Anselm, and the strange inbending of the wall beyond. Out of the city I walked eastwards, under great trees, and mounted the hill to the little Church of St. Martin, itself very old, and built, 'tis said, on the site, and partly on the walls, of an older church which stood here, already bearing St. Martin's name, when Augustine and his monks came to convert the pagan English; for the Keltic British were Christians, but their conquerors remained heathen.

Ethelbert—or, if you like, Æthelberht—King of Kent, Saxon' and pagan, married the Christian Bertha, daughter of Charibert, King of Paris, and for her and her attendant bishop was the little Christian chapel set on the slope of this hill near the capital of the kingdom of Kent, earliest permanent settlement of the Teutons in Britain. Ethelbert, moreover, as at this time 'Bretwalda,' exercised a supremacy, not exactly definable, over the other kings.

There are three good reasons why Augustine came first to Canterbury: Queen Bertha's Christianity, King Ethelbert's authority, and the nighness of the city to Rutupiæ, the usual landing-place of visitors to Britain. At Rutupiæ, now 'Richborough,' between Ramsgate and Sandwich, where the great fragments of Roman fortification still look forth from their low cliffs—but the sea has receded from them, and level green pastures now stretch below — at Rutupiæ Augustine and his monks landed, and sent a message to the king. He ordered them to stay where they were for the present, and that meanwhile they should be supplied with all necessaries. Some days after, the king came into Thanet, and received the missionaries in the open air, where he would be less subject to magical arts than in a house. After conference he said, ' You speak very fairly.

I cannot forsake my old worship; but you are free to come to Canterbury and teach whom you will.'[1]

A thousand years later, by-the-bye, there was (rightly or wrongly) much less toleration in England for new teaching.

So the monks from Rome travelled along the Roman road and reached this very hill, whence they looked down on the wooden and wicker city of the Cantuarii, with its earthworks of defence and palisades, in the broad vale among trees and thickets. It cannot be doubted that they stopped to worship at the little shrine of their faith; then lifting a tall silver cross they formed into a procession, and, with choristers chanting a Gregorian litany, descended into Canterbury, and were well received.

This little Church of St. Martin was handed over to Augustine, and some of these very stones and bricks (Roman bricks) that I touch may be part of the walls within which the first English king was baptised into Christianity, an event commonly spoken of as one of the most momentous in the history of the human race; and perhaps it may be allowable so to speak of it. Mighty temples (like this of Canterbury), establishments, Church-and-state conjunctions and rivalries, persecutions, wars, reformations and revolutions, creeds, books and art-works, civic and family arrangements,—all modes wherein human life, public and private, can manifest itself and send on its influences — have they not taken form and colour for a thousand years and more from that mystic sprinkling?

Missionaries have usually been the bearers not only of a theological creed, but of a superior civilisation and culture; and monasteries were long the refuges and nurseries of learning. These are facts which go far to account for success and authority; but also make more difficult the question to which the answer has never yet perhaps been

---

[1] Bede's *Ecclesiastical History.*

fairly sought), how much and in what ways any creed, as such, has modified human life and manners. What, for example, were Ethelbert's life and character like, whilst he was a pagan, and what afterwards? The English in general, from A.D. 500 to 1000, what were they as heathens, and what as Christians, say in the matters of truth, courage, humanity, purity, wise and happy life? Certainly the new rules had no effect of making men leave off fighting; that continued to be the main business of their lives; and, indeed, promises of success in battle and extension of territory were among the usual bribes (in addition to eternal salvation) employed to persuade men of note to be converted. The monkish chroniclers often record instances where these promises were fulfilled; but, after all, the pagan Jutes and Saxons and Angles beat the Christian British. The pagan Danes afterwards beat the Christian Saxons, who by that time had fallen, as a people, into a very weak and confused state. In short, the word 'Christianity,' as commonly and loosely used, is one of those vague and misleading terms for each of which it would be beneficial to substitute at least three or four of a more definite sort, to be used on their proper occasions. The very first thing that ought to be aimed at in language, and usually the very last thing aimed at, is definite expression of definite meaning. But since the latter is too often missing in writers and speakers, they can scarcely be expected to strive for the former.

After peeping in through the windows of this thrice-famous little Church of St. Martin, I mounted the hill behind, through a market-garden, and found atop a hawthorn in bloom—my first this year. With what a delicious soothing flowed the well-remembered fragrance over my sense! One has nothing to quarrel with in these lovely joys of nature. 'I love this hawthorn-bush,' I exclaimed aloud, 'twenty times more than Canterbury Cathedral, with all its pillars and arches, in every style of Gothic!' and, picking a pearly tuft, went over to the windmill, and stood awhile under its lee; now looking up with awe at one great sail after another swashing down like a Titan's sword, now looking forth on the prospect of green sloping corn-fields, with here and there a grove, and amid a shallow vale the simple city, with its one dominant edifice, three-towered, in the midst.

It was Saturday night, and I walked about the streets by gas-light, presenting them older and more picturesque than garish day; but the Cathedral yard was locked up, which did vex me. I remembered York last year, and that great pile by moonlight, and how I stood on the west steps and climbed with mine eyes into the stars by the ladder of those vast towers.

But the west gate of Canterbury is satisfactory, is mighty and massive. In the wider street outside are a good many old wood-fronted houses; one of which was formerly an inn, where pilgrims arriving after the gates were closed used to put up for the night. I enjoyed the little old-fashioned shops, with their low ceilings and miscellaneous jumble of articles, and often paused at a window or door to watch the friendly greetings and gossipings of vendor and customer, so characteristic of a country town not too large for everybody to know nearly everybody else. Countryfolk, their market-ings finished, got deliberately into their carts and drove away. I saw no tipsy person, or night prowler, or any sign of disorder, all along the main thoroughfare, from the tall dark foliage of St. George's Place to where the street of St. Dunstan melted into the darkness and solitude of a country road, with a white horse grazing on its hedge-side grass.

The last house at this end of the city stood alone, ancient and decayed, at its gable a dead tree seen weirdlike against the broken night-sky. It looked like a house with a history; at least, like every old house, it has the scene of many histories under its uneven roof, and behind its lead-latticed windows; not of people and events who are 'historic' in the usual sense (for this is but a small house, and never was a rich one), but of simple human beings, of infancy and maturity, old age and death. Many a child of the house must have played round that withered tree when it, too, was green and gay, and gone to sleep under those battered tiles in a garret more full of wonders than all the palaces and temples of the outside world. Could one but have the record—the real inner record—of the life of one of those unknown and for-ever-forgotten children, I would not give it for the best extant history of St. Thomas à Becket, and of St. Augustine to boot—two personages for whom, taking the reports of their admirers, I confess to feeling but moderate regard.

Wending northwards, I came into the neighbourhood of the barracks, and then first on some token of nocturnal revelry. From the 'Duke's Arms' and the 'British Grenadier' issued sounds of rude chorusing, in one case with some attempt at 'singing a second.' What a good little thing, I thought for the thousandth time, if part-singing were universally taught in schools, so that whenever two or more singers met, they might have a repertory of kindly song-music at their command. Elsewhere in the same street was the notice, 'A Free and Easy every night. Miss Adelina Villiers, lady dancer; Mr. Brown, pianist; singing.' In the dim road a few belated soldiers were making for their quarters; and presently the patrol came round the corner and marched past with a slow swing. At the barrack-gate paced the sentry with his gun; while inside lay quietly, each on his own pallet, hundreds of strong men, of coarse unruly natures many of them, ready to start up, one and all, at the bugle's sound to-morrow morning, and 'fall in,' each to his allotted place. The most wonderful of machines is an army, composed of that complicated and variable material, human nature; yet acting at its best with a powerful concert and regularity as of the heavenly spheres themselves. Might not men be trained to act with equal order and combination to peaceful ends? Undoubtedly. Let us manage that little business of part-singing to begin with; and go on to the organisation of labour.

Next day was Sunday, and I went to morning service in the Cathedral, heard the living river of choral harmony, heard the Athanasian Creed, and a sermon, or rather the noise of it, like the cawing of a rook, for the words slipped through my mind unheeded. In the quarto Prayer-Book on the ledge before me was a book-plate of old device, showing enclosed in scrollwork a cross with X at the centre, and written underneath, 'Christ Church, Canterbury.' On one side of the cross in this book some profane pencil had drawn (most likely at sermon-time) a grotesque face or mask. The nave and choir looked almost as new and fresh as though Pugin had built them yesterday; and one half-expected to see here and there a warning of 'Wet Paint.' It was only by turning to certain corners and details that the eyes assured themselves they were gazing on a thrice-venerable building Seen from where I sat, the uniformity of the newly cleaned pillars and groinings of the nave, and the uniformity of the panellings of the choir, along with the execrable modern stained-glass, made the general effect disappointing. There was a kind of dismal tidiness and smartness; no grand gloom anywhere. Even the oblique glimpses of the transepts (usually effective in cathedrals) were uncomfortable, showing, as it were, a jumbled museum of various kinds of arches.

I learned next day that most of the modern glass is the doing of a private gentleman of Canterbury, solicitor by profession, who having, first, a turn for designing painted windows, secondly, money to spare, thirdly, an ambition to distinguish himself, and fourthly, interest with the Cathedral authorities, has filled, not one or two, but perhaps a dozen or more of the great windows with his handiwork. Let me offer my contribution to his fame, by copying the inscription, ' *George Austin, dedicavit,* ' and add the remark of a virger on the subject : ' Well, sir, there they are, and we can't take 'em away, you see ; and the boys won't break 'em.'

I wished to ascend the great tower, but was told it was inaccessible to visitors, the stairs being out of repair. Most part of the crypt, also, is in a very disorderly condition.

Leaving closer examination for the morrow (which I duly accomplished : but *vide* Professor Willis, Dean Stanley, and many others), I went forth for a country walk, and was lucky in my course. Mounting by St. Thomas's Hill, a slope of the gentle ridge that shuts in Canterbury vale on the west, I took a field-path to the left. Zephyrus came over the flowery meads, and every breath carried conscious health and sweetness into the blood.

The path led me to the edge of a steep little dell, into which it sloped. On the right hand was a thick grove not yet in full leaf ; on the left stood, some fields off, a little church ; in the hollow, among orchards, peeped the brown roofs of an old hamlet, and thither I gladly descended ; nor was my pleasure lessened to find that this hamlet was Harbledown, formerly Herbaldown, the very place—at least I doubt it not—which Chaucer calls ' Bob-up-and-down, under the Blea ' (now the Blean, still a wild tract of half-forest land), and certainly where Erasmus was stopped to kiss St. Thomas's old shoe.

' Having set forth for London,' says Ogygius, ' we came, not far from Canterbury, to a place where the road descended, steep and narrow, into a hollow, hemmed in with banks on either side, so that there is no escape : you cannot take any other way. Here on the left hand is a little alms-house of old men. When they spy a horseman coming, one of them runs out, sprinkles the traveller with holy water, and then offers him the upper part of a shoe bound round with brass, in which is set a bit of glass by way of a gem. After kissing this, you give a small piece of money.' 'Well,' says Menedemus, 'I'd rather meet a set of old almsmen in such a place than a gang of sturdy robbers.' 'Gratian,' continues Ogygius, 'rode on my left, next to the little alms-house. He bore the sprinkling pretty well, but when the shoe was held out, he asked what was that? "St. Thomas's shoe," says the man. Upon which Gratian got angry, and turning to me exclaimed, "What do these animals [*pecudes*] want? would they have us kiss all good people's shoes? They might as well ask us to kiss their spittle, and so forth!" I pitied the old man, who was looking doleful at this, and consoled him with a little money.' *Menedemus*. 'In my opinion Gratian was not wholly unreasonable in being wroth. If such shoes or slippers be preserved, as proofs of the wearer's frugality, I don't object; but it seems to me a piece of impudence to thrust these things upon everybody to be kissed. If any-one liked of his own free will to kiss them out of a vehement impulse of piety, I should hold that pardonable enough.' *Ogygius*. ''Twere better these practices were given up, I confess; but from things which cannot suddenly be amended, it is my habit to extract what good I can find, if any good there be.' A sentence very characteristic of friend Erasmus.

And here is the very place—the hollow of two hills and the narrow way between steep banks where Erasmus and Colet rode by; and here is the almshouse or hospital of St. Nicholas, the very same charitable institution that harboured the old man who ran forth with his holy shoe, for the Reformation spared little Herbaldown Hospital. It is rebuilt as to its walls, and now stands in the form of a small group of trim red dwellings, wherein nine old brethren and seven old sisters abide.

In the first letter to John Colet in the collection (Epis. xli.) dated Oxford, 1498, Erasmus gives an interesting sketch of his own character, which has probably full as great a share of truth as is usual in such confessions. From this letter, along with Colet's previous one (Epis. xi.) already alluded to, I infer, contrary to the statements of biographers, that they had no personal intercourse until this visit of Erasmus to England. After much compliment and deprecation of Colet's too high estimation of him, Erasmus says, ' I will describe myself to you, and better than any other can, since no other knows me so well. You shall find in me a man of little fortune, nay, none at all ; averse from ambition ; most ready to affection ; but slightly skilled, it is true, in literature, yet a most *flagrant* admirer of it ; who religiously venerates another's goodness, though he has none of his own ; who easily yields to all in matters of doctrine, to none in matters of faith ; simple, open, free ; well-nigh ignorant of simulation and dissimulation ; pusillanimous, yet honest ; sparing of speech ; and in fine one from whom you must expect nothing but his soul [*animum*].'

Climbing the steep bank on the south side of the hollow way at Harbledown, I came to an old weedy churchyard with a little very old church with square tower and Norman door. The low side-wall is crumbling, the old high-pitched roof seems almost ready to fall in. As usual, everything has been let go to the verge of destruction for the want of a stone here, a tile there, till at the last moment shall step in the restorers (a clergyman most likely the ringleader) to make a grand job of it. Some such thing, I gathered, is about to happen to this little gray church also.

Mounting the hill westward, and catching sight, as the pilgrims used to do at this point, of the great cathedral, at the same moment a rich gurgle of song broke from a thicket close at hand—a nightingale! My first this year, and the song lifted me again to poetry and Chaucer.

'As I lay' awake (says Chaucer) 'the other night, I thought of the saying, that it was of good omen for lovers to hear the nightingale sing before the cuckoo; and anon I thought, as it was day, I would go somewhere to try if I might hear a nightingale; for I had heard none that year, and it was the third night of May. So as I espied the daylight, I would no longer stay in bed, but boldly went forth alone to a wood that was fast by, and held the way down by a brook-side, till I came to a land of white and green, the fairest I ever saw. The ground was green, and powdered with daisies; the flowers and the grass of the same height,—all green and white, and nothing else to be seen. There I sat down among the fair flowers, and saw the birds trip out of their bowers, where they had rested all night; and they were so joyous of the daylight, they began at once to do honour to May, singing with many voices, and in various songs. They pruned them, and danced, and leaped on the spray, and were all two and two in pairs as they had chosen each other on St. Valentine's Day. And the river whereby I sat made such a noise as it ran, accordant with the birds' harmony, methought it was the best melody that might be heard of any man.'

For very delight he fell into a half-slumber, not all asleep, not fully waking, and in this he heard a cuckoo sing, which vexed him, and made him say to the bird, 'Sorrow on thee! full little joy have I of thy cry!'

> And as I with the cuckoo thus 'gan chide
> I heard, in the next bush beside,
> A nightingale so lustely sing,
> That her clere voice she made ring
> Through all the greene wood wide.

Then followed a dispute between the birds, the nightingale praising love, and the cuckoo disparaging the same, till at

last the former cried out bitterly, ' Alas ! my heart will break,
to hear this lewd bird speak thus of Love, and his worshipful
service.' Then (says Chaucer) methought I started up and
ran to the brook, and got a stone and flung it heartily at the
cuckoo, who for dread flew away ; and glad was I when he
was gone. For this service the nightingale thanked the
Poet, saying,

> One avow to love make I now,
> That all this May I will thy singer be ;

and promising that next May he should hear her song first,
and meanwhile must believe no whit of the cuckoo's slanders
against love. Nothing (replies Chaucer) shall bring me to
that ;—and yet love hath done me much woe.

> ' Yea ? Use,' quoth she, ' this medicine,
> Every day this May or thou dine,—
> Go look upon the fresh daisie,
> And, though thou be for wo at point to die,
> That shall full greatly lessen thee of thy pine.
>
> And look alway that thou be good and true,
> And I will sing one of my songes new,
> For love of thee, as loud as I may cry.'
> And then she began this song full high,
> ' I shrew all them that be of love untrue ! '

and so she flew away.

Chaucer's hearty and untiring delight in grass and daisies
and birds' songs, and his sincere belief, which he preserved
into old age, in the curative balm for anxious thoughts which
is given to men in these simple joys, is one of those things
for which we dearly love the old poet. His very heart and
soul are soothed by a pleasant grove, a green field, a clump
of wild flowers. And so did these vernal sights and sounds
and odours soothe me that day as they soothed old Geoffrey
five centuries ago.

' The Flower and the Leaf,' by-the-bye, is certainly *not*
Chaucer's (say the experts), but later, and most likely by a
woman. In that case, the name and memory of a great

English poetess, able to write of these things as well as
Chaucer himself, lie buried among the dark centuries. She
too, whilst yet her eyes could see daylight, rejoiced greatly
in the

> —— branches broad, laden with leaves new,
> That springen out against the sunny sheen,
> Some very red, and some a glad light green—

of early spring, and the rich fields 'covered with corn and
grass,' and the fragrance of flowers.

> —Suddenly I felt so sweet an air
> Of the eglatere, that certainly
> There is no heart, I deem, in such despair,
> Nor with thoughts froward and contraire
> So overlaid, but it should soon have bote [relief],
> If it had once felte this savour sote [sweet].

By this time I had come back into the city, and here my
meditations took another turn. Close to the railway station
is a grass-field, and in a corner of it two or three children
were gathering handfuls of buttercups. 'Is this the field
where the people were burnt?' 'Yes, sir,' says a little maid
of four years, dropping a curtsy. 'And where did they
burn them?' 'Down there, please, sir,' pointing to a
grassy, weedy hollow. This, then, is the Martyrs' Field.

In the year 1556, on March 2, Cranmer was burnt alive at
Oxford, in front of Balliol College; and the same day
Queen Mary made Cardinal Pole Archbishop of Canterbury
in his room. Under his primacy about 2,000 Protestants,
men and women, were burnt alive; eighteen of them in this
hollow, within sight of the great Christ Church and the
monastery of the first English saint; such being the practical result of a thousand years of 'Christianity.' No shrine
covers the ashes of these 'martyrs;' only the spires of grass
spring above them; only the indiscriminate rain falls upon
the scene of their torture. Yet, if voluntary acceptance for
conscience' sake of the worst extremities of suffering con-
stitutes martyrdom, some of these poor men and women—

long since at peace—are better entitled to it than Thomas à
Becket, slain in a wrangle with fierce knights of his own
creed, on motives political and personal ; or Alphage (whose
church is here, close to the Palace), carried off a prisoner
by the heathen Danes when they sacked Canterbury in 1011,
and after seven months' captivity, slain by the stroke of an
axe. Alas! how men torment each other and themselves.
Is human life in its own nature too long and too happy?

The sun shone out gaily, the children gathered king-cups ;
a white butterfly came wandering into the Dell of Agony,
and poised for a moment on a tall stem of grass.

Another walk, that kindly afternoon, led me to the 'Dane
John,' where were many folk in Sunday clothes, enjoying,
according to their several measure, the grass and trees, and
the prospects from the battlements. Then I found the Old
Castle, a shapeless mass of pebbled wall. To one corner
telegraph wires are fastened, and the fortress is now a gas
factory. Behind it lurks the little old church of St. Mildred
with a quiet avenue of lindens. Thence by bye-streets,
such as set one meditating on life in a country town, both
to-day and in its past generations, for everywhere is the suggestion of peaceful continuity, I slipt into a field-path, among
young corn and hop-poles, and so came round by Long Port
to a quaint little space named 'Lady Wotton's Green,' and
facing upon it the great old gate, older than Chaucer's time,
of St. Augustine's Monastery.

Looking from the shade of a linden on the mullioned
window of the room above the gateway, I thought of it now
as the marriage-chamber of a happy bridegroom and bride,
he five-and-twenty, she not sixteen ; he an Englishman, tall,
slender, handsome, dignified, full of chivalrous courtesy and
grave tenderness ; she French, girlish, vivacious, *spirituelle*,
with clear brown complexion and soft black eyes, a sparkling
brunette, now timid in a foreign land and new condition ; he

a king, just come into his ancient heritage, she the daughter
of many kings. How gay was the old gateway with flags
and flowers as the young royal pair drove through, coming
from Dover to sup and sleep here!

Princess Henrietta Maria, daughter of King Henry the
Fourth of France, married by proxy in Nôtre Dame, May
21, 1625, to King Charles of England, was detained a month
by weather and else, during which time the King waited
much at Dover for his bride; but he was at Canterbury
when she landed, on Sunday evening, about eight o'clock,
June 23 (N.S.). Next morning about ten came the King to
Dover Castle, when his sweetheart was at breakfast.
Hearing of his arrival, she hurried down, and would have
knelt, but 'he wrapped her in his arms with many kisses.'
The trembling little bride began a set speech—' *Sire, je suis
venue dans ce pays*,' &c., but broke down in a burst of weeping.
The courteous tenderness of her bridegroom soon reassured
her; and when, finding her taller than he had expected, he
glanced towards her feet, she showed her shoes with a smile,
saying, ' Sir, I stand upon my own feet; I have no helps by
art;' and they drove off together to Canterbury. 'The
same night, having supped at Canterbury, her Majesty went
to bed, and some time after his Majesty followed her; but
having entered her bedchamber, he bolted all the doors with
his own hand. . . . The next morning he lay till seven
o'clock, and was very pleasant with the lords that he had
beguiled them, and hath ever since been very jocund.' [1] The
lords in waiting had planned, doubtless, not to exempt even
Majesty from some of the old-fashioned epithalamic
ceremonies.

Next morning at breakfast the young couple (' Mary ' is
the name he calls her by), looking out through that large
window, see before them in the June morning sky this same

[1] Contemporary Letters, given in *Court and Times of Charles I.*
London, 1848.

great tower, with its attendant pinnacles. The little Queen is unfortunately a ' Papist,' which may make some trouble by-and-by, when the priests and politicians get to work, but hardly in present circumstances. They say something, it is likely, of the past history of the city and the kingdom. Over the *future* history of England, over their own future, hangs for them a thick, impenetrable veil.

From Canterbury the happy young pair travelled to Rochester, the next day to Gravesend, and in the State barge they entered the capital,—the river banks, in spite of a heavy shower of rain, lined with loyal and applausive multitudes; and landed at *Whitehall.* Happy, thrice happy, young King and Queen!

Thence I passed to North Gate Street, and the Hospital of St. John (founded under Lanfranc, 1070-1089), ' twin-hospital of Herbaldown.' Through an old arched gateway, mostly of wood, I passed into a quiet quadrangle (rebuilt) with tall trees behind and a space of little garden-lots where the inmates cultivate their patches of peas and lettuce, mixed with many gay flowers and fragrant potherbs. Below this a meadow gently slopes to the winding Stour.

Coming back to the street I walked northwards to the barracks, and there a sideway led me to the river's brink beside a great mill, and a path that followed the watery windings by many a great old pollard-willow. Swallows skimmed the slow-flowing stream; on the other bank were little orchards and sleepy red houses, and for landmark rose ever the long roof and tall towers of the Cathedral. This predominance in visible form of a supernatural idea gives (even yet) the suggestion of a reverent unity pervading the life and thought of those who dwell within the compass of its immediate presence. Nor is there much in Canterbury to disturb this impression. Barrack and railway have in-truded themselves, but the old city is not swallowed up in the results of modern ' industry and prosperity.'

I returned by the Abbot's Mill, with its dam and rushing weir, fronted by a grass-field in which stand four mighty trees of the poplar kind, mountains of shivering leaves. Higher up, tanneries pollute the stream, and the cows' hoofs, for glue, hang up in ugly rows. In benighted pagan times a river was held sacred. Still, recollecting what the Medlock is like where it crawls with its inky load of foulness by Manchester Cathedral, one may be almost thankful for the Stour's condition.

I had walked a good many hours, but the calm starlight night drew me forth again, and approaching the dim bulk of the West Gate, I heard a nightingale singing on the left.

> There might you hear her kindle her soft voice.

Finding a path to the river, where it flowed down through the fields and into a shrubbery just before entering the city, I stood close to the unseen singer, sometimes whistling to him, and answered, I chose to think, with a louder and more triumphant strain.

'*She*,' our old poets always said, following the Greeks and Latins, and it was natural to make feminine this airy charm of sound; but we cannot now afford to disregard so broad a natural truth as that the male birds of every kind are always the chief and often the only singers. A poetic statement and a scientific statement are essentially different; yet they must both be statements of *truth*; and as scientific truths pass more and more into general apprehension, these, in place of old mistakes, will form the natural and proper vehicles and illustrations of poetry.

At midnight, through my open bedroom-window, came the distant song of the tireless bird, and I thought again of Chaucer. With eagerness and faith can I listen to bird or poet; not to bishop, or dean, dead or living. As to those old saints, their unscrupulous piety seems to have been capable of any lie—one might almost say of any crime;

and, with all their good intentions and self-denying labours, they left a terrible legacy to mankind, of which we also are heirs.

But all this is growing dreadfully wearisome even to think of, at our time of day. Better look at antique edifices and establishments with the mere eyes of an archæologist or an American tourist. The Americans enjoy English cathedrals so much that I believe they would keep them up by subscription if necessary. If they were in the market, Mr. Barnum would very likely buy Canterbury and York, to number the stones and set them up in Central Park and Boston Common, and perhaps make a handsome bid for the respective archbishops, deans, vicars-choral, and virgers.

We had better go to bed.

Chant on, dear bird, God's chorister,

and do thy might
The whole service to sing 'longing to May.

Ah, Chaucer, where now art thou, this new May night? If one could learn that, 'twere worth a pilgrimage. Good night!

RAMBLE THE ELEVENTH.

AT LIVERPOOL.

The Mersey—Irishism—Americanism—The Docks—Commerce and Credit
— The British Association—Mr. Huxley on Vital Germs—Mr. Tyndall on
Scientific Imagination—Physical and Moral Philosophy—Science and
Religion—Liverpool Architecture—Corn Stores—An Emigrant Ship—
Poor Streets—Birkenhead Park—In the Train.

I REMEMBER very clearly my first sight of England. I was eighteen years old. Awake in my berth in the steamer, the perturbation, external and internal, at an end, how delightful it was to look through the little round window, its bull's-eye open to a fresh morning breeze, and see, gliding past, the bank of a large river with numerous clusters of houses shining in the sunlight—first sight of English houses and English land. Seen from deck, the broad Mersey sparkled and danced, as though it had been a mere holiday river, between the terraces and villas of the Birkenhead shore on one hand, and on the other an endless line of huge warehouses with a forest of masts in front, and here and there a tower or cupola rising from the dark mass of houses behind. This was Liverpool. Large ships lay at anchor in the stream ; others, of all sizes, sailing or steaming, moved every way across the picture. At the great landing-stage rows of steamships sent their hissing clouds aloft, porters and sailors bustled and shouted, and passengers kept landing and embarking among heaps of baggage, each intent on his own affairs, crossing gangways and shifting and shoving to and fro among boys and bystanders, while on the pavement above waited the jarvies, with uplifted whip, crying ' Keb, sir, keb ! ' which I set down as my first experience of the true native English accent. Everything in Liverpool had the freshness of a foreign country (though I came no farther than from the Irish West), and I noted every point of English novelty, and found myself plunged in a torrent of new experiences.

Revisiting Liverpool this autumn, having in the meantime lived much in London and the south of England, it is my first impression that Liverpool is rather more Irish than Dublin. The huge station, slovenly and ill-kept, swarms with frowsy interlopers. Porters, coachmen, little boys, policemen, accost or answer you, in nine cases out of ten, in a rich Emerald brogue. Milesian names cover the sign-boards of shops and market-booths—Murphy and Duffy, Donovan and Conellan. Maguire's ' cars ' (even the word cab seems to be almost supplanted) are in chief request. The streets abound in barefooted, ragged children, wrinkled beldames with *dudeens*, stout wenches, loosely girt as Nora Creena, balancing baskets on their heads ; unshaven men in every variety of old hat lounge at corners; and if you venture into one of those byways which lead out of the best business streets, the foul gutters, the flung-out refuse under foot, the dangling clothes hung aloft to smoke-dry, the grimy houses, their broken panes stuffed with rags, the swarm of half-naked babes of dirt and poverty about the open doors, here suckled, here scolded by their intensely slatternly mothers, the universal squalor mixed with an indescribable devil-may-care-ishness, and the strong flavour of brogue that pervades the air, will all remind you forcibly (if you have ever been there) of that famous ' Liberty ' which surrounds the cathedral of St. Patrick.

The Irishism of Liverpool is a strong (in every sense) and all-pervading element : its Americanism, though much less marked, is sufficiently noticeable.   The big 'Washington Hotel,' the three-horse omnibuses trundling and jingling along their tramways, the United States journals at the newsvendors', the not unfrequent negroes, the unmistakable Transatlantic intonation which often strikes the ear in public rooms, the 'Oysters stewed in the American style,' with many other hints, remind one that here is a chief portal between Europe and the great West, and indeed the wide world.   Placards abound of the starting of ships and steamers for New York, Boston, Philadelphia, New Orleans, the West Indies, Valparaiso, Melbourne—wheresoever the salt wave washes; and looking down street after street, the vista ends in a crowd of masts and rigging.

Thus, underlying the Irish and the American elements, is everywhere visible the general seafaring character of the town, whereon rests the mighty line of docks and warehouses, and behind these the countless outfitting shops and nautical instrument shops, shops of every kind, polyglot hotels and taverns, drinking bars (with a glass barrel for sign), lodging-houses, sailors' dancing-rooms ; and moreover the crowds of comfortable and luxurious villas that besprinkle the country for miles around Liverpool, inhabited by ship-owners, ship-insurers, corn merchants, cotton brokers, emigrant agents, etc., etc., men with 'one foot on sea, and one on shore,' yet to one thing constant ever—namely, money-making—and therein duly successful; with the thick fringe of humbler houses in the immediate suburbs wherein their clerks abide.

Mostly in the filthy heart of Liverpool itself, the squalid byways and pestiferous alleys, dwell the dock labourers, carters, stevedores, all the grim hard-handed men, white with flour, black with coals, yellow with guano, fluffy with cotton, dusty with maize, who are hoisting and lowering, heaving and shovelling, dragging and hauling, carrying and trundling great bales, boxes, bags, barrels, weights of iron bars and pigs of lead, mountains of coal, mountains of corn, amid creaking of windlasses, rattling of chain-cables, roll of heavy wheels, trampling of great slow horses, and busy turmoil of a throng of grim human creatures like themselves, in that endless range of waterside sheds, with endless range of tall stores looking down across the long narrow street full of mud and noise, and over the prison-like line of the dock-wall.

Mortally oppressive is this whole region—the huge warehouses, the blank wall, the lumbering drays, the heavy weights swinging in mid air :

> What dreadful streets are these I tread !
> Bales, hogsheads, hang above my head—

boundless mud, smoke, stench, with perpetual grinding, rolling, clattering. Inside the dock gates is some little relief—not much : the water is usually foul, the ships lie jammed together like bullocks in a market pen ; the monotony of the long sheds and long walls and long paved causeways, crowded and dirty, the drays and horses and grim men and great burdens again at every step, the trap-like and ponderous bridges, the huge stonework of the docks and piers, the brutal and unfeeling bigness and ugliness of every instance of power, the uncertainty of getting out by any given route (for a bridge may be open or a gate locked), the certainty that you have no choice of direction, the stagnant water on this hand, the gray wall on that, and your sense of the dreary spaces which in any case you must traverse to escape—these oppressed me years ago, when I first walked in to see these famous things, and oppressed me this last time still more dismally. It was like a nightmare. The very memory of it is burdensome.

Such is part of the machinery of commerce on the large scale, a necessary detail in the grand scheme of modern civilisation, a department of life and work where a Rambler with tastes for the picturesque and sentimental cannot reasonably expect much pleasure. Would you have no dock for the ship, no wall for the dock, no store for the cargo, no hands to move it? Or would you wish to find the long wall painted in fresco, and each stevedore with a bunch of violets in his buttonhole? Well, I don't feel easy in my body among these grand docks, and will get out of the place as soon as I can; but neither do I feel easy in my mind. Suppose our modern commerce, rich and mighty as it appears, should prove some day to be based not on sound principles, but on unsound. Suppose the human race, or any community of it, to discover Credit, on which of late all trading transactions are built, to be not a rock, but a sandbank; Credit, with all its bourses and banks and bills, to be in the long run of maleficent effect to men in general (while enabling a few lucky and astute persons to sweep enormous gains into their pockets)—to be on the whole a pernicious thing, diminishing happiness, increasing misery, a huge loss, not a grand gain, to mankind. Commerce nowadays rests mainly on an artificial system of Credit, and is almost synonymous with 'Speculation;' and Speculation in a vast number of cases is something very like Gambling. With all trading put on a different basis—say a tripod of ready money, real securities, personal (not legal) credit— I doubt if huge Liverpool and huge Manchester could concentrate so much ill-organised human labour within their melancholy walls, overdriven when speculation is lucky, left to idleness and starvation when speculation is out of luck—could gather round them so widespread and close-packed, so dark and ugly a multitude of ill-fed, ill-taught, filthy, diseased, · vicious, helpless, hopeless human beings. And I also doubt if this concentrating process, as at present effected, be a blessing to England and the world.

If I were Lord Chancellor to-morrow I would frame a Bill to abolish all laws for the Recovery of Debt. Besides the check upon huge, unwholesome, inorganic conglomerations as aforesaid, a vast swarm of useless and worse than useless intermediaries in commerce would be nipped and suppressed by the no-recovery principle, and honest buyers would get their things purer and cheaper. Now they pay for the rogues, and get bad things to boot. Half the shops in London would shut up—far more than half of the luxury-shops, finery-shops, bauble-shops ; and those that remained would still perhaps be too many. It is a struggle for existence among the general body of shopkeepers now, spun out in the individual cases by credit received and credit given (debts to come in by-and-by, bills that may be renewed for three months longer), and the strugglers clutching in their bitter anxiety at all possible 'tricks of trade,' almost always including adulteration, and very often unjust charges and false weights and measures beside. Most of these are non-producers ; their sole business is transmission, and for this, I repeat, there are far too many ; and they do it dishonestly and expensively—give us worse things at higher cost.

I don't suppose that a ready-money system would reform all the evils of the mercantile and shopkeeping world ; but I do believe it would cut across many dishonesties, dry up a good deal of waste, and help to make life, national and individual, more wholesome.

The inconveniences would prove to be mainly imaginary. You do not go to a railway station without your fare in your pocket. If you have but a third-class fare, you do not ask for a second or a first-class ticket. That is the natural and wholesome arrangement, and applicable to every affair of buying and selling. The number or magnitude of the trans-

actions makes no real difference: if you are legitimately
engaged in large transactions, you will find or soon make
proportionate means and conveniences for buying and pay-
ing as you go. Neither would trust (*personal* trust) fail,
within proper limits,—which limits, however, would be
something very different from the present undefined, almost
boundless, area of 'Credit,' in whose soil and climate
Speculations and Peculations, upas-trees and poison-fungi,
do rankly grow and flourish, to the great moral and physical
detriment of mankind.

Contracts resting on real securities would be dealt with by
the law as such; and all *bonâ fide* business would soon
adjust itself and go on without difficulty. Certainly *malâ
fide* business would be checked, and that large department
of trade much discouraged which is only a kind of gambling;
which elbows fair trading out of the field; which produces
so many compositions with creditors, and ever and anon
culminates in a 'commercial crisis,' in which multitudes
of little people suffer who had no part in the 'speculations,' while the gamblers very usually set up again;
and then perhaps as 'trade revives,' they have a run of
luck, and all goes merrily forward—till the next crisis.
Details I will leave to the Lord Chancellor of the future
to work out.

Meanwhile, here is the huge town—Hibernico-American-
English Liverpool, seafaring, rough, busy, dirty, wealthy.
Hither converge in ceaseless streams the cotton of America,
India, Egypt, the wool of the Australian plains, the
elephants' tusks and palm oil of African forests, the
spermaceti of Arctic seas, the grain from the shores of
Mississippi, St. Lawrence, Elbe, Loire, Danube, Vistula,
and many another stream, the hides of South America, the
sugar, copper, tobacco, rice, timber, guano, etc., of every
land the sun's eye looks upon. Hence radiate to all quarters

of the globe, bales of cotton goods, linen, woollen, bulks of machinery, inexhaustible leather and hardware, salt and soap, coals and iron, copper and tin.

Liverpool at this time, busy as she seems, complains of bad times. The docks are full of ships—post horses in stable, eating their heads off. Nevertheless, Liverpool, portal and caravanserai of the human race, is thronged with visitors and passers-through. Americans who have been seeing Europe, now homeward-bound in the fall, swarm at all hotels, waiting for their steam-packets; and, moreover, the British Association is this year (1870) holding its seven-day congress in the Town of Ships.

Its presence makes a gala week in such a town as Norwich or Bath. Exeter last year was like a house made ready for guests, and busied in entertaining them. But the Scientific Congress, with its sections and savants and skirmishers, hardly quickens the pulse of a big, busy place like Liverpool. Ask your way to the Reception Room, your answer may be a shake of the head. The President himself pushes unnoticed through the hasty crowds of Lime Street or Bold Street, and his likeness has not supplanted Bismarck or the fallen Emperor at the photograph shops. But this apathy by no means extended to the hospitalities of Liverpool, civic and private; and the Town itself gradually became aware, in some degree, of the Association, under the influence of the long daily reports and comments of the local newspapers, and the splendid *soirées* at St. George's Hall, the Free Library and Museum, the Philharmonic Rooms, and his Worship the Mayor's two receptions at the Town Hall, embellished with a great show of modern pictures, lent by people round about. I should not be surprised to hear that Lancashire buys more modern pictures than any three other counties. Professor Huxley is President this year; his address was on the subject of 'vital germs.' Over and above the regular business of the meeting, the Association arranges to have two or three lectures of a popular or semi-popular character. This time the chief of these was given by Professor Tyndall to a very large audience in the Philharmonic Hall. It was long and without experiments, and more fit to be read at home than listened to amid the difficulties of a large public assembly. Still it is always something to see a man of note in the flesh, and hear his living voice; and this interest, over and above that of the topic and treatment, secured general attention for the best part of two hours. With clearness and originality, in an easy voice agreeing with his elastic bearing (he has light-ness without levity—a kind of agile earnestness, so to say), the Professor threw forth hint after hint on the nature of scientific investigation, and on the directions which it has taken in our own time (illustrating mainly from the study of *Light*), and connected all into a firm chain of thought.

Drawing towards the end of his discourse, the lecturer spoke of the well-known nebular hypothesis—fiery mist con-densing into suns, which throw off planets. When first detached from the sun, 'life, as we understand it, could hardly have been present on the earth. How, then, did it come there?' Life (he said towards the end of his dis-course, with a semi-apologetic reference to the English Clergy) was either 'potentially present in matter when in the nebulous form, and was unfolded from it by way of natural development, or it is a principle inserted into matter at a later date.' In brief, the first is the scientific, the second the theologic view; and those who hold the second call the first degrading, debasing, demoralising, destructive — all kinds of terrible names.

Now, whether or not 'emotion, intellect, will' were once 'latent in a fiery cloud,' I must own seems to me, P. Walker (whom it concerns as much as another), a question which, however interesting speculatively, is not of the slightest *practical* importance. Man is the highest being we know of. He is, somehow or other, what we term a spiritual being, but this we cannot explain or define. His understanding, imagination, judgment, æsthetic sense, moral instinct, will, personal consciousness are thoroughly real and effective manifestations of his nature; and it is by and in them that human life, in its truly comprehensive sense, really is. Its connection with atoms or fiery clouds, whatever mental steps may be taken in the direction of establishing it (and the complete journey, judging by all experience and all intuition, is for ever impossible to us)—that seeming, and possibly real connection is, I repeat, of no practical importance in any way. Whether we think of man at first as moulded at once out of clay, like a sculptor's figure, or developed gradually from a fiery cloud, how can it make any difference as to our place in the universe, our powers, our duties, our prospects? People are curious just now about protoplasm, development, spontaneous generation, and so forth; first, on account of the scientific novelty of some of the views put forth, and then, I suppose, because they vaguely expect some new light upon the nature of the universe and the duty and the destiny of man. They had better give up every shadow of such expectation for good and all.

The Evolution hypothesis (our Man of Science confessed) 'does not solve—it does not profess to solve—the ultimate mystery of this universe. *It leaves, in fact, that mystery untouched.* Its really philosophical defenders best know that questions offer themselves to thought which science, as now prosecuted, has not even the tendency to solve.'

Often, in the pauses of reflection, the scientific investigator finds himself overshadowed with awe—is aware of 'a power which gives fulness and tone to his existence, but which he can neither analyse nor comprehend.'

So ended our Professor, rising for a moment into that region which Immanuel Kant declared to be 'above all other spheres for the operations of reason,' and indeed the only philosophy deserving to be so called. The mathematician, the natural philosopher, and the logician (says Kant) are merely artists, engaged in formalising and arranging conceptions; they cannot be termed philosophers. They but furnish means. In view of the complete systematic unity of reason, there can only be one ultimate end of all the operations of the mind. To this all other aims are subordinate, and nothing more than means for its attainment. This ultimate end is the destination of man, and the philosophy which relates to *it* is termed Moral Philosophy. The superior position (he adds) occupied by moral philosophy above all other spheres for the operations of reason, shows why the ancients always included the idea of moralist in that of philosopher. 'Even still, we call a man who appears to have the power of self-government, even though his knowledge may be very limited, by the name of philosopher.'[1] These are practical and pregnant words of the old German, and worth meditating upon.

The mysteries of man's spiritual life, science has 'no tendency to solve.' Nay, far short of this our knowledge stops—even her wings of imagination fail her in the inner region of physical nature's profounder subtleties. We can trace sound-waves and light-waves into the auditory and optic nerves; but when we ask how this force is translated into the sensations of hearing and of seeing, Imagination itself does nothing for us—gives no least hint of help. We examine in every case, not nature itself, but our conceptions of nature; and the very link which connects us as thinkers with the world, as we conceive it in thought, is utterly beyond our cognition. Physical science attempts to explain

[1] *Kritik der Reinen Vernunft.* (Second edition, last chapter but one).

by formulæ certain facts given by human consciousness, and the explanations are no more than a tracing of connections. The least approach to a discovery of origins has never been made. Endless curiosity and investigation are proper to man. So also are awe, and reverence, and humility. It was Newton who compared himself to a child picking up pebbles on the shore of the great sea of Truth; and in this he only referred, I think, to the extent of *comprehensible* truth, beyond which lie the measureless regions of truth incomprehensible to man.

Theories of Atoms and Motion, Evolution, Natural Selection, etc.; from these vantage points, carefully built up of observation and reasoning, we get wonderful glimpses into the workings of wide physical nature in its relations to our intellect. True conceptions of cause and effect we also glean here and there, some of them applicable most beneficially to the external conditions of our earthly existence. As to the nature of human life, all the accumulated science of mankind up to this hour has not one word to say.

Let us take heart, then, brethren—do our work, gather knowledge, tell truth, say our prayers, be kind and helpful to each other, enjoy landscapes and flowers, books and pictures, music and poetry, and fear no protoplasmic philosophies. For my part I believe neither Huxley nor Darwin will hurt a hair of our heads.

The work of Modern Science as regards the mixture of moral philosophy and mythology which goes by the name of religion has been one with that of historical and literary criticism—demolition; troublesome and vexatious but necessary work, already we hope almost complete. What remains is that the attained results be publicly and practically recognised, and that life, social and national, should adapt itself to admitted facts, getting rid of a huge lumber of individual and incorporated obstructiveness. After this

we may at length hope for some *constructive* work on a large
scale. Obstruction—Destruction—Construction. May the
era of Construction soon arrive !

We cannot roam for ever through a boundless universe
of vibrating atoms. The human soul (whatever the
human soul may be—' soul ' is one of the faint efforts of
language in the region of the inexpressible) is as little to
be satisfied with ' a vibrating atom ' as with ' a multiple
proportion.'

What boots it to send our thoughts wandering into
the empty wilderness of a material world ? What wisdom
or comfort bring we back into our inner life ? Socrates
(as Aulus Gellius reports) used very frequently to repeat,
with an application of his own, a certain line from the
Odyssey : [1]

ὅττι τοι ἐν μεγάροισι κακόν τ' ἀγαθόν τε τέτυκται.

The evil and the good that have befallen in thy own house.

Mankind must sooner or later, I am deeply convinced,
come back to a simple faith and trust—personal trust in a
personal Ruler of us and all things; finding Him first
within, not without.

Out of the brilliant Hall we pass again into the dirty
labyrinthine streets of this windy, tarry, briny Town of
Ships, full everywhere of the indescribable seaport briskness
and shabbiness on a great scale. In a moment of ill-
humour I was inclined to describe it thus to a Londoner :
Take Thames Street and the Docks, set Islington behind
them, with here and there some huge gray stone building of
brutal bulk ; put in a great deal of dirt and clatter and
Irish brogue, and make the natives say ' oop ' for ' up,'
and you have some notion of Liverpool. Well, this would
not be a fair description, I admit. The Mersey with its

[1] iv. 392.

shipping is grand in its own way. So in *its* way (ludicrously
unsuitable as it is to the place, the purpose, and the climate)
is that vast Greek temple called St. George's Hall. The ,
region of the Exchange has a busy and wealthy aspect of
civic importance, befitting one of the commercial centres of
the globe. Considered architecturally, however, the Exchange buildings give little delight, and perhaps the new
part of the quadrangle is the very worst thing I have yet
seen in modern architecture, the most pretentiously mean—
true cork-cutter's Renaissance. The old part is stately in
comparison. The central monument with its black figures
in chains, might once have well seemed an allegory of Liverpool Commerce supported by Negro Slavery. It used to be
said that every brick in the town was cemented with human
blood. To come back to our own day, what opportunities
are thrown away, what sums of money misspent every year,
in our modern architectural exploits! Look once more at
his new Railway Station and Hotel in Lime Street, and
wonder by what ingenuity of stupidity so huge an edifice, of
uch costly materials and workmanship—fine yellow stone
ut and fitted to perfection—is contrived to look paltry and
unsubstantial.

After these pretentious failures, there is comfort to the
eye in the great corn stores, based on iron pillars of Egyptian girth, rising in storey after storey of grain-lofts, broad,
lofty, and airy, and enclosing three sides of the docks in
which their ships lie quiet after thousands of miles of stormy
water, sending grain, grown in California, Canada, or on
the shores of the Danube, up an 'American lift,' from the
hold to the top loft, whence it flows in rivers of maize, rivers
of wheat, on endless horizontal bands, about eighteen inches
wide, worked by hydraulic power, to every part of the stores.
In this great corn warehouse, the greatest in the world, they
say, Liverpool commerce showed itself in its most pleasing

aspect. It was dealing with the first of bodily necessaries, man's bread of life ; and though the processes (of unlading, cleaning, transferring, etc.) were on a great scale, they were managed with so much ingenuity and simplicity combined, worked so smoothly to these ends with a minimum of dust and noise, as to give one a comfortable and even pleasurable sense of perfect adaptation, such as one finds in Nature's own doings. Neither was there here any hint of *cheating* —a suspicion, alas ! which the known usages of commerce so often infuse. What the baker does, is done outside these walls. If corn-dealers ever mix good corn with worse— avaunt ! Thou canst not say these do it ! No : but it is done, not seldom.

In another dock I found the ' Great Britain,' at first unlucky in Dundrum Bay, lucky since in many voyages, and now preparing for another, to carry half across the globe her 750 passengers and 150 sailors, and hoping to come to anchor under the warm summer sky of Melbourne harbour a month at least before Christmas. Strange reading our ' Christmas books ' and picture-papers must be to an Anglo-Australian child. And then I went with a Government official on board the ' Holland,' at anchor in the river, just starting for New York, and saw the mustering of her emigrants. She can carry 1,250 full-grown passengers, all of one class. This time she had much cargo, and only 300 passengers, of whom many were Swedes and Norwegians, who reach England by way of Hull. The sturdy figures, and homely, honest, flaxen-haired faces of the Scandinavians, were pleasant to see, telling of steady, unambitious industry and domestic faith. Yet here is the stout miner of Fahlun, or boatman of Saltenfiord, or farm-worker of Fossdal, in his big boots and fur cap, with his flaxen-haired wife, and flaxen-haired oys in woollen night-caps, and girls with long rat-tail plaits f flaxen hair, and not seldom with an old wrinkled grand-

mother whose once flaxen hair is now snow-white, all bound
to the new hopes, new labours, and new fortunes of the
Great Republic, where land is as yet of less value than men
and women. Now and again a slim Norse *piye* steps shyly
up to the inspector, answering to her name, and hurries past
with glad smile to join the crowd 'for'ad' who stand watch-
ing those 'aft' that have still to pass muster. The Government doctor stops any one who has symptoms of fever, small-
pox, measles, etc., and the master of the ship takes care to
carry no one whom the American authorities might turn
back to the Old World as obviously unable to earn a living.
All on board to-day passed with little question, save a boy
about four years old, who, with his parents and two younger
children, was forced to wait till all the others were disposed
of. The child was heavy-eyed, and suspected of measles.
The poor father and mother—they were from South Wales,
and seemed scarcely able to speak a word of English—sat
very doleful in fear of being turned back on the threshold to
which they had no doubt painfully struggled; and it was a
great relief at last when the doctor, after turning up the
boy's eyelids with his thumb, said, carelessly, 'That'll do—
pass on.'

I hear there are no few Welsh in the United States,
and they often live grouped together, and continue to
speak their old Kymric in that conglomerate of races and
nationalities. There were few Irish emigrants in the
'Holland,' and Liverpool is no longer so much their transit
port as it used to be, for many of the Liverpool passenger
steamers to the States call either at Cork or Derry. The
arrangements of the ship seemed very good as to berths,
cooking, hospital accommodation, etc., except that unmarried women and married couples are placed in the same
division of the ship—a plan, the Government inspector
agreed with me, not free from objection. Away slid our
steam tender, and soon I saw the big ship steadily following

her busy, puffing tug-boat down river, her deck crowded with gazing passengers.

Less pleasant than the river experience was a walk of several hours through some of the worst and poorest parts of the town of Liverpool—Scotland Road, Vauxhall Road, and their cross-ways. The names on the corners were suggestive of all pleasant things: the streets of Meadow, Rose, Arden, Paradise, and then of Chaucer, of Ben Jonson, of Addison (with its ' Morning Star ' whisky shop)—irony of nomenclature! What foul vistas are these crowded streets? The garments, *quasi*-washed, which dangle overhead on clothes-lines stretched across, draw one's eyes upward, and lo, far above the chimneys, through the veil of smoke, is evidence of a cloudless blue sky, filled with sunshine and sweet air. Below, all is squalor and stifle, rags and drunkenness, an atmosphere thick with fever. Many Irish are here. At one dirty corner I came on the Church of St. Joseph, and I have no doubt the priests do their appointed functions diligently and fearlessly. Elsewhere was a dirty crowd round a dirty door, with two dirty women talking vehemently to a policeman, and another policeman bearing down leisurely on the scene of action. The shops were mostly for drink, cheap provisions, and cheap haberdashery, with here and there a petty newsvendor's, in which the ' Flag of Ireland ' kept company with ' Reynolds' and sheets of comic songs. A great many police cases, another constable told me, come from this quarter, ' but nothing very bad mostly ' (he added with toleration) — ' only drunkenness and assault.' The Hospitals and other charitable establishments of Liverpool are liberally and well managed, I believe. I visited the General Infirmary and the Nurses' Home connected with it, and found them apparently models in their kind. But alas! here in Meadow Street and Paradise Street are the *roots* of the evils, ever germinating and spreading.

After this one wants a little fresh air, so away again to the landing-stage and across the broad Mersey, and by a mile or two of tramway to Birkenhead Park, whose smooth-winding bowery walks and clear pools, and trees that now lattice a red and gold sunset—the seeming threshold of a purer world—have few this evening besides myself to' enjoy their peaceful beauty. Returning after dusk, the ferry steamer shows a striking night-picture of the river, dotted with interminable lamps stretching eastward and westward, ships at anchor with their lights dimly reflected in the dark stream, and over Liverpool a lurid gleaming arch, *Aurora Urbana*, the gaseous halo crowning Modern Civilization.

Next day the triumphal car of that Power carried me away from the great Seaport, for whose present condition the lonely bird by the water brink, and '*Deus nobis hæc otia fecit*,' are by no means the most fitting crest and motto.

River, ships, docks, landing-stages, the big, murky town, with its struggling and striving, business and wealth, ignorance, disease, and vice, charities and hospitals and free libraries, vile and dark human swarms, noble and generous lives—all these, now that visible Liverpool also is gliding away from me into a distance of space and time, shape themselves into one memorial impression, sombre and pathetic.

> And we have sped our wondrous course
> Athwart a busy, peaceful land,
> Subdued by long and painful force
> Of planning head and plodding hand.
> How much by labour can
> Poor feeble, timid man !

I am in the midst of another busy scene of England's daily life, a huge inland manufacturing town. Poor laborious generations of feeble men, blindly working on from day to day, what seek ye? what find ye? Great and wonderful are the visible effects of your persistent labours: are you steadily increasing the value and happiness of all human existence?

END OF VOL. I.

PRINTED BY DALZIEL BROTHERS, CAMDEN PRESS, LONDON, N.W.